# the bad seed

OTHER BOOKS *by* WILLIAM MARCH

Company K

Come in at the Door

The Little Wife & Other Stories

The Tallons

Some Like Them Short

The Looking-Glass

Trial Balance

October Island

# the bad seed

a novel by

- - - - - - - - - - - -

## WILLIAM MARCH

*with a new introduction by*
ELAINE SHOWALTER

**ecco**

*An Imprint of* HarperCollins*Publishers*

All the characters in this book are fictitious, including the principals and subordinate characters in the Denker and Ponder cases. The other cases cited are true.

FIRST ECCO PAPERBACK EDITION 1997

*Designed by Susanna Gilbert, The Typeworks*

The Library of Congress has catalogued the previous edition as follows:

March, William, 1893–1954
  The bad seed / by William March
    p.  cm.
  ISBN 0-88001-540-3
  I. Title.
PS3505.A53157B36   1997
813'.52—dc20          96-41686

ISBN 0-06-079548-4 (pbk.)

07  08  09  ❖/RRD  10  9  8  7  6  5  4  3

# introduction

by ELAINE SHOWALTER

IN APRIL 1954, when it was first published by Rinehart, *The Bad Seed* was an instant sensation. The *Atlantic Monthly* called it "an almost impeccable novel of suspense," *The New Yorker* declared it "undoubtedly one of the year's best," and the *New York Times Book Review* predicted that "no more satisfactory novel will be written in 1954 or has turned up in recent memory." Ernest Hemingway, John Dos Passos, Carson McCullers, and Eudora Welty wrote William March with praise and congratulations; British reviewers called the book "terrifyingly good." *The Bad Seed* quickly turned up on the bestseller list (it would ultimately go on to sell over a million copies). Even before the end of the year, Maxwell Anderson's hit stage version, starring Nancy Kelly and Patty McCormack, opened on Broadway, and ran for 322 performances. Two years later, Mervyn LeRoy used most of the original cast in a Warner Brothers film version, which annoyed critics by substituting a happy ending for March's grim, ironic one, but it nonetheless received four Academy Award nominations. Today, even those who have never read the book, and never seen the play or film, use March's image of the "bad seed" as a proverbial term for an evil child.

Although William March himself regarded *The Bad Seed* as a potboiler, he would have been thrilled by his book's artistic and commercial success. Ironically, he was already ill when it was published and died of a heart attack soon after, on May 15, 1954, at the age of sixty. Throughout a long literary career as a novelist and short-story writer, he had chafed against his marginal status as a figure the critic Gilbert Milstein, in the *New York Times*, called "a sport, a mutation," "entirely out of the main stream of American letters." Even his loyal friend Alistair Cooke, who edited *A William March Omnibus* (1954), and regarded him as a neglected genius, acknowledged March's reputation as "a journeyman realist, a third-rate Sherwood Anderson . . . a minor connoisseur of morbidity."

But in *The Bad Seed*, March finally managed to make the most of his talents, obsessions, and stylistic affinities. Of his six novels, only this last book, wrote Milstein, "was a true artistic achievement." In the 1990s, the sensational plot of a cold-blooded child serial killer is more familiar to readers and audiences than it was in the 1950s, and indeed tabloid headlines, movies of satanically-possessed kiddies like *The Exorcist* and *The Omen*, and TV talk show hosts like Geraldo Rivera and Sally Jessy Raphael, may even have made the theme conventional. In some respects, however, the story is even more strange and compelling now than when it was first published. Information about March himself, especially Roy S. Simmonds's critical biography, *The Two Worlds of William March* (1984), offers fresh insights into the subtexts of the novel, particularly its fascination with sexual violence and perversity.

*The Bad Seed* made its debut during the golden age of psycho-analysis in America, at a moment when not just urban sophisticates but audiences generally were sympathetic to Freudian interpretation. Yet discussions of homosexuality were still taboo, and March's sophisticated allusions to gay men and to castrating wives and mothers must have either gone over the heads of readers in the fifties, or seemed merely witty. In the context of contemporary understanding, his fascination with the murderous child, victim of hereditary blight, seems much more personal, autobiographical, and metaphorical than it did five decades ago.

In order to understand the novel more fully, we need to take a look at March himself. He was born William Edward Campbell in 1893 in Mobile, Alabama, the recognizable setting for *The Bad Seed*. The precocious second child and eldest son in a family of eleven children, March won prizes for writing, music, and acting, but his education was abruptly terminated on the brink of high school, when the family moved to a small Alabama sawmill town where he had to work as a filing clerk. March left home at the age of sixteen and never returned. A family legend held that he had been rejected by a rich girl named Bessie Riles; the name "Bessie" certainly turns up in much of his fiction whenever a particularly monstrous woman is imagined. In *The Bad Seed*, Bessie Denker is the original mass murderer and breeder of the bad seed of violence. But more likely, March, like Dickens, whose father sent him to work in a blacking factory, resented being deprived not just of education and opportunity, but also of status as a Southern gentleman. He often made harsh remarks about his family, telling his friend Nicholas McGowin, for example, that he would never commit incest, since his relatives were too ugly. He also said that he had been made to feel "depraved" by his strict, god-fearing parents; his biographer reported that March's father burned one of his early literary efforts and then thrashed him. Edward Glover, who psychoanalyzed March in the 1930s, enigmatically observed that he grew up "rather lamed in emotional respects. . . . He was half-afraid to embark on emotional relationships with people and half in dire need to do so." Later, March's friends—among them, Alistair Cooke and Lincoln Kirstein—said that he had been "warped" and traumatized by an unhappy childhood.

March's adult life certainly showed signs of warping if not trauma. He was never married or known to have a relationship with a woman; he had at least two severe psychological breakdowns; and despite business success and some literary recognition, he became increasingly eccentric, isolated, and obsessed with sexuality and crime. Friends of March who spoke about him to Roy Simmonds were guarded about his emotional conflicts; his art dealer and confidant Klaus Perls observed that they "ended in the tragedy of his having to go on his sexual pursuits into areas where tragedy in those days was bound to happen."

The overall picture of March's life suggests repressed homosexuality, which March himself discusses in *The Bad Seed*. Monica Breedlove, the society matron who owns half the town and has been briefly analyzed by Freud himself, is forthcoming both about her own penis envy and incestuous fantasies, and her middle-aged bachelor brother Emory's "larvated homosexuality." "What does 'larvated' mean?" asks Emory. "It means covered, as with a mask," Mrs. Breedlove replies. "It means concealed." Although she adds that her analyst, Dr. Kettlebaum, regards homosexuality as "a matter of personal preference," the sense in the book is very different, especially in the nuances of Breedlove's repulsive terminology. Indeed, the plump, balding Emory has a larval quality; this image also implies immaturity and an insect-like monstrosity. Emory is not the only character in the novel whose identity is masked; Rhoda, Leroy the janitor, and Christine Penmark herself, are also larvated personalities, concealing or repressing their secret worlds.

Outwardly, the two worlds of William March were his role as a businessman and his career as a writer. After leaving home, March took business courses, made up his high-school deficiencies, and briefly attended the University of Alabama Law School.

In 1916 he joined his older sister Marion in New York, and then enlisted in the Marines during World War I. By 1918, he was at the French front and slightly wounded at Belleau Wood. He finished his military career with the Distinguished Service Cross, the Navy Cross, and the Croix de Guerre. Upon his discharge, he took advantage of the military's educational benefits, spending four months at the University of Toulouse.

March's war experience eventually became the basis for his first published novel, *Company K* (1933). But he began almost immediately to embroider upon and mystify his military career, claiming that his bronchial passages had been permanently damaged by mustard gas, although there was no evidence in his military record that he had ever been exposed or treated. His family believed that he had been recommended for the Congressional Medal of Honor, but disdained the award out of pacifist sentiments. Some friends had the impression that March came home with only six months to live, although he was actually in excellent physical condition. He also told and retold a story of coming face-to-face with a handsome young German soldier, whom he stabbed with his bayonet. After the war, he blamed that event for recurrent episodes of conversion hysteria in which his emotional trauma was converted in physical symptoms, including the loss of his voice, throat problems, and visual disorders.

Despite any aftereffects of the war, March found a job working for Waterman, the shipping firm. By working and investing in stock, he made enough money to support himself and help family members throughout his life. In the early thirties, March represented his company in Berlin but had a mysterious breakdown and left Germany for London, where he sought the help of the analyst Edward Glover, who encouraged him to return to New York and to continue writing. Although his Southern

Gothic stories and novels, including *Come In at the Door* (1934), *The Tallons* (1936), *Some Like Them Short* (1939), *The Looking-Glass* (1943), and *Trial Balance* (1945), were not commercially success-ful, March became involved with New York's literary and artistic circles, made a name for himself as a party-giver, and decided in 1946 to leave his job to write full time. He also began to buy modern French paintings from the dealer Klaus Perls. Perls re-called that during the many years March was planning *The Bad Seed*, they often discussed the character of Rhoda, and that March purchased a small painting by the modern French artist Claude Bombois "that to him seemed to incarnate some Rhoda feeling." He was especially fond of the work of Chaim Soutine, with whose turbulent life he felt a "kinship of spirit": he inter-preted Soutine's "Jeune homme dans un fauteuil" as depicting a young man masturbating. By the end of his life, he owned nine Soutines and nineteen other paintings, including works by Pi-casso, Modigliani, Rouault, Braque, and Klee. The collection was sold at auction after his death.

March became a mysterious, disturbed, and disturbing pres-ence in literary New York. One friend, Lombard Jones, recalled March's long-standing obsession with other people's sex lives, and his reticence about his own: "He was an avid student of the works of Sigmund Freud and an analyst in the Freudian frames of reference of people he had met and observed." Beginning in the mid-1930s, he declared himself an authority on handwriting analysis and often volunteered to display his talents at parties; the name Penmark in *The Bad Seed*, and Rhoda's desire for the medal in handwriting, allude to this fascination with penman-ship as a clue to personality.

March's literary friends also began to notice Freudian themes in his published stories and conversational anecdotes. The writer

Kay Boyle often spent time with March walking in Central Park in the early 1940s and remembered his indifference or even hostility toward children, and his accounts of spying on neighbors and strangers. "His obsession then," she recalled, "was with still another alien world: the bizarre world of sexual and largely 'perverted' encounters which took place in the remote sections of the park. From his window on  Central Park West, Bill was able to observe through a pair of binoculars the random encounters and subsequent sexual activities of these lonely wanderers. He would tell me in detail of all he had witnessed, but the stories were never gleefully or viciously recounted, but in something like wild despair, his face tight as a fist with concern. At times, I believe that he told me these things out of apprehension, out of the fear of his own loneliness, and that this kind of love was all that was available to those who were alone."

His fiction also tended to focus on the perverse and the violent. He wrote about a serial sex murderer; about an eight-year-old boy who is traumatized and humiliated when a wasp stings him on the penis; and, in "Cinderella's Slipper," about a shoe fetishist named Verne Hollings:

> It seemed incomprehensible to him . . . that another man
> would embrace a mass of flesh, stuffed with disgusting
> food, when there were shoes to be loved, shoes as imper-
> sonal and beautiful as the one he now held against his
> lips; and yet there were: in fact, you couldn't go to the
> theater or the movies, or even a walk in a public park,
> without seeing men and women locked in each other's
> arms, their lips pressed together.
>
> He lifted his head, his eyes burning with the pure,
> fierce light of a crusader. A shoe was also flesh in a way,

he thought; but it was flesh with the disgusting things taken out.

In 1946, March had a serious breakdown and spent six months in a sanitarium in the South. In 1950, he moved to New Orleans and established a quiet, stable life on the fringe of the bohemian French Quarter community. His friends were surprised when he finished *The Bad Seed*, because he had been talking about it for years, and they had come to believe it would never be written. The manuscript was rejected by his longtime publisher Little, Brown as too shocking, but Rinehart accepted it with only minor suggestions. The editors there felt that the book's many true-life case studies interrupted the suspense; March had used his reading and research to surround the story of Rhoda Penmark with accounts of real mass-murderers, homicidal sociopaths, and amoral women and children. At the heart of the novel is Christine Penmark's recovered memory of her real childhood and genealogy, and her fear that she has passed on a hereditary blight to her daughter and must take responsibility for it.

As in much of March's writing, women in *The Bad Seed* are more sinister than men, and the idea that the propensity for violence and evil is passed on through the female line dovetails with other recurring March themes: that of smothering mothers like Mrs. Daigle, and lurid rape fantasies like those of the janitor Leroy. At the same time, March's narrative reveals a masked attraction to and identification with the little girl who so cleverly conceals her murderous impulses and crimes. In the novel, the mystery writer Reginald Trasker argues that serial killers can be precocious geniuses: "Some murderers, particularly the distinguished ones who were going to make great names for themselves, usually started in childhood; they showed their genius early, just as outstanding poets, mathematicians and musicians did." Even more telling, the novel's narrator points out that despite Leroy's sadistic teasing and threatening of Rhoda, he is attracted to her: "In a sense he was in love with the little girl, and . . . his persecution of her, his nagging concern with everything she did, was part of a perverse and frightened courtship."

Psychologists and sociologists who have studied the small numbers of children who kill have noted that girls are rarely killers, and that children who murder come from violent, chaotic, negligent families. A Rhoda Penmark would not be the product of heredity, but might fall into the category psychologist James Sorrell calls "nonempathic," a child who is "fiercely protective of people who satisfy her own narcissistic needs, but otherwise oblivious to other people." In the hands of a writer like Nabokov, Rhoda Penmark would be a kind of Lolita: these undercurrents and images of powerful, merciless females and weak, lustful men make *The Bad Seed* more than a thriller. Read on this level, *The Bad Seed* can still send shivers up the spine. On another level, William March's mask concealed a man who felt that in his creative and sexual desires he himself was a bad seed. Contemporary readers may sense that the tale of Rhoda Penmark is more complex than it first appeared.

# the bad seed

# one

LATER THAT SUMMER, when Mrs. Penmark looked back and remembered, when she was caught up in despair so deep that she knew there was no way out, no solution whatever for the circumstances that encompassed her, it seemed to her that June seventh, the day of the Fern Grammar School picnic, was the day of her last happiness, for never since then had she known contentment or felt peace.

The picnic was an annual, traditional affair held on the beach and among the oaks of Benedict, the old Fern summer place at Pelican Bay. It was here that the impeccable Fern sisters had been born and had lived through their languid, eventless summers. They had refused to sell the old place, and had kept it up faithfully as a gesture of love even when necessity made them turn their town house into a school for the children of their friends. The picnic was always held on the first Saturday of June since the eldest of the three sisters, Miss Octavia, was convinced, despite the occasions on which it had rained that particular day, and the picnic had to be held inside after all, that the first Saturday of June was invariably a fine one.

"When I was a little girl, as young as many of you are today," she would say each season to her pupils, "we always planned a picnic at Benedict for the first Saturday of June. All our relatives and friends came—some of whom we'd not seen for months. It was a sort of reunion, really, with laughter and surprises and gentle, excited voices everywhere. Everyone had a happy, beautiful day. There was no dissension in those days; a quarrel was unknown in the society of the well-bred, a cross word never exchanged between ladies and gentlemen. My sisters and I remember those days with love and great longing."

At this point Miss Burgess Fern, the middle sister, the practical one who handled the business affairs of the school, said, "It was so much easier in those days, with a houseful of servants and everybody helpful and anxious to please. Mother and some of the servants would drive down to Benedict a few days in advance of the picnic, sometimes as early as the first of June, when the season was officially open, although the established residents of the coast didn't consider the season really in swing until the day of our picnic."

"Benedict is such a beautiful spot," said Miss Claudia Fern. "Little Lost River bounds our property on the Gulf side, and flows into the bay there." Miss Claudia taught art in the school, and automatically she added, "The landscape at that point reminds one so much of those charming river scenes by Bombois." Then, feeling that some of her pupils might not know who Bombois was, she went on. "For the sake of some of the younger groups, Bombois is a modern French primitive. Oh, he is so *cunning* in his artlessness! So right in his composition, and in the handling of green! You'll learn much about Bombois later on."

It was from the Fern town house, the school itself, that the picnickers were to begin their long day of pleasure; and the parents of each pupil had been asked to have their particular child on the school lawn not later than eight o'clock, when the chartered busses were scheduled to leave. Thus it was that Mrs. Christine Penmark, who disliked being late or keeping others waiting, set her clock for six, which, she felt, would allow time for her ordinary tasks of the morning and for the remembrance of those last-minute, hurried things which are so easily overlooked.

She had impressed the hour on her mind, saying to herself as she fell asleep, "You will awake precisely at six o'clock, even if something happens to the alarm"; but the alarm went off promptly, and, yawning a little, she sat up in bed. It was, she saw instantly, to be a beautiful day—the day Miss Octavia had promised. She pushed back her blond, almost flaxen, hair and went at once to the bathroom, staring at herself in the mirror for a long moment, her toothbrush held languidly in her hand, as though she were not quite decided what to do with it. Her eyes were gray, wide-set, and serene; her skin tanned and firm. She drew back her lips in that first tentative, trial smile of the day; and standing thus in front of her mirror, she listened absently to the sounds outside her window: an automobile starting in the distance, the twittering of sparrows in the live oaks that lined the quiet street, the sound of a child's voice raised suddenly and then hushed. Then, coming awake quickly, in possession once more of her usual energy, she bathed and dressed and went to her kitchen to begin breakfast.

Later she went to her daughter's room to waken her. The room was empty, and it was so tidy that it gave the impression of not having been used for a long time. The bed was neatly remade, the dressing-table immaculate, with each object in its accustomed place, turned at its usual angle. On a table near the window was one of the jigsaw puzzles that her daughter delighted in, a puzzle only half completed. Mrs. Penmark smiled to herself and went into the child's bathroom. The bathroom was as orderly as the bedroom had been, with the bath towel spread out precisely to dry; and Christine, seeing these things, laughed softly, thinking: *I never deserved such a capable child. When I was eight years old, I doubt if I could do anything.* She went into the wide, elaborate hall with its elegant, old-fashioned parquetry

floors of contrasting woods, and called gaily, "Rhoda! Rhoda! . . .
Where are you, darling? Are you up and dressed so soon?"

The child answered in her slow, cautious voice, as though the
speaking of words were a perilous thing to be debated. "Here I
am," she said. "Here, in the living-room."

When speaking of her daughter, the adjectives that others
most often used were "quaint," or "modest," or "old-fashioned";
and Mrs. Penmark, standing in the doorway, smiled in agreement and wondered from what source the child had inherited
her repose, her neatness, her cool self-sufficiency. She said, coming into the room, "Were you really able to comb and plait your
hair without my helping you?"

The child half turned, so that her mother could inspect her
hair, which was straight, finespun, and of a dark, dull brown: her
hair was plaited precisely in two narrow braids which were
looped back into two thin hangman-nooses, and were secured,
in turn, with two small bows of ribbon. Mrs. Penmark examined
the bows, but seeing they were compact and firmly tied, she
brushed her lips over the child's brown bangs, and said, "Breakfast will be ready in a moment. I think you'd better eat a good
breakfast today as there's nothing more uncertain about a picnic
than the arrival of lunch."

Rhoda sat down at the table, her face fixed in an expression of
solemn innocence; then she smiled at some secret thought of her
own, and at once there was a shallow dimple in her left cheek. She
lowered her chin and raised it thoughtfully; she smiled again, but
very softly, an odd, hesitant smile that parted her lips this time
and showed the small, natural gap between her front teeth.

"I adore that little gap between dear Rhoda's teeth," Mrs.
Monica Breedlove, who lived on the floor above, had said only
the day before. "You know, Rhoda's such an *outmoded* little girl

with her bangs and pigtails and that single dimple. She reminds me of the way children looked when my grandmother was young. Now there was a colored print in my grandmother's house that I've always remembered; it was a little girl skating— oh, such an immaculate, self-possessed little girl with flowing hair, striped stockings, laced boots, and a fur toque that matched a little fur muff. She was smiling as she skated, and there was a darling gap between her teeth, too. The more I think of it, the more that child reminds me of Rhoda."

She had stopped talking suddenly, wondering if her affection for the little Penmark girl had somehow been determined by her reaction so many years ago to her grandmother's skating print, for Mrs. Breedlove denied the existence of the meaningless thought; everything said, she maintained, no matter how casually, was related, was tied together, was part of a logical and quite comprehensible pattern if others could find the clues or glimpse the design. She came to the conclusion that her admiration of the colored print was the genesis of her admiration for the child. There was no doubt about it! . . . None at all! . . . Then she remembered that her brother Emory, with whom she lived, loved the little girl quite as much as she did. Now, Emory's affection was *certainly* not the associative end result of an old lithograph, for he was nine years younger than herself, and there was no reason whatever to assume that he'd even *seen* the old skating print. In fact, her grandmother had died, and her effects had been scattered, two years before Emory was born. . . . So it was very doubtful that—In other words, there was no reason to suppose—She waited, wondering if her system of associative wisdom were as effective as she had believed, her brows puckered in perturbation.

She had said these things, and had thought these thoughts the morning before, while returning leisurely with Mrs. Penmark and her daughter from the closing exercises of the Fern School. There had been the customary recitations with the customary lapses of memory and the usual flow of tears; the fumbling application of parental handkerchiefs; the traditional caresses and words of comfort. Miss Burgess Fern (the middle one) had made her expected speech on honor and the need for fair play; there was the harp solo by Miss Fern herself, who had once studied in Rome.

When these preliminaries were done with and the chorus of children had sung the school song, the prizes for the different excellencies displayed were awarded. At the very end, the most important prize of all, in the minds of the pupils, was given: the gold medal awarded annually to the child who showed the greatest improvement in penmanship during the school year. ("The hallmark of the lady or gentleman is the quality of his penmanship," Miss Octavia Fern so often said. "The clarity, elegance, and refinement of one's penmanship establishes the true character and background of the individual when all other tests are inconclusive.")

Rhoda had wanted the penmanship medal from the first, and from the first she had thought she would win it. She had practiced faithfully, the tip of her tongue protruding between her teeth, the pen clutched in her determined hand; but as it happened, the beautiful medal had gone not to herself but to a thin, timid little boy named Claude Daigle, who was in her class and who was her age.

When the exercises were over, and the pupils and their parents were strolling under the live oaks of the Fern lawn, Miss Claudia came up, rested her hand on Rhoda's shoulder, and said, "You mustn't feel badly about not winning the medal, although I know how important these things are at your age. It was a very close race this year." Then, turning to Mrs. Breedlove, she added, "Rhoda worked so hard; she labored so diligently to improve her penmanship. We all knew how badly she wanted the medal, and I, for one, was sure she'd win it. But our judges, who are entirely impartial, who don't even know the identity of the children whose work they inspect, decided that the little Daigle boy, while not writing the clear neat hand that Rhoda used, did show the greatest *improvement* for the term, and improvement is what the medal is given for, after all."

Remembering these things of the day before, knowing how disappointed the child was, the reason for her quietness now, Christine said gaily, "You must have a perfectly wonderful day! When you're as old as I am, and perhaps have a little girl of your own who goes on school picnics, you can look back on today and remember it with pleasure."

Rhoda sipped her orange juice, turning her mother's words over in her mind; then, with no emotion in her voice, as though repeating a thing which did not really concern her, she said, "I don't see why Claude Daigle got the medal. It was mine. Everybody knew it was mine."

Christine touched the child's cheek with her finger. "These things happen to us all the time," she said; "and when they do, we simply accept them. If I were you, I'd forget the whole thing." She drew the child's head toward her, and Rhoda submitted to the caress with that tolerant but withdrawn patience of the pet that can never be quite domesticated; then, smoothing down her bangs, she impatiently pulled away from her mother. But feeling, perhaps, that she had been inconsiderate or unwise, she smiled her quick, placating smile, her pink, pointed tongue darting toward her glass.

Christine laughed softly and said, "I know you don't like to have people paw at you. I'm sorry."

"It was mine," said Rhoda stubbornly. "The medal was mine." Her round, light-brown eyes were stretched and unyielding. "It was mine," she said. "The medal was mine."

Christine sighed and went into the living-room; and kneeling on the window seat, she hooked back the heavy, old-fashioned shutters, allowing the soft morning sunlight to flood the room. It was almost seven o'clock, and the street was rapidly waking up. Old Mr. Middleton came onto his front porch, yawned, scratched his stomach, and, stooping cautiously, picked up the morning paper; the cooks for the Truby and the Kunkel families, approaching from opposite directions, nodded, raised their hands in greeting, and disappeared, almost at the same instant, around the corners of their respective houses; a half-grown girl, with legs as shapeless and almost as thin as the lines in a child's drawing of a girl, pulled her scarf more tightly about her head and ran for her bus with a clumsy, loping motion, her ankles turning inward a little like the ankles of an inexperienced skater. . . .

Mrs. Penmark, seeing these familiar things, turned back to her living-room and began to straighten it up. When her husband's work had brought them to this particular town, they had looked forward to a house of their own, having spent their entire married life in apartments; but not having at once found what they wanted, they had taken another apartment after all, deciding vaguely to build later on.

The apartment house itself consisted of three floors of ponderous Victorian elegance. It was of red brick, and its turrets, oriel windows, spires, and ornamental spouts balanced and matched one another in a sort of impressive architectural mad-ness. It was set on a little natural hillock, well back from the street, and it was banked with shrubs and flanked by a well-tended lawn. When the house was planned, the lot at the back had been bought as a playground for the children who might some day live in the apartment itself, and it had been turned into a sort of private park enclosed by a high brick wall. It was the playground rather than the big, inefficient apartment which had attracted the Penmarks to the place.

The bell rang at that moment, and Christine went to answer it. It was Mrs. Monica Breedlove from the floor above, and she called out gaily, "I wanted to make sure that you hadn't overslept on such an important morning. I thought my brother Emory was coming along, too, but he's still fast asleep. No power in the world can get him up before eight o'clock, but he did open his eyes long enough to tell me that his car is parked in front of the building, and to suggest we use it this morning. So I'm going to drive you and Rhoda to the Fern School, if you haven't any objections. Anyway, it'll save you the trouble of getting your car out of the garage." Then, turning to the child, and tossing her head a little, she added, "I have two gifts for you, my darling. The first is from Emory. It's a pair of dark glasses with rhinestone decorations, and he says tell you that it's intended to keep the sun out of those pretty brown eyes."

The child moved quickly toward Mrs. Breedlove, with the expression on her face which Christine had come to think of as "Rhoda's acquisitive look." She stood obediently while Mrs. Breedlove adjusted the glasses, then turning, she examined herself in the mirror. Monica stood back, clasped her hands together, and cried out in an enraptured voice, "Now, who *is* this glamorous Hollywood actress? Can it really be little Rhoda Penmark who lives with her delightful parents on the first floor of my apartment house? Is it possible that this lovely, sophisticated creature is the little Rhoda Penmark that everybody loves and admires so greatly?"

She paused for effect, and then, continuing in a lower key, she went on. "And now for the second prize, which is from *me*." She took from her purse a gold heart with a finely wrought chain attached to it. She explained that the locket had been given her when she, too, was eight; and it had waited all these years in her jewelry case just for this occasion. The locket had been a birthday present originally, and in one side of the heart there was set a garnet, which was her birthstone, since she'd been born in January. At the first opportunity, she meant to take the locket to the jeweler and have the garnet taken out and a turquoise, which was Rhoda's own birthstone, put in instead. She planned, too, to have the locket cleaned and the little chain fixed; the clasp didn't seem to be as firm as it should be, which was hardly surprising when you considered that she, Mrs. Breedlove, had had the locket for more than fifty years.

"Can I have both stones?" asked Rhoda. "Can I have the little garnet, too?"

Christine smiled, shook her head disapprovingly, and said, "Rhoda! Rhoda! How can you say such a thing?"

But Mrs. Breedlove went into peals of pleased, hysterical laughter. "But of *course* you may! Why, *certainly* my dearest!" She seated herself, and went on. "How wonderful it is to meet such a *natural* little girl. Why, when I was given that same locket by my Uncle Thomas Lightfoot, I just stood tongue-tied in the parlor and twisted my plaid dress, a quivering little mass of anxiety and frustration."

The child went to her, put her arms around her neck, and kissed her with an intensity that seemed to engage all her consciousness. She laughed softly and rubbed her cheek against the cheek of the entranced woman. "Aunt Monica," she said in a sweet, shy voice, drawing the name out slowly, as though her mind could not bear to relinquish it. "Oh, Aunt *Monica*."

Christine turned and went into the dining-room. She thought, half-amused, half-concerned: *What an actress Rhoda is. She knows exactly how to handle people when it's to her advantage to do so.*

When she returned to the living-room, Mrs. Breedlove was inspecting the child's dress. "You look like you're going to a fashionable afternoon tea, not to a picnic at the beach," she said gaily. "I know I'm behind the times, but I thought children wore coveralls and playsuits to picnics. But you, my love, look like a princess in that red-and-white dotted-Swiss dress you're wearing. Now, tell me, aren't you afraid you'll get it dirty? Aren't you afraid you'll fall down and scuff those new shoes?"

"She won't soil the dress, and she won't scuff the shoes," said Christine. She waited a moment, as though debating with herself, and then added, "Rhoda never gets anything dirty, although I don't know how she manages it." Then, seeing the question in Mrs. Breedlove's eyes, she said, "I wanted her to dress like the other children, but she felt so strongly about it that—well, if she wanted to wear one of her best dresses, I didn't see any real objection."

"I don't like coveralls," said Rhoda in an earnest, hesitant voice. "They're not—" She waited, as though unwilling to finish her sentence, and Mrs. Breedlove laughed with pleasure, and said, "You mean coveralls aren't quite *ladylike*, don't you, my darling?" She embraced the tolerant child once more, and said in a delighted voice, "Oh, my old-fashioned little darling! Oh, my absolutely quaint little darling!"

Presently, when the preparation for departure was completed, Rhoda went to her bedroom to put her locket away for safekeeping, and as she stepped off the rug, her shoes made a sharp, staccato sound on the hardwood floor. "You sound like Mr. Fred Astaire tap-tapping up and down stairs," said Mrs. Breedlove. "What have you got on your shoes? Is this something entirely new? Is this something I haven't heard about?"

Rhoda returned, put one hand on Monica's shoulder for support, and stood obediently while Mrs. Breedlove lifted each of her feet and examined the new shoes. They were heavier than average, designed for the play of childhood, with thick leather heels which had been reinforced with metal cleats in the shape of half-moons. In explanation, Rhoda said, "I run over my heels all the time, so Mother had those iron pieces put on this pair so they'd last longer. Don't you think it was a good idea?"

"It was Rhoda's suggestion, not mine," said Christine. "I can't take any credit, I'm afraid. You know how vague and impractical I am most of the time. It would never have occurred to me at all. It was Rhoda's idea entirely."

"I think they're nice," said Rhoda solemnly. "They save money."

"Oh, my penurious little sweetheart," said Monica in delight. "Oh, my thrifty little housewife." She embraced the child exuberantly, and added, "What are we going to *do* with her, Christine? Tell me, what are we going to do with this remarkable little creature?"

Later, when they came out of the apartment house, they paused on the marble steps that led to the foyer, for Leroy Jessup, the janitor, was hosing down the walk that ran from the house to the street beyond. He worked with that aggrieved persistence, as though calling on heaven to witness the injustice done him, which the sullen everywhere bring to their trivial tasks; and as he worked, his lips moved in unison with his hands to shape his petulant thoughts for his pleasure, for his mind rehearsed eternally the inequities that had been forced upon him—inequities which he must endure in silence, since he was one of the underprivileged ones of the world, the unfortunate son of an unfortunate sharecropper, the pathetic victim of an oppressive system, as everyone who knew anything at all admitted, and had admitted for a long time.

He was conscious that the two women and the little girl had stopped on the steps, but he pretended that he did not see them, and he did not lift his hose from the flooded flagstone so that they could pass; instead, he turned toward the street, and with eyes carefully averted, he guided the stream of water so far up the flagstones that the group had to move quickly onto the porch once more. He covered his mouth with one hand to hide his amusement at their consternation.

Mrs. Breedlove said patiently, "Leroy, will you kindly move that hose? We're going to my brother's car. We're late as it is."

He pretended that he did not hear her; he wanted to prolong the scene to its limit, but Monica, losing patience with him, called out, "Leroy! Have you completely lost your senses this time?"

He stared insolently at her, as though undecided what his next move should be; then, regretfully, he shifted the hose so that the water fell on the lawn. "I got work to do," he mumbled. "But I guess you don't know nothing about that, now, do you? I haven't got no time to go bus-riding and picnicking. I got plenty work to do."

He stood, hand on hip, thinking how unjustly others used him. He didn't live in no big apartment house with servants to wait on him hand and foot; and he didn't have no nice automobile to ride around in; he didn't have nothing to ride in but an old broke-down wreck that you couldn't even give to the junk man. He didn't have no fine clothes to wear, neither; and when he was little, he didn't go to no private school that cost a pile of money and was always giving picnics and frolics for its worthless pupils. No, sir! He'd walked to school himself! In all sorts of weather, too; and mostly without no shoes on his feet. But at that he was a lot smarter than most of those dumbbells that had all the advantages in the world; he could make monkeys out of them dumbbells any time he wanted to. . . .

He felt infinitely sorry for himself. No, sir! He didn't have nothing now, and he didn't have nothing when he was a boy about Rhoda's age. The world was in a plot to cheat him out of what was rightfully his, he thought. He watched as the women and the little girl picked their way across the dripping flagstones; but when they had reached the sidewalk, he wheeled abruptly so that the hose lifted, and water splashed over the feet of the people he so deeply despised.

Mrs. Breedlove's hand, which had been on the door of the car, dropped with a dramatic suddenness. She closed her eyes, her face and neck turning a deep coral-pink as she counted calmly to ten; then, in her well-bred voice she diagnosed Leroy's emotional condition in a detailed manner: in the past, she had thought of him as emotionally immature, obsessed, torn by irrational rages and, in a sense, a bit on the constitutional psychopathic side; but now, after the demonstration she'd just witnessed, she wondered if her diagnosis hadn't been too mild; she thought now that he was definitely a schizophrenic with well-defined paranoid overtones. And another thing: she'd had quite enough of his discourtesy and surliness—a feeling that the other tenants in the building enthusiastically shared. He might not know it, but it was due to her intervention that he now had a job: the other tenants, including her brother Emory, who was hardly a man to take liberties with, had been in favor of demanding his discharge, but she had pleaded for him, not because she condoned his actions, but because she considered him disturbed and hardly responsible for some of his irrational acts.

Christine touched Mrs. Breedlove's sleeve with a mild, placating gesture. "He didn't mean to wet us," she said. "It was an accident. I'm sure it was."

"He meant it," said Rhoda. "I know Leroy well."

Mrs. Breedlove shook her shoulders in indignation. "It was no accident, dear Christine! I assure you, it was no accident." But already her anger was subsiding and, extending her hands tolerantly, she added, "It was deliberately done—the spiteful act of a neurotic child."

"He meant to do it," said Rhoda. Her voice was cold and thoughtful, and she stared at Leroy with her round, calculating eyes as though she could see into his quivering mind. Then, speaking directly to the man, she added, "You made up your mind to do it when we were standing on the steps. I was looking at you when you made up your mind to wet us."

Then Leroy, knowing that he had gone too far this time, that his contempt and his fantasies of injustice had betrayed him into an action which his intelligence had not entirely sanctioned, became very humble and apologetic. He dropped to his knees on the wet pavement, and, bending down, he took out his handkerchief; and, as a token of his humility and surrender, he passed it over the shoes of Mrs. Breedlove and her guests.

Mrs. Penmark pulled back quickly, as though embarrassed, and said, "Oh, please! Oh, no—please!"

Monica opened the door of her car. Her anger was gone now, and, already ashamed of her outburst, she sighed ruefully and said, "Oh, very well! Very well! But my patience has a limit, and you may as well realize it."

Leroy crumpled the handkerchief he had used and threw it into the street. He stood erect, feeling a sense of power returning, a knowledge that he could handle this situation or any other that arose. . . . That good-looking Mrs. Penmark, that dizzy blonde, didn't know what it was all about. She was too dumb, when you came right down to it, to understand his contempt for her. She was one of them soft, easy-taken-in ones that went around feeling sorry for people. She was one of the ones that was eat up with kindness. You could do that one a dirty trick, but instead of hitting back, or hating the hell out of you, she'd feel guilty, instead, thinking she must be the one that was wrong. He spat on the lawn, insolent and sure of himself once more.

Now, that Breedlove dame, that big-talking bitch, was something else again. She'd feel in the wrong, too, but for another reason. She thought she was so smart; she thought she knew everything there was to know; she thought there wasn't nobody as tricky as she was. She'd feel guilty, all right—not because she was humble, but because she was so stuck on herself. She didn't expect other people to come up to her standards; it wasn't fair to expect ordinary people to be as delicate and fine and smart as she was. She'd feel bad, all right, when she thought things over, and to ease her conscience, she'd send her maid down with a ten-dollar bill to pay him off for the things he'd done to her. That one was really something!

He picked up the hose again. The triumph would be his in the end this time, just as it had always been in the past, with these dumbbells. Just wait and see, that was all. Just wait. . . . And then

Rhoda said, "You did it on purpose. I know the way you are. You knew you were going to do it all the time."

There was no resentment in the child's face; there was not even disapproval; there was only a stubborn appraisal of his character that startled him. He knew then that the little girl understood him entirely; that nothing he could say or do, that none of the acts which misled others, and got him his way with them, would affect her at all. He turned away in confusion before the cold knowledge in her eyes, as though his weapons had failed him where she was concerned; and as the automobile pulled away from the curb and turned the corner, with the morning sunlight flashing for an instant on Mrs. Breedlove's extended, bejeweled hand, he said under his breath, not of Mrs. Breedlove, but of the child, "That bitch! That nasty little bitch! There's nothing I wouldn't put past her. That one would put a knife between your ribs and watch the blood spurt."

Rhoda said softly, "Sometimes when Leroy is feeling mean, he says he's lost the key to the park gate, and won't open it so the children can come in and play. He wants to make people wait and beg him to open it for them. Leroy is a very mean man, I think."

Mrs. Breedlove's usual good humor was now completely restored, and she said, "I simply adore little Rhoda's twang." She touched the child's earlobe in affection. "It's such a wonderful twang. It's such a fascinating twang, my darling. Won't you teach it to me sometime?"

Christine laughed softly, and, touching her child's hand, she said, "With my shocking Midwestern twang, and Kenneth's New England one, the poor child didn't have a chance, really."

Leroy unscrewed the hose from its faucet and prepared to put it away in the basement, thinking: *Nobody can put nothing over on*

*Rhoda, I'll say that much for her. And nobody can put nothing over on
me, neither. I guess Rhoda and me are just alike.*

But in this he was mistaken, as we shall see in time, for Rhoda
was able to put into action the things that he could only turn
over in his mind as fantasies.

# two

MRS. PENMARK HAD ENTERED her daughter in the Fern
School the previous August; and Miss Burgess Fern, who handled enrollments, said shrewdly, "You must not get the impression that ours is a so-called 'progressive' school. We teach the
niceties, even some of the elegancies, of fastidious living; but we
give our pupils a solid groundwork in practical matters, too. We
teach our children to spell accurately, to read with fluency and,
where possible, with some expression, as well. We teach arithmetic in the way arithmetic should be taught—from a book and
from a blackboard, not on a sandpile in the garden with shells
and flower petals for counters."

"Yes, I know," said Christine. "My husband and I talked with
one of our neighbors at the Florabelle Apartments, a Mrs.
Breedlove, and from what she's told us, we feel your school is
ideal for a child of Rhoda's temperament." Miss Claudia Fern entered at that moment, and went to one of the filing-cabinets, as
Mrs. Penmark continued in an uncertain voice, "You know Mrs.
Breedlove, of course?"

The sisters looked quickly at each other, as though surprised
anyone could ask such a question. "*Monica* Breedlove?" asked

Miss Burgess Fern in astonishment. "Why, everybody in town knows Monica. She's one of our most active citizens. She won the Civic Association award a couple of winters ago as the most valuable citizen of the year."

Miss Octavia Fern came in and sat at her desk. She said, smiling gently, "I'm afraid I'm not familiar with the name Penmark. It's an unusual name, and I'm sure I'd remember it. Have you been here long?"

"No, not long at all. My husband is with the Callendar Steamship people, and we were transferred here from Baltimore only a week or so ago. We hardly know anyone so far." Miss Fern sighed, as though approaching an unwelcome task, and Christine, seeing the direction her mind was taking, said in a propitiating voice, "My husband's people are from New England. The name Penmark is better known there, I'm told."

"Ours is not an inexpensive school," said Miss Burgess Fern. "Our tuition is high, which is to accord with the standards we use in choosing our pupils. We reject far more than we select."

Miss Octavia said, "You will find neither false pride nor snobbery here. We are sympathetic with the problems of children, and we operate on a basis of complete nonprejudice; but we do not consider the best interests of a child are served through minimizing the standards of excellence his ancestors have established, a course of action fashionable in some quarters during the reign of the Roosevelts; and we do not believe it wise to play down what his forbears have accomplished, or to belittle what they have collected in the way of prestige, fame, or worldly possessions." She waited, and then said, "In other words, while we advocate the democratic ideal, we are convinced that such an ideal is possible only where all members of a particular group come from the same level of society, preferably a high one."

Mrs. Penmark turned these remarkable statements over in her mind, and said, "I think you'll find our family background acceptable." In a more careful voice she added that she herself had been born in the Midwest, and as a child had lived pretty much all over the country; she had taken a degree at the University of Minnesota, graduating the summer before Pearl Harbor. Her scholastic record had not been distinguished; she had got by reasonably well and that was about all. She hesitated, looked down at her hands, and then said, "My father, to whom I was devoted, was killed in a plane crash during the second world war. His name was Richard Bravo, and he was quite well known at one time as a columnist and war correspondent."

"Of course, of course!" said Miss Octavia. "I'm familiar with his work. He had imagination and a beautiful prose style." She turned to her sisters, they nodded in agreement, and she went on. "He was a man of depth and understanding. His death was a great loss."

"There's a book of his collected pieces in the library," said Miss Burgess; but Miss Octavia raised her hand, as though the matter were settled, as though Mrs. Penmark had now established beyond question the eligibility of her daughter, and said, "Our enrollment is limited, as you probably know; and already we have our quota for next term; but my sisters and I will surely find a place for the little granddaughter of Richard Bravo." Then, rising, she bowed and went out of the room.

Miss Claudia, the youngest of the sisters, found what she sought in the files, and said, "So Monica Breedlove is a neighbor of yours? . . . At one of the carnival balls—it was the year I came out—she stepped on my train, and pulled it off. I was so embarrassed! I went home and didn't dare come back!"

"Monica was the first woman in town to bob her hair," said

Miss Burgess. "And she was the first woman, at least the first respectable one, to smoke in public."

"When you see her," continued Miss Claudia, "tell her I think
she stepped on my train because Colonel Glass had danced with
me three times that evening, and hadn't danced with her once."

Christine nodded, and promised to do so; but she forgot until
the morning of the picnic, when, as she approached the school,
she saw Miss Claudia trailing a paper-filled burlap bag across the
lawn. She smiled, remembering, and after Mrs. Breedlove had
parked her car, and Rhoda had joined a group near the fig trees,
she repeated Miss Claudia's words. At once Mrs. Breedlove
laughed and said she remembered perfectly.

It had happened at the annual fancy-dress ball of the Pegasus
Society, and all she'd done, really, was put the toe of her dancing
slipper on poor, frowzy Claudia's train and exert just the tiniest
bit of pressure as Claudia giggled and walked away on the arm of
Colonel Glass; and, as she'd expected, the train detached itself
and pulled away, like something out of an old Marx Brothers
movie. The trouble was that the Fern girls, in those days at least,
were so hard up for ready cash that their wardrobe was a joint
one—a sort of grab-bag which each felt free to use when occasion demanded it. And so they were always arranging, and rearranging, the parts of their wardrobe in different patterns, in
different color contrasts, hoping to achieve somehow the illusion of freshness; but since everything was borrowed for the one
occasion only, nothing was sewed firmly together, as the clothes
of others were sewed; instead, everything was tied and pinned
and basted hurriedly, so that it all could be taken apart the next
day and used again.

Mrs. Breedlove laughed gaily and fanned herself for a moment in silence; then she went on to say that Claudia had been

quite correct in suspecting her motive. She'd done it on purpose, all right, but not because Claudia had danced three times with Colonel Glass—whom she remembered as a pompous and most tiresome man interested in fishing and the regenerative power of discipline impersonally applied—but because Claudia was making such a play for her brother, Emory, and she'd determined, no matter what else happened to the Wages family, there wasn't going to be a disarranged, cowlike Claudia Fern in it!

The two busses were drawn up to the curb, and already some of the children had taken their places. Mrs. Breedlove, looking about her, called to Rhoda, and when the child joined her, she said, "Where is the little Daigle boy, the one who won the penmanship medal? Has he arrived? I haven't seen him."

"There he is," said Rhoda. "Standing there at the gate."

The boy was pale and remarkably thin, with a long, wedge-shaped face, and a full, pink underlip that puckered with an inappropriate sensuousness. His mother stood possessively beside him—an intense woman with protruding eyes. She plucked anxiously at her passive son, adjusting his cap, smoothing his tie, fiddling with his socks, or dabbing at his face with a handkerchief. He was wearing the penmanship medal pinned to the pocket of his shirt, and his mother, as if knowing somehow that the medal was being discussed, put her arm nervously about his shoulders and lifted the medal in her palm as though it were she, and not her son, who had won it.

Mrs. Breedlove said to Rhoda in an amused, coaxing voice, "Don't you think it would be a lovely little gesture if you went over and offered your congratulations? If you told him that since you didn't win the medal, you're most happy that he did?" She took the child's hand, as if to guide her toward the gate, but Rhoda pulled back and said, "No! No!" She shook her head with determination, and added, "I'm not glad he won it. It was mine. The medal was mine, but he got it."

Mrs. Breedlove was startled at the cold intensity of the child's voice, but she laughed after a moment and said, "Oh, I wish my instincts were as natural as yours, my dear." She turned, as though for verification, to Christine, and said gaily, "A child's mind is so wonderfully innocent. So lacking in guile or deceit." But Mrs. Penmark had already moved away to speak to Miss Octavia Fern, who had nodded and beckoned to her.

They stood together beside the small side porch where the star jasmine bushes were, and Miss Octavia said, "My sisters and I are so disappointed that Mr. Penmark didn't come with you today. We've never met him, although we're anxious to do so, since we've heard so many pleasant things about him. Everyone says he's such a capable young man. Actually, we'd hoped to see him yesterday at the closing exercises, but I suppose he was too busy to get away."

Christine explained that, at this period of his career, her husband's work kept him away from home much of the time. Currently, he was in South America to make a survey of port facilities along the West Coast. He'd embarked only the week before; the only news she'd had of him thus far was the cable that announced his arrival. She missed him, of course; but she'd resigned herself to the inevitable fact that this time he'd be gone all summer. Had it been possible, he most certainly would have come to the closing exercises of the day before, as he, in turn, had heard much about the Misses Fern, and had often expressed a wish to know them personally.

They seated themselves in rockers on the porch, and after a time Miss Octavia, long used to the unasked questions of parents, said, "Are you interested in what we think of Rhoda, and of what she's accomplished since she's been with us?"

Mrs. Penmark said that she was, adding that the child, almost from babyhood, had been something of a riddle both to herself and her husband. It was a thing difficult to isolate, or identify, but there was a strangely mature quality in the child's character which they found disturbing. Both she and her husband had thought that a school like their own, a school whose accent fell on discipline and the old-fashioned virtues, would be the ideal school for Rhoda—would eliminate, or at least modify, some of the upsetting factors of her temperament.

Miss Fern nodded to a new arrival, pressed one hand against her forehead, as though marshaling her thoughts, and said that, in some ways, Rhoda was one of the most satisfactory pupils the school had ever had. She'd never been absent a single day; she'd never once been tardy; she was the only child in the history of the school who'd made a hundred in deportment, each month, in the classrooms, and a hundred in self-reliance and conservation, each month, on the playgrounds, for a full school year; and if Mrs. Penmark had dealt with as many children as Miss Fern had in her long career as a teacher, she'd realize what a remarkable record that was. She put on her tattered straw hat, and adjusted it over her eyes as protection against the strong morning sun which was now sifting itself insistently through the lifting leaves of the camphor tree. "Rhoda is a conservative, thrifty child," she went on, "and she's perhaps the *neatest* little girl I've ever encountered."

Christine laughed and said, "Rhoda is certainly neat. My husband says he doesn't know where she gets her tidiness—certainly not from either of us."

Miss Burgess Fern came up, sat in the chair beside her sister, and, after listening a moment, said, "I think the secret of Rhoda's temperament is the simple fact that she doesn't need others, the way most of us do. She is such a self-sufficient little girl! Never in all my life have I seen anybody so completely all-of-one-piece!"

Mrs. Penmark sighed, raised her hands with humorous exaggeration, and said, "Sometimes I wish she were more dependent on others. Sometimes I wish she were less practical and more affectionate."

Miss Octavia, from the depth of her experience with children, spoke gently. "You will not be able to change her. The child lives in her own particular world, and I'm sure it isn't anything at all like the world you and I live in."

Miss Burgess said, "The little girl, even at eight, seems able to stand alone, and that is certainly not common at any age." She got up, walked down the steps, but paused to add, "Rhoda has many qualities remarkable in a child. In the first place, her courage is most unusual. She seems almost without physical fear; she'll stand up calmly to things that frighten the average child and make them cry, or run away, and she's certainly no tattletale; that we've already found out. Last winter one of our boys threw a stone through Mrs. Nixon's window across the street, and—"

"You'd have thought the hydrogen bomb had been released on us, from the commotion Adelaide Nixon made," said Miss Octavia genially.

"*Anyway,*" continued Miss Burgess, "Rhoda saw the whole thing, and, of course, she knew who the guilty boy was. But when we questioned her, telling her it was her duty as an honorable little citizen to *report* the culprit, we got precisely nowhere. She just went on eating her apple, shaking her head, and looking us over with that calculating, almost contemptuous, look she has at certain times."

"Oh, I know! I know!" said Christine. "I've seen that look so many times!"

"We would never have found out the truth," said Miss Burgess, "if the little boy hadn't broken down in tears the next day and confessed his crime." At this point Miss Octavia, as head of the school, took up the story and said, "At first, my sisters and I thought Rhoda should be punished for willfulness and lack of cooperation; but we came to the conclusion that her attitude was really a demonstration of loyalty, and that she should not be given a demerit—which would have spoiled her perfect record—for refusing to be a little sneak."

Christine put her hand impulsively on Miss Octavia's forearm. "Is she popular?" she asked. "Do the others like her?"

But before Miss Octavia could reply, before she was faced with the choice of telling an untruth or admitting that the other pupils both feared and detested Rhoda, her sister Claudia, on watch at the sidewalk, called out that the last of the children had come, and had been checked off the roster. The busses were now ready to start, the picnic to begin, and Miss Fern and her sisters, their arms loaded with those last-minute things which somebody might, after all, find a use for, walked with Mrs. Penmark down the long, flag-paved path to the gate.

For a time there was milling about, laughter, and awkward movement; then, at length, the Fern sisters, their assistants, and their pupils, were all stowed safely away, and the first bus pulled out from the curb, the driver turning his head, listening, and turning his head again, with the quick movement of a suspicious bird. The lead bus had been parked in the driveway beneath the low-hanging limbs of the camphor tree, and as the driver moved his bus forward, it scraped the green branches of the tree, causing a rain of fluttering, aromatic leaves to fall to the pavement below.

At the first movement of the lead bus, at the first holiday note

of departure, two Airedales who had lain contentedly with muz-
zles resting on their outthrust paws, sprang up from the lawn of
the house across the street and barked hysterically, springing
into the air in frenzy, whirling, and running along the fence. The
cap of one little boy blew off and rolled into the street, and the
lead bus stopped while Monica Breedlove, flushed and laughing,
ran forward and restored the cap to its owner; a little girl in the
following bus dropped her slate—which for reasons of her own
she had thought appropriate to bring along on a picnic—out of
the window; and the driver of that bus, to the accompaniment of
shouts, catcalls, and piercing finger-whistles, stopped his bus,
went back, and retrieved it. In that interval, Mrs. Daigle rushed
to the bus side for a final clutch at her son. She caressed the
damp, unresisting hand he held out to her, and said, "Has your
headache gone? Have you got a clean handkerchief?"

The driver, returning with the slate, said with exaggerated
patience, "Watch it! Watch that window, lady!"

"You must not overexert yourself," said Mrs. Daigle in a tense,
anxious voice. "And keep out of the sun as much as you can."

Slowly the busses moved forward again, and people came to
their doors to smile and call out to the travelers; then the drivers
turned the corner, but cautiously, remembering Miss Octavia's
repeated admonitions, and the street was calm once more; the
picnic had begun in earnest. It was then that Rhoda moved from
her seat and took possession of one nearer the little Daigle boy.
Her eyes were fixed steadily on the penmanship medal, but she
did not speak at all; then a moment later, when she felt more sure
of herself, she stood in the aisle beside the boy, stretched out her
hand and touched the medal, but Claude pulled away petulantly
and said, "Why don't you go some place else? Why don't you
leave me alone?"

After the busses had disappeared, Mrs. Penmark moved in the direction of Mrs. Breedlove's automobile. She turned her head to look for her friend, and saw that Monica was, as usual, the center of a group of people—old acquaintances, plainly, whom she'd not seen in a long time; and, as usual, she was talking with animation, moving her hands and her shoulders, tossing her neck wildly for emphasis. When she saw this, Mrs. Penmark moved to the strip of lawn that was between the sidewalk and the street to wait until her friend had finished her story. Two men came up and stood under the crepe-myrtle tree behind her, both looking at their watches at the same instant.

"I was reading the other day," said the taller of the two, "that the age we live in is an age of anxiety. You know what? I thought that was pretty good—a pretty fair judgment. I told Ruth about it when I got home, and she said, 'You can say *that* again!'"

"Every age that people live in is an age of anxiety," said the other man. "If anybody asks me, I'd say the age we live in is an age of violence. It looks to me like violence is in everybody's mind these days. It looks like we're just going to keep on until there's nothing left to ruin. If you stop and think about it, it scares you."

"Well, maybe we live in an age of anxiety *and* violence."

"Now, that sounds more like it. Come to think about it, I guess that's what our age is really like."

They shook hands, made a date to meet for lunch the following week, and walked toward their beckoning wives, while Mrs. Penmark stood quietly, turning over in her mind the things she had heard. It seemed to her suddenly that violence was an inescapable factor of the heart, perhaps the most important factor of all—an ineradicable thing that lay, like a bad seed, behind kindness, behind compassion, behind the embrace of love itself.

Sometimes it lay deeply hidden, sometimes it lay close to the surface; but always it was there, ready to appear, under the right conditions, in all its irrational dreadfulness.

Mrs. Breedlove came up a little later and joined Christine on the grass, then, moving majestically toward her parked car, she said, "The incident of Claudia Fern's lost train is loaded with symbolism, so I'm not surprised she remembered it all these years, and spoke of it to you. When I was in analysis, Claudia's train kept coming up again and again; in fact, it became one of the key situations in my anxiety neurosis." She tossed her head, waved vaguely to passers-by, and went on. "My incestuous fixation on poor Emory is so obvious that it doesn't need elaboration; so I won't attempt any, incest being so *trite*. What was more interesting in the eyes of my analyst was that the detaching of the train revealed latent penis hostility and penis envy; and it showed, besides, my impulse to mar and castrate men and women both."

She talked with animation, nodding her head for emphasis; there was much she'd like to say, but she knew how circumspect one must be in discussing, even with the completest scientific detachment, even with those as objective and intelligent as Christine had proved herself to be, these emotionally charged matters—these primitive taboos of the half-civilized tribe—if one were not to be considered depraved, or, at best, a bit on the peculiar side; but just the same, there were many associations, many implications, some of them quite amusing, in the simple, seemingly innocent, rupture of poor Claudia's train. But she'd restrain herself; she'd button up her big lip and omit these other things, although they were plain enough, heaven knew, to the unbiased and perceptive listener. . . .

But Christine heard little that she said, for her mind was still concerned with the conversation she had listened to, still fixed on the theme of violence. Her father, whom she'd loved so deeply, had himself died through the uncaring violence of others, and, remembering again, she thought: *He was much too young; there should have been many years before him. If that had not happened, he might be alive today to comfort me as he did when I was a child, and frightened.* She remembered the last time she had seen him; it was a week before the plane that carried him was brought down by enemy fire somewhere in the South Pacific. She had gone alone to the airport with him, her mother being ill at the time, where he was to embark on the initial leg of what was to be his final journey, and while she was seeing about his luggage, an unnecessary task which she had always insisted on doing for him, he put his arms about her and held her cheek tightly against his own. It seemed to her now that he must have had some precognition of his own end, some knowledge that this was the journey from which he would never return, for he had kissed her and had said softly in her ear, "You are the bright thing in my life. You were the thing I loved more than all others. I want you to remember that, no matter what happens. I want you to remember that always. And never change from what you are at this moment."

Remembering now, Christine turned her head away, so that Monica's discerning eye could not detect her emotion, and said under her breath, "I remember, Father. I remember."

Mrs. Breedlove parked her car under the live oak, and, raising her eyes, she caught sight of Leroy polishing brass at the back of the house. She made a rueful gesture with her lips and said, "I'm sorry I made an issue about the hose, but Leroy can try the patience of a saint. I remind myself that he hasn't had our opportunities or advantages, and that I have no right to expect too much from him, but, of course, I go on losing my temper and forgetting my fine sentiments."

Hearing Mrs. Breedlove's voice, Leroy looked up and caught her eye. She nodded and waved gaily to him, to show that their misunderstanding was a thing of the past, that she no longer cherished hard feelings, nor bore him malice; that she had found it in herself to pardon his rude behavior. But Leroy was not to be placated so easily, now that victory so plainly was his. He did not return the greeting; he only stared at her, shrugged his shoulders, and disappeared around the side of the building, in the direction of the courtyard where the new garages, once the old carriage houses, were. He rested against the building and spat on the cement, his mouth twisting with the sourness of his discontent.

That know-it-all, that Monica Breedlove; that loud-mouthed bitch. She didn't think nobody knew anything, but her. Going around insulting people; going around looking down on people just as good as she was, and thinking she knew it all. Well, he'd show her a thing or two one of these days. He'd show that bitch *plenty*—and good. It wouldn't surprise him none if she turned out to be one of them lady-lovers you read about these days. . . . His mind flooded with the obscenities his lips shaped under his breath; then he walked away, his eyes darting from side to side, his hands making little slashing gestures against the air. He heard the door of Mrs. Breedlove's car close, and the two women coming up the walk, chatting together. He stood concealed behind the big japonica bush, peering at them through the leaves.

Now, that dizzy blonde—that trough-fed Christine Penmark—was something else again. He'd like to get her down in the basement some day. He'd let her have it, all right. He'd turn her every way but loose. He'd put it to her all the ways there were in the book, and he'd think up some extra ways besides.

He'd make her holler calf-rope. And when he got done with her, she'd follow him about like a begging bitch. He'd make her cry and beg him for it again, that's what. And sometimes he'd give it to her, and sometimes he wouldn't, depending on how he felt.

Mrs. Breedlove, her hand on the door, glanced at her watch and cried out, "Heaven and earth—it's eight-fifteen already!" She sped upstairs to get her brother out of bed, and off to work. Christine, once in her apartment, made herself a pot of coffee and brought it into the living-room, where she sipped it, and skimmed the morning paper; but her mind accepted little that she read, for her thoughts kept turning to her past.

She had met her husband in New York, the year she was twenty-four, at a time when she had come to the conclusion that she would never marry at all. She had been living with her mother on Gramercy Park that year. Her mother had been ill with a heart condition, and she had devoted herself to her as best she could. She was glad now that she had had this opportunity to return, even in so small a fashion, some of the things her mother had done for her; but her mother, although she knew she was dying, refused to become an invalid, or to make nagging demands upon others, and as a result, Christine had taken a job in an art gallery where the hours were not too long, and where her mother could get in touch with her quickly if she were needed.

That winter a Mrs. Bogardus, one of her mother's old friends, asked Christine to a dinner party she was giving for her nephew Kenneth Penmark, a young naval lieutenant, and she had accepted more to please her mother, who felt she was too serious, that she did not go out often enough, than for any other reason. She had liked the lieutenant at once, and for a little while, before they were overwhelmed by the boisterous wholesomeness of the other guests, they had sat before the fire and discussed the painters of the Paris School. She had left early, thinking she'd made no impression on him at all, but the next afternoon he came to the gallery and said, "I want to see the Modigliani drawing you were admiring so much last night." She showed it to him, and he said, "I'm thinking about getting it for the girl I'm going to marry. Do you suppose she'd like it?" Christine was positive the girl would like it; but if, incredibly, she did not, then she'd advise the lieutenant to waste no more time on a creature so dull. He bought the drawing and took it away with him.

That night before dinner he telephoned her at home. He was devoting the evening to Aunt Clara and family reminiscences, he said, so he wouldn't be able to see her, as he'd hoped; but at eleven he telephoned again to say he'd got his aunt to bed at last, and that the remainder of the evening was his own. He suggested that they go dancing somewhere. She came home tired and contented, knowing that Kenneth Penmark was the one man in the world for her. The next day was Sunday, and when he telephoned, she asked him to tea, to meet her mother; later they went to the Museum of Natural History, of all places.

On Monday he sent her mother roses and herself an orchid.

His leave was up on Tuesday, and that morning he came by the gallery to tell her good-by. He gave her the Modigliani, and said, "I hope you understand the implications, my lass!" Then, in front of all those people, he took her in his arms and kissed her, turned, and went calmly through the door. Her mother died that same winter; the following spring Lieutenant Penmark came to see her, and they were married. Hers had been a most successful marriage, she thought. If she had not married Kenneth, she would not have married at all.

She put away the paper, and went about cleaning her apartment. Already she missed her husband, and although she had become reconciled to these necessary absences, she had never become used to them; and standing quietly in her living-room she thought that all her life she had waited for someone—first her father, and now her husband.

This time, since the trip was to be a long one, they had considered the idea of her accompanying her husband; but regretfully they had abandoned the notion. They told each other it was merely a question of additional expense, that the money could be better used toward the house they planned to build later on. The true reason had been deeper and had been concerned with their daughter. They felt that they could not take the child with them, and they knew that leaving her with another, even another as tolerant and doting as Mrs. Breedlove, was out of the question.

There had always been something strange about the child, but they had ignored her oddities, hoping she would become more like other children in time, although this had not happened; then, when she was six and they were living in Baltimore, they entered her in a progressive school which was widely recommended; but a year later the principal of the school asked that the child be removed. Mrs. Penmark called for an explanation, and the principal, her eyes fixed steadily on the decorative, gold-and-silver sea horse her visitor wore on the lapel of her pale-gray coat, said abruptly, as though both tact and patience had long since been exhausted, that Rhoda was a cold, self-sufficient, difficult child who lived by rules of her own, and not by the rules of others. She was a fluent and a most convincing liar, as they'd soon discovered. In some ways, she was far more mature than average; in others, she was hardly developed at all. But these things had only slightly affected the school's decision; the real reason for the child's expulsion was the fact that she had turned out to be an ordinary, but quite accomplished, little thief.

Mrs. Penmark closed her eyes, and then said quietly, "Has it occurred to you that you could be wrong—that your judgment isn't necessarily infallible?"

The principal admitted that the thought of her fallibility had occurred to her not once, but many times. It bothered her, in fact, at this precise moment, but not in reference to the thefts, for there was no doubt on that point at all; they had set a trap for the thief and had caught Rhoda red-handed. Her reaction to the child's acts had not been one of condemnation, but one of sympathy. "We've had similar problems in the school before," she finished, "and so I took Rhoda at once to the school psychiatrist for his opinion."

Christine sighed, covered her face with her hands, and said in a weak voice, "What was his opinion? What did he suggest?"

The principal waited, and then went on to say that in many respects the psychiatrist considered Rhoda the most precocious child he'd ever seen, her quality of shrewd, mature calculation was remarkable indeed; she had none of the guilts and none of the anxieties of childhood; and of course she had no capacity of affection, either, being concerned only with herself. But perhaps the thing that was most remarkable about her was her unending acquisitiveness. She was like a charming little animal that can never be trained to fit into the conventional patterns of existence. . . .

At ten o'clock the postman came. There was a letter from her husband, and as Christine read the closely written pages, she said, "Oh, Kenneth! Oh, Kenneth!" in the soft, deprecating voice with which the pleased accept their flattery. Resolutely she dismissed from her mind the things that troubled her. She felt a wave of irrational happiness, for it seemed to her at that moment that she had everything a woman could desire. She seated herself at her desk to answer the letter, but first she rested her hands against her cheeks, and looked out at the soft, green street, holding on to her happiness, which was wise, for it was the last she was ever to feel.

# three

_ _ _·_ _·_ _·_ _

MRS. BREEDLOVE LIVED with her brother on the floor above the Penmarks. There had been a great event in her life, one which she had not been able to forget. In the middle twenties, her husband, not knowing what else to do with her, acceded to her wish that she go to Vienna and be psychoanalyzed by Professor Freud. The story of her analysis was one which she never tired of telling— one whose possibilities she never succeeded in exhausting. It seemed that after her intense initial session with the professor, he had said frankly that her particular temperament was beyond his skill, and had suggested that she go to London and seek the aid of his pupil Dr. Aaron Kettlebaum. This she had done.

"It was a fortunate suggestion," she often said; "not that I'm minimizing Doctor Freud's professional standing in any manner, shape, or form, for I still consider him, in spite of his peculiarities, the great genius of our time; but Doctor Kettlebaum was more—more _sympatico_, if you know what I mean. Freud was so committed to nineteenth-century materialism that it warped his viewpoint, it seemed to me. Then, too, he loathed American women, particularly the ones who were able to stand on their own feet and slug it out on equal terms with men. Now, Doctor Kettlebaum believed in the power of the individual soul, and he considered sex of only trivial interest. His mind was mystic rather than literal—the same as my own. He did much for me, and when he died several years ago, I cabled flowers and cried for a week."

She had returned to her husband three years later, and at once began proceedings for a divorce, an action which he made no effort to oppose. When she was free again, she decided it was her duty to make a home for her brother Emory, and she did so. She took pleasure in the analysis of his character, analyses that he endured mostly in silence. Of late, she had come to the conclusion, through a series of her own deductions, that Emory was, as she termed it, a "larvated homosexual"; and once during the preceding spring, at one of her big dinner parties, she seized on the new theme and discussed it so freely that the only unembarrassed person at the table was herself.

"What does 'larvated' mean?" asked Emory. "That's one I haven't heard so far."

"It means covered, as with a mask," said Mrs. Breedlove. "It means concealed."

"It means something that hasn't come to the surface as yet," said Kenneth Penmark.

"You can say *that* again!" said Emory, laughing weakly.

He was a plump, ruddy man, a few years younger than his sister. His hair had receded far back on his pink, domed forehead. His belly was small and hard; it had a taut, rounded quality, as though designed by nature as a background for the massive watch chain and emblem. Frank Billings, whom Monica always referred to as "Emory's canasta friend," said, "Well, where did you get that idea, Monica? What makes you think that?"

"My opinion," said Mrs. Breedlove, "is based on the evidence of pure association, and that's the best evidence of all." She sipped her wine, puffed her lips thoughtfully, and went on in an earnest voice. "To begin with, Emory is fifty-two years old, and he's never married. I doubt if he's ever had a serious love affair." Then, seeing that she was about to be interrupted by Reginald Tasker, "one of Emory's true-murder-mystery friends," she raised her hand and said, "Please! Please!" in a placating voice; and then went on quickly. "Now, let's look at things objectively. What are Emory's deepest interests in life; what are the things that occupy his psyche? They are fishing, murder mysteries that involve the dismemberment of faithful housewives, canasta, baseball games, and singing in male quartettes." She paused and then said, "And how does Emory spend his Sundays? He spends them on a boat with other men—fishing. And are there *ladies* present on such occasions? I can answer that question at once—there are not."

"You're damned right there aren't!" said Emory.

Mrs. Breedlove looked about her, and then realizing for the first time the effect she'd created among her guests, she tossed her head and said in a surprised voice, "I don't see why the idea shocks you so. A thing so commonplace as *that*! Actually, homosexuality is triter than *incest*! Doctor Kettlebaum considered it was all a matter of personal preference."

But it would be a mistake to think of this obsessed, garrulous old woman as a fool in most matters. She had taken the lump settlement that her husband had so cheerfully given her and invested it in real estate, following a system based both on sexual symbolism and the unalterable fact that if the town continued to grow, as everyone predicted, it had to go in the direction of her holdings. She had been successful from the first. She had written a successful cookbook; she was responsible for the city's psychiatric clinic; she was thought of as the tireless civic worker, the logical, efficient chairman of the charitable drive for funds.

On the day of the school picnic, Mrs. Breedlove telephoned Christine and asked her to lunch. One of Emory's fishing friends had sent him a beautiful, seven-pound redfish. Emory himself had just called to say that, since it was Saturday, he was closing the plant at noon and would be home for lunch. He'd asked her to fix redfish Gelpi, which she hadn't done in a long time, and she said she would. "Emory is inviting his friend Reggie Tasker, that true-crime writer you and Kenneth met last spring in our apartment, and he wants you to help entertain him. Now, why don't you come up early, say around noon, and I'll show you how to fix the redfish? It's in the sauce, mostly."

Later, Mrs. Breedlove decided to serve lunch not in her gloomy, paneled dining-room, but in the little alcove off her living-room where she kept her ferns and African violets; and when her brother and his guest arrived, the table was set there, and ready. The men were talking about a recent murder, one which was being featured in the local papers. Reginald Tasker, it appeared, was going to do it for one of his murder magazines, and was now gathering his preliminary facts. Mrs. Breedlove, hearing fragments of the talk, laughed, tossed her head, and said, "We're off to the races again!"

The case concerned a middle-aged hospital nurse, a Mrs. Dennison, who had been indicted for the murder, on May first, of her heavily insured two-year-old niece, Shirley. It was then the town remembered that another niece, a sister of the 1952 victim, had died in 1950, in the same manner, when she had been two years old as well. Nurse Dennison, a woman dedicated to the benefits of insurance, had collected five thousand dollars on the death of the first child; the second niece she had insured for six.

Mrs. Breedlove came into the living-room to welcome her visitor; Christine followed immediately and put a pitcher of Martinis on the coffee table; a moment later they went to the alcove for a final checkup of the luncheon table, and Reggie went on quickly to say that Nurse Dennison's husband, conventionally true to the family tradition of nausea, burning throat, and convulsions, had passed on in the autumn of 1951, with, of course, the conventional policies on his life.

Christine laughed a little, put her hands over her ears, and said so softly the men could not hear her, that she did not like to listen to such stories. Anything concerning crime, particularly murder, depressed her and made her anxious. She had seen the accounts of the Dennison case, but she could not bring herself to read them; she had merely turned the page, and had gone on to something more cheerful.

"You have a little psychic *block* there!" said Mrs. Breedlove in an intense, pleased whisper. "Now, if you'll associate to the situation, maybe we can get at the roots of your anxiety." She straightened her centerpiece, and when Christine did not answer at once, she went on earnestly. "Tell me the first thing that comes into your mind! Tell me, no matter how silly it seems to you!"

Reginald Tasker went on to say that in the forenoon of May first of that year, Nurse Dennison had visited her sister-in-law's family. She got there in time for lunch. At once she picked up her niece Shirley and began playing with the child. She had meant to bring Shirley a present, she said, but had forgotten, a thing which distressed her so greatly that she went to the country store near by and bought candy and soda pop for the family.

"Nothing comes into my mind," said Christine. "It's entirely blank."

"Actually, Nurse Dennison *had* brought her niece a present," said Reginald Tasker. "It was the ten cents' worth of arsenic she'd bought on her way to her sister-in-law's home. In a way it was more a present for herself than for her niece, since she stood to benefit so greatly if she succeeded in administering it."

"But what's on your mind at this moment?" insisted Mrs. Breedlove. They returned to the kitchen, and as Mrs. Breedlove agitated the salad in her big wooden bowl, Christine said presently, "I was thinking how much the Fern sisters are impressed by my father's reputation. Miss Burgess thinks I look very much like him, although she never saw him in person, and is familiar only with his photographs."

Mrs. Breedlove said in an uncertain voice, "That's an unusual association, I must say. I don't understand it so far." She narrowed her eyes, pursed her lips, and listened absently to the conversation in the living-room. According to Reggie Tasker's notes, Nurse Dennison returned with her treat and immediately prepared a drink of orange pop for her niece Shirley. For the next hour or so she observed the child's convulsions with a most flattering concern; later on, perhaps because the child's stamina seemed about to triumph over her aunt's intention, Nurse Dennison said that, in her opinion, what little Shirley needed at this point in her illness was another sip or two of orange pop; it was sure to settle her stomach and return her to her customary bouncing health. She tendered the cup, and Shirley, a sweet, obedient child, drank at her aunt's bidding.

"Now, what's your *second* association?" insisted Mrs. Breedlove. "Maybe your second association will be clearer."

"It's even sillier," said Christine. For a moment she turned her past over in her mind, then impulsively she said, "I've always had a feeling I was an adopted child, that the Bravos weren't my real parents. I asked my mother about it once—it was in Chicago, the year I finished high school—but she kept saying, 'Who have you been talking to? Who's been putting such ideas in your head?' The thing upset her so much that I never mentioned it again."

"Oh, you poor, innocent darling!" said Monica. "Don't you

know that the changeling fantasy is one of the commonest of childhood? I once believed I was a foundling with royal blood—Plantagenet, I think it was. I don't know how I managed to get on my parents' doorstep, but I had it worked out well enough when I was five years old. The myths and folklore of all people simply teem with such fantasies."

Her laughter died suddenly. In the silence, Reginald Tasker's voice came through once more. After the child had accepted her second dose of arsenic, and it was plain she could not rally again, Nurse Dennison announced that she must hurry back to town in order to take care of a matter of her own. This errand, as it turned out, was a trip to the agent from whom she'd bought the smaller of the two policies she carried on the life of her niece; she'd failed to pay the current premium, and this particular day was her last day of grace. She paid the premium in time, and ate her supper in the knowledge that a good piece of business had been accomplished that day. She was certain the child could not last until midnight, and in this she was correct, for the little girl died about eight, making both policies operative.

Mrs. Breedlove who had been listening, nodding her head from time to time, said that, in her opinion, Reginald Tasker wasn't at all bad in his specialty. It was true that she ranked him miles below an inspired psychiatrist like Dr. Wertham. She did not even consider him on a par with men like Bolitho and Roughead; but there was a quality of compassionate irony in his best work that distinguished him and made him stand out in his field; then, their preparations for lunch completed, Mrs. Breedlove and Christine joined the men in the living-room. They each took a cocktail, and Monica, her competent ankles crossed firmly, said, "Can't you two find something else to talk about?"

"When she says 'something else' she means sex," said Emory.

He turned to Christine as though seeking support, but she only smiled and lowered her eyes, her thoughts turning once more to the past. There were unfocused, shapeless things which had troubled her childhood, even when she had been happiest; there was the half-memory of some dreadful event which she had never understood, even at the time of its occurrence, but these things were so formless and far away that they existed in her mind less as certainty than as a feeling of unreasoning dread. She sighed, pressed back her hair, and thought: *I think I once lived on a farm somewhere, and that I had brothers and sisters I played with.*

Monica thrust her jaw forward, and then in a quick, spasmodic movement, she jerked her head to the left, as though there were a pebble balanced on her chin, and she strove to toss it over her shoulder. "My tic is annoying today," she said. "I don't know why, I'm sure." She lit a cigarette and then went on. "I talked to Doctor Kettlebaum about my tic, and how to overcome it; but he looked at me in surprise, and said, 'But, dear lady, it's such a young, such an intriguing gesture. Why not leave it the way it is?'"

"That Kettlebaum must have been quite a boy," said Emory.

Monica agreed placidly. Dr. Kettlebaum had been a wise and a most useful man, she said, her brown eyes swimming with light. Certainly he would have instantly understood both her brother's and Reginald's attempts to transform their unconscious violence into something more acceptable to society: the odd thing was that neither of them had become a *surgeon*, which would have been far more dramatic than reading and writing murder stories. She had considered these matters thoughtfully in the past, and had come to the conclusion that the greater the impulse, the greater must be the defense against the impulse, if one were to survive as a social animal.

She got up to change the angle of the Venetian blind, and Reginald, who had known her all his life, leered horribly and pinched her well-stuffed buttocks. Instantly she went into gales of merriment, her laughter resounding through the apartment. She poured him another cocktail, and when he had taken it, he wound up his facts quickly.

Later the child had been taken to a hospital, but only to die there. The doctors, seeing her condition, asked for an autopsy, and the arsenic was quickly found. Again Christine put her hands over her ears. She thought: *I'm very vulnerable. I have no strength of character at all.* She laughed nervously and said, "Oh, please! Please!"

Reginald laughed with her, patted her shoulder in sympathy, and said that, in his opinion, the case was destined to become one of the classics of its kind. For one thing, there was the thrifty reasoning of Nurse Dennison about payment of the lapsed policy, a circumstance which gave the dreadful affair the wholesome, ordinary note it needed; for another, there was one of those unconsciously humorous asides which seem to distinguish the classic from the lesser crime, for after the autopsy, when her guilt had been established and confessed, Nurse Dennison, in a moment of contrition, said that she regretted the poisoning of her niece far more than she could ever say; she wept and said that she would never have done such a terrible thing, either, if she'd known in advance that such a little bitty old pinch of arsenic could be found later. . . .

At half past two, when lunch had been eaten, Reginald said that he had to go, and while the women straightened up the kitchen, Emory turned on the radio to get the three-o'clock news. The commentator spoke briskly of world conditions for a time, then lowering his voice, he continued gravely. "I have been asked to announce that one of the children on the annual outing of the Fern Grammar School was accidentally drowned in the bay this afternoon. The name of the victim has been withheld until the parents are first notified. More news of the tragic affair is expected momentarily."

Mrs. Breedlove and Christine came into the living-room at once, and stood anxiously beside the radio. "It was not Rhoda," said Mrs. Breedlove in a positive voice. "Rhoda is too self-reliant a child." She put her arm around Christine's waist and continued. "It was somebody more like myself when I was a child. It was some timid, confused child who was afraid of its own shadow, as I was, and had no self-confidence at all. That does not sound like Rhoda."

A little later, toward the end of the broadcast, the announcer returned to the local tragedy; he was now authorized to say that the little victim was Claude Daigle, the only child of Mr. and Mrs. Dwight Daigle of 126 Willow Street. He added details to the story; there was an old wharf on the Fern property, a wharf which had not been used for a long time. It was a mystery how the little boy got on the wharf, for the children had been explicitly told not to go there; but apparently he had managed somehow, for his body had been found there, after the routine check at lunchtime had shown him missing, wedged among the old pilings. The discovery had been made by one of the guards who brought the body ashore, and applied artificial respiration. One mysterious element of the affair was the fact that there were bruises on the forehead and hands of the boy, but these bruises, it was assumed, were caused by the body washing against the pilings.

Christine said, "Poor child! Poor little boy!"

The announcer continued. "Only a few days before, the little Daigle boy won a gold medal at the closing exercises of the Fern

School. He was wearing the medal when last seen, but when his body was discovered, the medal was not found. It was thought the medal had become detached in some manner from his shirt; but although the bottom was searched at that place, the medal had not been located."

Christine went to her own apartment immediately. She hoped her child had neither seen the boy brought to shore, nor had watched the efforts of the guards to revive him. If the child were frightened or upset emotionally, she wanted to be there at the door to comfort her. Rhoda was not a sensitive child—certainly, she was not an imaginative one—but the inevitableness of death, she felt, if knowledge came too suddenly, without a proper preparation, could make an impression on even the calmest person; but when Rhoda came in at length, she was as placid, as unruffled, as she had been that morning. She entered so coolly, she asked for a glass of milk and a peanut-butter sandwich with such unconcern, that her mother wondered if she fully understood what had happened. She asked the question in her gentle, serene voice, and Rhoda said yes, she knew all about it, in fact, it was she who suggested that the guards look among the pilings. She had been present when the body was taken from the water; she had seen it laid out on the lawn.

Christine put her arms about the stolid child, and said, "You must try to get these pictures out of your mind. I don't want you to be frightened or bothered at all. These things happen, and we accept them."

Rhoda, enduring her mother's embrace, said in a surprised voice that she wasn't disturbed in the least. She had found the discovery exciting, and the efforts at resuscitation, since she'd never seen such a thing before, had interested her greatly. Christine thought: *She's so cool, so impersonal about things that bother others.* It was the thing she'd never been able to understand; it was the thing she and Kenneth had once smiled about and called "the Rhoda reaction" between themselves; but this time she felt uneasiness, a depression she could neither define nor fit into any pattern of reality that she knew.

Rhoda pulled away from her mother. She went into her room and began working on her jigsaw puzzle. Later Christine came into the room and put the sandwich and milk on the table. Her face was still puzzled, her brows puckered a little. She said, "Just the same, it was an unfortunate thing to see and remember." She kissed the child on the top of her head, and continued. "I understand how you really feel, my darling."

Rhoda moved a bit of her puzzle into its proper place on the board; then, looking up, she said in a surprised voice, "I don't know what you're talking about, Mother. I don't feel any way at all."

Christine sighed and went back to the living-room. She tried to read, but she could not concentrate; then Rhoda, as though feeling, if dimly, that she had somehow erred, had done something which, though incomprehensible to her, had strongly displeased her mother, abandoned her puzzle, and approaching the chair where Christine was sitting, she smiled her charming, hesitant smile, her single dimple appearing suddenly. She rubbed her cheek against her mother's in a calculated simulation of affection, laughed coquettishly, and moved away.

*She's done something naughty,* thought Christine; *something very naughty indeed to make her go to such trouble to please me.*

It seemed to her then that her child, as though sensing for the first time that some factor of body or spirit separated her from those around her, tried to conceal the difference by aping the values of others; but since there was nothing spontaneous in her heart to instruct her, she must, instead, consider, debate, experiment, and feel her way cautiously through the values and minds of her models.

She approached her mother once more, made an eager sound with her mouth, and kissed Christine on the lips, a thing she had not voluntarily done for a long time. Then, her eyes narrowed, her head thrown back as though for a final glance of affection, she said, "What will you give me, if I give you a basket of kisses?" It was a game the child had sometimes played with her father, and Christine, knowing the rules so well, feeling a rush of both tenderness and pity, took the little girl in her arms and gave the expected answer: "I'll give you a basket of hugs."

Later on, when she was bored with her puzzle, Rhoda got out her skates and said she'd like to go to the park. Her mother said she could, and not long afterward, hearing Leroy's scolding, illiterate voice, she went at once to her kitchen window. The man was saying, "How come you go skating and enjoying yourself when your poor little schoolmate is still damp from drowning in the bay? Looks to me like you'd be in the house crying your eyes out; either that, or be in church burning a candle in a blue cup."

Rhoda stared at the man, but she did not answer. She moved in the direction of the park, and stood there fumbling at the heavy iron gates; but Leroy would not leave her alone. He followed her and said, "Ask me, and I'll say you don't even feel sorry about what happened to that little boy." Rhoda, surprised for a moment out of her perpetual calmness, swung her skates from side to side, and said, "Why should I feel sorry? It was Claude Daigle that got drowned, not me."

Leroy shook his head, smiled with a wry appreciation, and walked away. It was now close to quitting time, and mechanically he began to do those small chores that were required of him before he left for the day, the child's words echoing in his brain. He swept the courtyard and made sure that the basement door was locked securely, and as he did so, he kept repeating to himself, mimicking the child's voice as best he could, "Why should I feel sorry? It was Claude Daigle that got drowned, not me." That Rhoda was really *something*! That little Rhoda didn't care nothing about nobody that lived, not even her good-looking mamma! That Rhoda was a mean little girl if he ever seen one! That little Rhoda was like him in a lot of ways; nobody could put nothing over on her, and nobody could put nothing over on him, either! That was sure. That was something you could bet on. . . .

He lived on General Jackson Street, a good two miles from where he worked, in an unpainted frame house, with his wife Thelma and his three gaunt, whining children. The building was on a lot a little lower than the street, and when it rained water stood undrained in a shallow pool under the house. Against the porch, Thelma had made flower beds of beer bottles driven into the earth, but the ground was too damp, and there was too much shade from the big sycamore and the flowering althea bush at the end of the porch, and nothing seemed to grow very well.

That night, before he had his supper, he sat on the porch with his wife, his feet resting on the rickety railing. At once he began to tell his wife about the death of the Daigle boy, but Thelma slapped at mosquitoes, yawned and said, "Don't bother to tell me about it. I heard it on the radio." Then, as though his words had reminded her of something, as though silence were a thing she could not endure, she went inside and turned on the radio, selecting one of the dance programs she liked so well. When she returned to the porch, Leroy said, "Jesus Christ, can't you turn that thing down some? Can't a man have quiet even in his own house?"

"I like it that way," she said. "I like to hear music loud."

She was a big, dull woman with the empty face of a fat baby, and as she sat again in her rocking chair, she said petulantly, "Quit spitting on them petunias. It was hard enough to coax them up as high as they are now. If you got to spit, sit on the steps."

He moved to the steps, grumbling a little. Then, as though he'd forgotten for a moment that his present audience was not one he could impress with his tales of injustice, he said, "Pick on me. Pick on me and belittle me like everybody else does. I'm used to it. I can take it. I know I'm nothing but a poor sharecropper."

"Listen, Leroy," said Thelma patiently. "Don't try to tell me them lies, because I know better. You never was a sharecropper; you never even lived in the country, like I did when I was a girl. Your papa wasn't any sharecropper, either. Your papa was a longshoreman, and you know that as well as I do. Your papa made good money doing it, too. Nobody went hungry or wanted for anything in your papa's house. It's a pity you didn't turn out like him."

"I didn't have a chance," he said. "I didn't have a chance to accomplish nothing."

"You had chances. You had plenty chances. You're lazy."

She fanned herself languidly, pulling down the yoke of her dress; then, thrusting her legs against the banisters, she went on to berate him for his laziness, his lying, his dirtiness, his unwillingness to play up to people that could help him along, her voice carrying well over the radio. The way he acted, the way he insulted people, was about as silly a way as a man could act. No wonder he was always losing his job. For instance, she knew some of the people at the Florabelle that he was always belittling, and they wasn't no way at all like the way he said they was—that Mrs. Breedlove, for instance, was a real nice, jolly woman, and a kindhearted one, too. Maybe if he started doing nice things for people instead of griping all the time; maybe if—

Then, in the middle of a sentence, she said quickly, as though bored with her own moral advice, "How about a can of beer before I start supper?" She got the beer and brought it to the porch. It was still not dark, and the children were playing a game in the back yard, a game that seemed to require a great deal of bickering and screaming. Their voices interfered with the music, and Thelma went into the house and turned up the radio a little more. "Jesus Christ!" said Leroy draining his beer. "Can't a man get no quietness even at home? If I catch them kids, I'll tan the tar out of them."

"You won't catch them, though," said Thelma placidly. "Them kids run too fast."

It was then that Leroy repeated Rhoda's remark about the death of the Daigle boy, and Thelma, laughing a little, threw her empty can high over the fence and into the street. She got up from her chair, pulled her dress away from her sweating buttocks, and said, "I think that was a real cute thing to say."

"That's a real mean little girl," said Leroy. "I never seen a little girl like that one in all my born days." He got out his pipe, lit it, and smoked in silence, thinking how the other children who played in the park—them other ones that wasn't mean—were all afraid of him, just like he wanted them to be. He could make them jump and run out of the park if he barked at them loud enough; he could even make the little girls cry, and run off to tell their mammas on him, although he had always got out of it so far by being humble, and saying it wasn't so, or that the little girl had been acting ugly—like trampling down the flowers, or trying to scoop goldfish in the lily pond. But that little Rhoda Pen-mark he couldn't make no impression on at all—at least not so far. But give him time and he would. Give him a little time and he'd make her jump and run from him like the others. He chuck-led in anticipation of that pleasant day, and then, defiantly, he spat into his wife's flower bed again.

Thelma, slapping at mosquitoes with her palmetto fan, said, "Your papa made good money all his life. Your papa was a good provider. That I can say for him, and do so gladly."

"That little Rhoda Penmark is a mean little girl," said Leroy aloud. "But one thing you can say for her, and it's this: she don't blab nothing. Anything that happens, happens between me and her."

"Listen to me," said Thelma. "You leave that little girl alone. You hear me, Leroy? You going to get yourself in trouble if you don't quit messing around with those rich folks and their chil-dren. I'm telling you, you going to get yourself in a mess of trouble."

"I don't do nothing to her," said Leroy, "except maybe plague her and tease her a little."

"I'm telling you," said Thelma. "I'm telling you right now."

She got up from her chair, called her children, and went into the kitchen to start supper, but Leroy remained on the steps for a time, smoking his pipe and thinking of the little Penmark girl. He would have been surprised to know that, in a sense, he was in love with the little girl, and that his persecution of her, his nag-ging concern with everything she did, was part of a perverse and frightened courtship.

That night after dinner Christine went to the Daigle home on Willow Street, her purpose still not clear in her mind. It was not quite dark when she came up the steps. The sky was soft, dark blue, with only the early stars against the horizon. Mr. Daigle answered the bell. He was a larger image of his son; there was the same pale, blue-veined forehead, the same outthrust jaw and small, puckered underlip. The hand he offered Christine was cold and damp. She gave her name and explained her mission; she wanted to offer her sympathy, and to ask if there were anything she could do; and he said in a voice that trembled in spite of himself, "Anyone who knew our son is welcome in this house." Then, opening the door wider, he added, "You are the first to call. We are not people who entertain a great deal, and we have not made many friends."

The living-room had that depressing look of expensive bad taste. There were beads and bows of ribbon everywhere. Everything was wrong, she thought, the furniture, the colors, the paintings; even the big Oriental rug somehow offended. Mr. Daigle said, "You must excuse the looks of the place. We have just returned from the funeral home where they've taken him. Everything is a little disarranged and lacks Mrs. Daigle's touch."

Then, standing there beside his visitor in the hall, he said, "You must go in and speak to my wife. Perhaps something you say will—perhaps, in some way you can—" He knocked on his wife's door, whispering, "Hortense! Here's a visitor. It's someone who knew Claude. Her little girl was his classmate, and was with him at the picnic."

He went away silently, and Mrs. Daigle sat up on the sofa where she had been resting. Her hair was disarranged, her eyes red and swollen, her mind still a little drugged from the sedatives she had been given. She said, "It's not true that Claude was timid and lacked confidence in himself, as some people have said. I'm not saying he was a pushing, aggressive boy, because that wouldn't be true, either. What I mean is, he was a sensitive boy, an artistic child, really. I'd like to show you some of the flower drawings he did so beautifully, but I can't bear to look at them again so soon."

She broke off and pressed her face into her pillow. Christine sat beside her and took Mrs. Daigle's plump, ringed hand in her own, pressing it in sympathy. "We were so close to each other," Claude's mother said. "He said I was his sweetheart, and he would put his little arms about my neck and tell me every thought he had."

She paused, unable to go on, and then said, "I don't see why they couldn't find the medal. I'm sure the men didn't look hard enough. It was the only thing he'd ever won in his life, and he valued it so much." Then, as though the loss of the medal were more terrible to her than the loss of her son, she wept without constraint, her face pale and bloated, her hair falling limply over her eyes. When she could speak again, she continued. "Somebody said the medal must have fallen off his shirt and sunk down into the sand, but as I told my husband, I don't think so. I don't see how the medal could possibly have come off by itself. I pinned the medal on him myself, and the clasp was strong and tight."

She wiped her face with a damp towel, and in the silence, Christine said softly, "I know. I know so well."

"The men simply didn't look hard enough," said Mrs. Daigle. "They said they'd looked over and over, but I told them to go back and look again. There was such a wonderful bond between us. We were so close to each other. He said I was his only sweetheart, and that he was going to marry me when he grew up. He obeyed me completely. He wouldn't even go to the corner until he'd discussed the matter with me, and I'd told him it was all right. He'd want to be buried with his medal. I know that without being told. I want to please him in every way I can— Will you tell the men to please look for the medal again?"

# four

————

WHEN CHRISTINE RETURNED HOME, Rhoda was curled up in one of the big chairs studying her Sunday school lesson for the following day, her lips shaping aloud the text that she read. She went each Sunday, with the little Truby girls who lived across the street, to the Presbyterian church on Lowell Street; and she was ardent in study, and faithful in attendance as well. Her teacher, Miss Belle Blackwell, believed in encouraging both attendance at her class and seriousness of purpose in her pupils, through a series of small rewards. Each time a child came promptly to the Sunday school room when the second bell rang, and knew the lesson printed on the back of the illustrated card which had been distributed in class the previous Sunday, she surrendered the card temporarily, and Miss Blackwell pasted a golden butterfly on it as a testimonial of piety and application. When a child had twelve of these cards with their twelve golden butterflies, she was given "a pleasant and instructive reward" in return.

The lesson this particular Sunday was concerned with one of the bloodier precepts of the Old Testament; it centered around the damnation and most cruel destruction of those who had been unable, or unwilling, to conform blindly to some Hebraic party line of that day; and when Christine sat quietly beside her daughter under the lamp, her mind still fixed on the suffering of the Daigles, Rhoda passed the card, on which she was to be examined next morning, to her, and asked that her mother question her about it. Christine read the text slowly, shook her head and thought: *Is there nothing but violence everywhere? Is there no real peace anywhere in the world?* She wondered if her daughter should be taught such things, but sighing in a gentle protest, feeling that others surely knew more about these matters of faith than she did, she asked her daughter the questions required. Rhoda had learned her lesson well and, smiling her charming, shallow smile, she nodded in triumph, and, going to her treasure box, she returned with the eleven butterfly-starred cards she'd already earned.

"I'm sure to get a prize tomorrow," she said. "I'm just *sure* to."

"What do you think it will be? Will it be something quite nice?"

"It'll be a book, I guess," said Rhoda. "Miss Belle almost always gives a book that improves the mind."

The anticipation of possession was already in her face, and, gathering her cards together, she returned them to their original place in her dresser drawer.

Later, Mrs. Penmark read the afternoon paper, and went to bed early; but she found it hard to sleep, for Hortense Daigle's tear-stained, disintegrating face kept coming in the dark before her eyes; but at last she did fall asleep, and had a dream which disturbed her, but which she could not remember afterward. She got up earlier than she usually did on a Sunday morning, the liquid, triumphant sound of church bells in her ears, and fixed breakfast for herself and her child.

Later that day, when Rhoda returned from church, she had her prize tucked under her arm; it was a copy of *Elsie Dinsmore*, and, going at once to the park, she opened her book and began eagerly to read, as though she hoped to find there an understanding of those puzzling values she saw in others—values which, though she tried her best to simulate them, were so curiously absent from herself. But the book bored her after a while, and returning to the apartment, she sat at the piano to practice her scales. Her teacher said she had almost no musical ability, in the true sense of the word—she had only patience and tenacity. But she would play acceptably some day, more accurately, perhaps, than children with talent.

At noon, old Mrs. Forsythe, who lived across the hall, brought over a tray of lemon meringue tarts she'd just baked. She knew that often a woman didn't feel in the mood to prepare for herself or her child, particularly if the child were a little girl, with the man of the house not there, these little extra treats, and she thought perhaps that Christine and Rhoda would enjoy the tarts for lunch, since they'd turned out quite well this time. It was such a pretty day, too; and if Mrs. Penmark had planned to go out, she'd be glad to keep an eye on Rhoda. It would be no trouble, really, for her grandchildren were coming over that afternoon, and one more would hardly make any difference.

Mrs. Penmark, the depressed direction of her thoughts broken for a time, bent forward impulsively and kissed the old woman on her forehead. And Mrs. Forsythe, returning to her own apartment, said softly to her husband, "Christine is a very kind, gentle woman. She's a nice neighbor to have."

The funeral of the Daigle boy was held on Monday, and an account of it was in the afternoon paper. The grave had been "banked with floral tributes," but the most imposing tribute of all had come from the children of the Fern Grammar School, which he had attended; each of his little classmates had contributed to the beautiful blanket of gardenias which had lain first on the coffin, and later on the grave itself.

Mrs. Penmark folded the paper and put it on the hall table, thinking it strange that nobody had asked for a contribution from Rhoda. She wondered if the oversight had been a deliberate one, and then she thought: *I'm paying too much attention to this thing. There was no intention back of it.* Perhaps one of the Misses Fern had telephoned when she was out, although that did not seem likely; perhaps Rhoda's name had been accidentally left off the list. Perhaps. . . .

She decided to ignore the slight, although the implications hurt her a little, and, turning away, she told herself that she would not speak of it, not even to Monica and Emory. That afternoon she decided to go shopping, and taking Rhoda with her, she drove in to town. She selected a pale-blue evening gown for herself, and she bought material for Rhoda's fall school dresses; but when she was home again, and Rhoda was skating in the park, up the walks, and around the cement path that circled the lily pond, the matter was still on her mind, and upon impulse she dialed the Fern School.

Miss Octavia answered, and Christine said, "I read about the Daigle boy's funeral, and the beautiful gardenias the children sent him. I'm sorry I wasn't in when you telephoned about Rhoda's share."

There was no answer for a time; she could almost feel Miss Fern's embarrassment over the phone; but at last the old woman said in a voice scarcely audible, "There are so many children in the school. The blanket wasn't nearly so costly as the papers seem to think. Please don't worry. The money has already been collected, and the flowers paid for."

"Did you telephone me about the flowers?" asked Christine. "If you did not, I think I should know."

Miss Fern said in a soft, placating voice, "No, my dear, we did not telephone you. My sisters and I thought it better not to."

Christine said, "I see!" She waited, and then went on. "Were there other children left out, or was it simply that you didn't telephone me?"

"My sisters and I thought you'd prefer to send flowers individually," said Miss Fern. She waited again, as though shaping her words with the greatest care, and then went on in a voice that carried no conviction at all. "It isn't as though you'd been here a long time; this is Rhoda's first term with us, as you know."

Christine said, "I see. I see." Then, softly, she added, "But why did you think we'd prefer to send flowers individually? Rhoda wasn't friendly with the boy, and my husband and I didn't even know the Daigles."

Miss Fern said, "I don't know, my dear. I couldn't answer truthfully if my life depended on it." Then, as though pleading forgiveness, she said so quietly that her voice was almost a whisper, "I must go now. We have guests, and they'll think it strange."

Mrs. Penmark turned away from the telephone, a frown on her usually serene brow. If there were overtones she did not understand, if there were implications her mind could not take in, she would tell herself that they were meaningless, of no significance at all. She would tell herself it was a simple oversight; she would not even refer to it when she wrote her husband. After all, she reminded herself, Kenneth had his problems, too; and this, certainly, should not be one of them. She sat at her desk and wrote him a bright letter full of gossip about the people they both knew; she missed him greatly, as always, but was consoled in the knowledge that their lives held many years in which they would not be separated at all, years of contentment and peace. She affirmed the unalterable fact that she loved him. "I'll dismiss the Daigle drowning and everything connected with it from my mind," she said to herself. "It was sad and unfortunate, but, after all, how can it concern me very deeply?"

A week later Mrs. Penmark got a letter from the Fern School. The letter was brief, courteous, and to the point; it said in substance that the school to its regret found its membership filled, its rolls closed, for the term commencing in September, and it would not, therefore, be able to make a place for Rhoda. The writer was sure that Mr. and Mrs. Penmark would experience little difficulty in making other arrangements for the child; and again with regrets, and sincere good wishes, she was most cordially, Burgess Witherspoon Fern.

That day Christine went about in a preoccupied manner, the note constantly in her mind. In the afternoon, she showed the note to Mrs. Breedlove, asking her advice. Mrs. Breedlove said, "The longer I live, the more I see, the more I'm unable to understand the tight little minds of people like the Fern girls!" She tossed her pebble over her shoulder, and went on. "The truth of the matter is, Rhoda is much too charming, too clever, too unusual, for them! She isn't like those simpering little neurotics who believe everything that's told them, and never have an original thought of their own. Rhoda stands on her own feet, and makes her own decisions, I may add. She's all-of-one-piece. She makes those others look stupid and stodgy by comparison. That's the *real* complaint, I assure you!" She lit a cigarette, and in the silence Christine thought: *Monica loves Rhoda, and she loves me, too. When she loves anybody, she can never see any wrong in them. She's completely loyal. She's a wonderful friend to have.*

Mrs. Breedlove said, "If I were you, I'd send Rhoda to public school next term; but if you think she won't meet the right sort of companions there, then we must arrange a private tutor for her. Anyway, I'd forget the matter for the time being. I wouldn't even answer Burgess Fern's insolent note."

But Christine went about with a feeling of panic in her breast, as though the incident of the Baltimore school were about to be renewed. To herself, she said for reassurance, "It's nothing like that. If it were, they'd have said so long ago." Nevertheless, she felt there were things she did not understand, facts which the Fern sisters had, perhaps, but which had been withheld from her, and on the third afternoon, as though the matter were a most casual one, she telephoned the school and asked for an appointment in order that she might talk things over with the sisters.

Miss Claudia ushered her into the big formal parlor, and said, as though in reproach, "As a usual thing, we'd be at Benedict this time of year, but the death of the Daigle child has ruined the summer for us."

"I'll never go there again," said Octavia firmly. "The place is spoiled for me now." She pulled a bell cord, and almost at once a maid came in with tea and bread and butter. When the servant had gone, Christine said, too abruptly, she felt, that she couldn't get the thought out of her mind that the drowning of the boy and the dismissal of Rhoda from the school were somehow connected. The thing puzzled her, and she wished they'd tell her frankly if this were, or were not, true.

"But why do you think there's a connection between the two events?" asked Miss Octavia primly. "My sisters and I haven't intimated such a thing, I'm sure."

"Then may I assume there is no connection?"

Miss Octavia sipped her tea and said that this particular situation was one she had earnestly hoped to avoid. She could not see what was to be gained, how anyone could really be served, by discussing it further; but since Mrs. Penmark had brought up the matter and wanted the truth, she had to confess there was a connection, a most definite one, between the two things.

Miss Burgess said, "The busses hadn't even started before Rhoda began teasing the boy. She wouldn't give him any peace. She hung over his seat and breathed down his neck, staring at the medal all the time. The child sitting with Claude got up and moved finally, and Rhoda took the vacated place at once. She wanted Claude to take off the medal and let her hold it for him; but he covered the medal with his hand and said, 'Let me alone! Let me alone!'"

"She became so insistent," said Claudia Fern, "that I finally had to take her by the arm and make her sit by herself, up near the driver—as far away from Claude as I could get her. But even then she twisted her neck around and looked at the medal the whole time."

Mrs. Penmark sighed and said, "Rhoda is certainly an aggressive child, and a selfish one, too, I'm sure. But then our world seems to be full of selfish and aggressive people. My husband and I hope that she'll outgrow these things in time."

"That isn't all, I'm afraid," said Burgess Fern. "When we were at the bay, and the other children were shouting and playing games together, Rhoda did nothing but follow the boy about, making his life miserable. She didn't say anything to him—she only stared at the medal, and at last the little boy, who was nervous and not at all strong, as we know, began to tremble so badly that I called him to me, and told him to pay no attention to Rhoda. Then he did a peculiar thing which I've thought about a great deal since his death. He took off his medal and asked me to keep it until the picnic was over."

"Did you do it? Perhaps the medal isn't lost, after all."

Miss Octavia rang for more hot water, and after the maid had gone, Miss Burgess continued. "No, I didn't do what he asked. I pinned the medal back on his shirt, and told him to develop more confidence in himself. I reminded him that the medal belonged to him, and nobody else. He had won it fairly. It was his. He had every right to wear it." She walked to the window and looked out at the garden beyond. "I called Rhoda, and talked to her as well. I told her that her behavior was unpardonably rude, and not what we expected from our pupils."

Miss Claudia took up the story. "I joined my sisters about that time and gave Rhoda a talk on courtesy and fair play; but she only looked at me with that puzzled, calculating expression we've all come to know so well, and said nothing."

"She's not an easy child to understand," said Christine. "If we went wrong with her somehow, it isn't surprising, I suppose."

"I hoped my talk would make some impression on her," said Claudia, "but not an hour afterward one of our older pupils came on Rhoda and the little Daigle boy at the far end of the grounds. The boy was upset and crying, and Rhoda was standing in front of him, blocking his path. The older girl was standing among the trees, and neither of the children saw her. She was just at the point of intervening, when Rhoda shoved the little boy and snatched at his medal; but he broke away and ran down the beach in the direction of the old wharf where he was later found, with Rhoda following him, although she wasn't running. She was walking along taking her time, the big girl said."

"Did it occur to you that the big girl you mentioned might not be telling the truth?"

"That isn't at all likely," said Miss Claudia. "She was one of the monitors we'd appointed to keep an eye on the younger children; she's almost fifteen, and she's been with us since her kindergarten days. We're familiar with her character by this time, and it's excellent. No, Mrs. Penmark. She was telling precisely what she saw."

Miss Octavia said, "A little later—it must have been around noon, really—one of the guards saw Rhoda coming off the wharf. He shouted a warning, and was on the point of going to her, but by then she was on the beach again, and he decided to forget the matter, as it didn't seem very important under the circumstances."

It was true, she went on, the guard had not identified Rhoda by *name*; he knew the names of none of the children, actually; and at that distance he couldn't have identified anyone positively, whether he'd known them or not. He'd only mentioned a girl in a red dress, and since Rhoda was the only girl who had worn a dress that day, they had reasonably assumed that she was the one he had seen.

Miss Octavia's old tottering spaniel came wheezing across the room. She picked the dog up and held it on her lap while the animal thrust its tongue out weakly and tried to touch her cheek. "The guard saw Rhoda on the wharf about noon, as I've said," continued Miss Octavia. "At one o'clock the lunch bell rang, and when roll call was made, Claude was missing. You know the rest, I think."

Christine said, "Yes. Yes. I heard it on the air." She opened and closed the catch on her bag, and then, against her will, she remembered an incident which had taken place in Baltimore the year before. One of the children in the apartment house where they'd lived had had a puppy, and Rhoda, seeing it, wanted one, too. They had bought the dog she selected, a little wire-haired terrier, happy to see the child was showing an interest, at last, in some object other than herself. At first she had been delighted with her dog; she had taken it everywhere, even exhibiting it to people in the lobby and boasting of its cost and pedigree; but later, when she found she was expected to take care of her pet herself—Kenneth had thought this excellent training for her, an object lesson in responsibility and kindness—when she found she must feed the dog and take it out, even though these things interfered with her reading, her jigsaw puzzles, her piano practice, the dog had somehow managed to fall from a window ledge onto the courtyard below.

Christine had heard the dying whimpering of the dog, and going into her daughter's room, she had seen Rhoda leaning out of the window, dispassionately watching some object below. She had joined her daughter, and there, three stories below, was the little terrier with its spine crushed. She said, "What happened? What happened to the dog?" But Rhoda had walked away, as though the matter concerned her not at all. At the door she paused and said, "It fell out of the window, I think."

It was the only explanation that either she or Kenneth had ever got out of the child. But now, remembering the incident, sensing some vague connection between the two accidents, Mrs. Penmark felt a sudden anger rising in her. Her hand trembled, and her teacup rattled in its saucer. She looked around her, as though somebody were about to attack her. Carefully she put down her cup, closed her eyes, waited until she knew her voice would be as detached, as soft, as gentle as the voices of the Fern sisters, and said, "Are you hinting that Rhoda had anything to do with the boy's death? Is that the purpose of all this?"

Her words had an odd effect on the Fern girls. They glanced

at one another in astonishment, as though their guest were demented. "Why, of course not!" said Miss Octavia in horror. "That would be impossible! An eight-year-old child mixed up in a thing like *that*? Oh, no! Such a thing never entered our minds."

"If we thought anything like that," said Miss Claudia, "we would have been compelled to notify the proper authorities."

Burgess smiled and said, "Oh, nothing so melodramatic as that, Mrs. Penmark. Our complaint is that Rhoda is evasive, and didn't tell us the whole truth. We feel she has knowledge that she's told nobody."

Miss Octavia broke off a piece of sandwich, fed it to her dog, and said that they'd been very fair to the child, and had given her every chance to explain. They had questioned her at length after the tragedy, and she had denied everything with a straight face; she'd denied harassing the boy in the bus, she'd denied trying to take the medal in the woods; she'd denied being on the old wharf at any time. She had been so innocent, so plausible in her denials that for a time the sisters had doubted the evidence of their own senses.

Christine said, "I see. I see." Then, as the Fern sisters continued to talk of the affair, her mind went back to the child's expulsion from the school in Baltimore. Her husband had made light of the matter, perhaps for his comfort as well as her own. Many children took things, he said; he had taken things himself as a child, and he'd turned out all right—at least reasonably so. It was nothing to be concerned about, even if true; and insofar as lying was concerned, that was a part of the growing-up process of children—particularly imaginative children. They had comforted each other, and had accepted these solutions, but in their hearts they both knew the differences; children took fruits from orchards and flowers from lawns; and the lies they told were the magical lies of the imaginary worlds they live in at the moment. There were none of these qualities in her own child. Rhoda was interested in material things for their own sake, and the lies she told were the hard, objective lies of an adult whose purpose was to confound and mislead.

She came back to the reality that surrounded her. Miss Burgess was saying, "We're sorry all this had to come up, or that Rhoda's connection with our school had to end this way; but we feel that Rhoda is not a good influence on our other pupils, whose interests we must consider, too."

"We feel that we're not able to understand or cope with a child of Rhoda's temperament," said Claudia Fern. "We feel we can do nothing further for her."

Miss Octavia rose, as though bringing the interview to a close, and said, "We feel your little girl would be happier somewhere else. Frankly, we do not want her in our school any longer."

Christine was depressed and a little anxious when she returned home; to calm herself, she made a cup of tea which she drank at her kitchen table. From where she sat, she could see both the playground and the wide, paved courtyard at the back of the building. In the park, the children of the house and the children of neighbors, who were permitted to use the playground, swung, splashed in the lily pond, skated, or played the running and shrieking games of childhood. Rhoda was in the park, too; but she kept herself away from the boisterous children; she sat on a bench beneath the old white pomegranate, reading the copy of *Elsie Dinsmore* she'd won for attendance and application. Then Leroy Jessup came out of the basement carrying a bucket of ashes from the incinerator. He stopped at the gate to scold the children wading in the pond, to warn them that if they tore up them lilies again, he was going to have their mothers whup them good with a buggywhup; then, lifting his eyes toward the skies, as though asking heaven to witness the things he endured, he disappeared into the alley beyond Mrs. Penmark's arc of vision.

She began to feel better, her depression dissolving itself in the warmth of the tea. After all, there was nothing the Fern sisters had told her about Rhoda that she had not already known, and for a much longer time. The child's singleness of purpose, her evasiveness, her innocent plausibility when trapped, her incessant lying, were things which had long since ceased to surprise either herself or Kenneth, and when she considered the factors of the affair in quietness, those things, really, were all the Fern sisters had intimated.

The charges they had brought, if one could call such vague dissatisfactions charges, were susceptible of more than one interpretation. She had little doubt that Rhoda had worried the Daigle boy, or that she had tried to take the medal from him in the woods, even though the child had denied these things with such earnestness. But Claude Daigle, as anyone could see, was the born victim of others—the one who, in a sense, went about the world to invite his own destruction. Rhoda's violence with him was unusual for her, greatly out of character. She would never have tried such an approach on a child with more courage and self-reliance, one who would cheerfully turn and slap her down.

She was not trying to justify her child, for she could not condone the things the child had done; she was only saying to herself that matters were not so bad as she had feared. Rhoda was her child, and she loved her. It was her duty to protect the child, to make every allowance for her, to give her the benefit of every doubt. She washed her cup and put it away. She would make the best of the matter. She would trust in the future. She would hope that everything turned out all right in time.

Then, returning to her living-room, she telephoned Monica to tell her she'd decided to take her advice and put Rhoda in public school next season. Mrs. Breedlove's cheerful voice came through the receiver, approving the decision; then, lowering her voice, she explained that Mildred Trellis and Edith Marcusson were in her apartment at the moment. They had called to discuss a clinic for the treatment of alcoholics which she was trying to establish. She had known Mrs. Trellis and Mrs. Marcusson all her life; they were charming girls of excellent families; but what was more important for her present purpose, they were stinking with money. The trouble was, Emory had come home earlier than she had expected, bringing with him that Reginald Tasker, and they were interfering with her plans. They'd been in town drinking, and Emory, at least, was high. It wasn't that they were acting common or using objectionable words; this wouldn't bother her friends in the slightest, for they were both well-read ladies; they were simply sitting together over by the ferns, making silly comments behind their hands; and at regular intervals, Emory would get the sherry decanter and fill the glasses of her visitors. She giggled and wondered if Christine would come up and divert the attention of the boys until she could put the squeeze on her wealthy friends.

"Put on your new high-heel pumps with the little leather bows in front, and see that the seams of your stockings are straight. Emory admires you to distraction. He says you've got the best legs in town."

The men met her at the door, took her into the kitchen, and

fixed her a drink. "Why is it," asked Reggie, "that real pretty girls like Christine never go around talking about their unconscious minds?"

Emory kissed her loudly on the cheek and said, "This one's got it, hasn't she, boy? This one's really stacked."

In the living-room, Monica was saying, "I'm so tired of novels about sensitive boys and their first sex experiences. You know how it is, Edith; they slink home in disgust, feeling degraded and guilty. Sometimes they flip their lids, sometimes they jump out of windows, they're all so delicately adjusted and refined."

Mrs. Marcusson took a swallow of sherry and said solemnly, "Sex is a wholesome and normal experience."

One of Reginald's long, pale eyes was set a little lower than its mate, like the migrating eye of a flounder at the beginning of its journey. He patted Christine's shoulder and said, "Is everything under that black satin dress really *you?*"

Christine took her drink and said, "I get it from the upholsterer. He comes in twice a week and fluffs me out." She laughed and pulled away, thinking: *Rhoda probably did follow the boy down the beach. Maybe he ran out on the wharf to get away from her, and she followed him. Maybe he backed away from her and fell among the pilings. I don't know whether this happened or not. But anyway it's the worst thing I have to face—*

"Now, the sort of book I'd like to read," continued Mrs. Breedlove, "is one about a boy who hasn't a smidgen of delicacy in him." She took a sip from her glass, giggled, and went on. "My little boy is an ordinary, nasty little boy who's going to be an ordinary, nasty little man when he's grown. He works in a grocery store after school, I think; and he saves his nickels and dimes until he's got enough for his first visit to the town whore, who's old and fat, and hasn't had a bath all over since Armistice Day."

Mrs. Trellis laughed shrilly; then, as though realizing how loud her voice sounded in the room, she composed herself, sat up in her chair, and said, "If you'll write it, I'll buy a thousand copies."

Christine thought: *But if the boy backed off into the water, and Rhoda was there, why didn't she call out to the guard who saw her on the wharf? Why did she run away? Why did she leave the boy to die?* She turned her head and shuddered inwardly. "But I won't keep going over this," she said to herself. "It's strange and terrible. I won't think about it again."

"My nasty, average little boy," said Mrs. Breedlove, "came out of the place smirking and rolling his eyes. He whistled and swaggered from side to side. He's wondering if he can talk his old man into letting him quit school and take a full time job at the bag factory. That way, he can make more money, and pay more visits to the greasy old whore who's just taken his virginity. My boy's going to be such a dear, *normal* boy!"

Emory stuck his head out and said, "If you girls are going to talk dirty, Reggie and I'll have to leave the room."

The girls went into whirlwinds of laughter, and Monica, catching his eye, shouted for him to open another bottle of the good sherry as her guests wanted another sip before they got down to business; then, turning to Mrs. Marcusson, she said, "I want to apologize for Emory's condition, my dear. Emory's drunk." Emory dropped an ice cube, kicked it under the stove, and said, "Well, look who's talking!"

While he got out the sherry, Christine and Reginald came into the living-room and sat down. Christine said she'd been thinking about the conversation they'd had the last time she'd seen him. He'd told a story then of a woman who'd poisoned her niece for insurance. What she wanted to know now was when did such people start their careers? Did children ever commit murders, or was she correct in assuming that only grown people did such dreadful things?

Reginald thought that this was not the best time for a discussion of such serious matters; but if she was really interested, why not telephone him, or drop by his apartment for lunch some day? However, he would say now, in spite of all the giggling and confusion, that children quite often committed murders, and clever ones, too, at times. Some murderers, particularly the distinguished ones who were going to make great names for themselves, usually started in childhood; they showed their genius early, just as outstanding poets, mathematicians, and musicians did.

He paused, and in the silence Monica said distinctly, "I've often wondered why I married Norman Breedlove. Lately, I've come to the conclusion that it was his name that attracted me." She glanced at her brother and continued. "Now, my first association to Norman is 'normal'; after all, there's only the difference of a consonant. 'Normal' is such a reassuring word. It's the word the worried people of my generation were looking for."

Mrs. Trellis wagged her finger and said, "Where's the sherry? What have you done with the sherry, Emory?"

Mrs. Marcusson, who looked more like a dowdy old farm woman in town to sell her vegetables than a woman of wealth, tilted her battered old hat with the back of her hand, and said, "I wonder what young people talk about these days? When we were young, at least we had sex and social betterment to occupy our minds. I've got a feeling that young people now don't talk about anything except television and canasta."

Monica waited tolerantly until her guest had finished, and then went on. "Now 'breed' is associated in my mind with increase, and 'love' is associated with love, naturally. So the combination Norman Breedlove brings to mind one who would not only be well adjusted and normal, but one of constantly increasing affection, too. The thing is so simple in retrospect, although it never occurred to me at all at the time."

Emory said, "I thought you married Norman Breedlove because he was the only man that asked you to."

Before she could answer, he laughed and said, "Now I bet Christine with those big gray eyes and yellow hair had to beat the boys off with an umbrella."

Christine said, "You couldn't be more wrong. I was never popular. I was too earnest and literal for the boys."

Mrs. Trellis began to laugh, and Mrs. Marcusson joined in the merriment. Mrs. Trellis said, "This has been such a stimulating afternoon, Monica. Now, just relax and sit back and quit worrying about how much you're going to get out of Edith and me. You're going to get plenty. Edith and I talked the matter over on our way here. You're not going to get as much as you figured on, maybe—but you're going to get quite a bit."

Emory said in a voice audible to all, "Those three old bags are as drunk as owls. They got away with a quart and a half of sherry." The three rose and stared at him coldly. Monica steadied herself, put on her glasses, and said, "Let's go into the library girls, where we can be by ourselves. We have pens and paper and blank checks on every bank in town." They put their arms about one another's waists and walked away, but as they passed through the big, old-fashioned folding doors, they turned their heads at the same moment, looked back, and screamed with laughter.

Christine put down the drink she had hardly touched, thinking: *But suppose she followed him to the end of the wharf, and Claude,*

*rather than let her take the medal, threw it into the bay. Suppose she*
*picked up a stick or something and hit with it, knocking him into the*
*water, stunning him and leaving him to die there. Suppose—*

She lowered her head and gripped the arms of her chair, for already despair and guilt were nibbling like mice at her mind. She got up and said she must go back to her apartment. It was almost five o'clock, and Rhoda should be returning from the playground soon. She called out to Monica that she was leaving, and Mrs. Breedlove, abandoning her friends in the library, came back into the living-room at once.

"Aren't you afraid, a pretty little thing like you, to live on the first floor without a man to protect you?" asked Reggie.

"It isn't really the first floor," said Monica. "Those front stairs rise quite a bit, if you'll notice. And underneath there's an enormous basement that's mostly above ground. Christine's window is about ten feet from the ground, really."

"I'm not at all afraid," said Christine. "Kenneth bought a pistol for me, and I know how to use it, incidentally." She smiled and said, "I was surprised that anyone can have a pistol here, if he wants it. In New York, having a pistol is one of the worst things you can possibly do."

"You have to have a permit," said Emory. "That is, everybody but the crook that shoots you has to have one. Now, we're more civilized in this state; we believe in giving the victim a chance, too."

Mrs. Penmark came into her apartment and stood there idly. She kept repeating under her breath, as though her denials were a charm to save her, "Everything is all right. There's absolutely nothing to worry about. I'm making a lot out of nothing at all, as I usually do. I'm being quite silly." It was getting dark in the rooms that faced the east, and she turned on the light, thinking:

*My mother used to laugh and say I could make a mountain out of a molehill without half trying. I remember once in a hotel in London, my mother was talking with some people she knew and she put her arms around my skinny shoulders—my mother was always such an affectionate, gentle woman—and said, "Christine bothers about the strangest things!" . . . I don't remember what she was referring to now, but I did know at the time, of course.*

She went about her house, performing the usual automatic tasks of late afternoon, and then, standing still in her living-room, she shook her head stubbornly and thought: *There's no reason to think Rhoda had anything to do with the death of the little Daigle boy. There's no real evidence against her at all. I don't know why I'm behaving so strangely. You'd think I was trying to build up a damaging case against my own child out of nothing but my own silliness. . . .*

Suddenly she sat down, as though too weak to stand any more, and rested her head on the arm of her chair, for she knew then that the thing she had determined never to remember again—that affair with its mysterious overtones which she'd never brought herself to face honestly—had entered her mind once more, despite all her resistances. Oh, no! It was not alone the unexplained death of the little boy that had so greatly disrupted the attitude of poised serenity which she had with such difficulty established for herself; it was really the unexplained death of the boy added to another most peculiar death, a death also unexplained, which, too, had involved her daughter—the only person to witness it. Either instance, taken alone, could probably be dismissed as one of those unfortunate but unavoidable accidents that happen everywhere, to everyone; but taken together, with the similarities of their mysteries combined, the effect was more compelling, more difficult to explain away with casual reasoning. . . .

The first death had taken place in Baltimore more than a year ago, when Rhoda was just seven. At that time, there had been living in the same apartment house with them a Mrs. Clara Post, a very old woman, and her widowed daughter, Edna. The old lady had become inordinately attached to Rhoda (It was strange, Mrs. Penmark thought, how greatly Rhoda was admired by older people, when children her own age could not abide her.) and when she came home from school in the afternoon, she often went up to visit her ancient friend. The old lady was in her middle eighties, and a little childish, and she took delight in showing her possessions to the child. The one thing she valued most of all her trinkets was a crystal ball filled with transparent fluid, a little ball in which fragments of opals floated, glistened, and changed with a movement of the wrist, into bright and varying patterns. There was a small gold ring sunk in the top of the crystal, like a miniature hitching post, and through it the old lady had run a black ribbon in order that she might wear her opal pendant about her neck.

Often she said that when she could not sleep, she loved to look at the changing ball and watch the varied pictures the floating opals made for her pleasure. Her daughter Edna often shook her head and said, when talking to the neighbors, "Mamma thinks she can see her childhood in the opals. I don't discourage her. I humor her as much as I can. She hasn't got much to enjoy these days."

Rhoda had also admired the floating opal ball, and when she and the old lady were together, Mrs. Post would sometimes pick it up from the table beside her chair and say, "Now, isn't that quite pretty, my dear? I'll wager you'd like to have it for your own."

Rhoda said eagerly that she would, and Mrs. Post laughed mildly and said, "It's going to be yours some day, my love. I'm going to leave it to you in my will when I die—that much I solemnly promise. Edna, you heard me say it, didn't you?"

"Yes, Mamma, I heard you."

Then, cackling in triumph, the old lady added, "But don't go and get your hopes high, honey, because I haven't any idea whatever of dying real soon. We come from a long-lived family, don't we, Edna?"

"Yes, Mamma, we certainly do. But you're going to live longer than any of them, I always think."

The old lady smiled with pleasure, and said, "My dear father lived to be ninety-three, and he wouldn't have died that young if a tree hadn't blown down on him."

"I know it," said Rhoda. "You told me."

"Mamma even beat Papa's record," said the old lady. "Mamma died at ninety-seven, and many claim she'd be alive today if she hadn't got her feet wet that cold night when she went over to visit the Pendletons and then came down with the pneumonia."

And then one afternoon, when Edna was shopping at the supermarket, and the old lady and Rhoda were alone together, Mrs. Post somehow fell down the spiral back stairs and broke her neck. When Edna returned, Rhoda met her at the door to tell her the news. She had an innocent, plausible explanation of the accident. The old lady had heard a kitten mewing like it was lost on the back stairs landing. She had insisted on going outside to see about it, the child following her. Then somehow she had miscalculated distance, missed her step, and had fallen the five flights to the little cement courtyard below. Rhoda pointed out where the body was laying, and Mrs. Penmark joined her neighbors beside the body in time to hear her daughter repeat her story of the accident.

Edna looked at the child with a strange, intense look. She said, "Mamma hated cats. She was afraid of them all her life. All the kittens in Baltimore could have been on the landing mewing and she wouldn't have gone near them."

Rhoda's eyes opened wide in surprise. "But she did, though, Miss Edna. She went out there to look for the little kitten just like I said."

"Where's the kitten now?" asked Edna.

"It ran away," said Rhoda earnestly. "I saw it running down the steps. It was a little gray kitten with white feet."

Then, in sudden alarm, she tugged at Edna's sleeve and said, "She promised me the little glass ball when she died. It's mine now, isn't it?"

Mrs. Penmark said, "Rhoda! Rhoda! How can you say such a thing?"

"But she did, Mother," said Rhoda patiently. "She promised it to me. Miss Edna heard her do it."

Edna looked strangely at the child and said, "Yes, she promised it to you. It's yours now. I'll go get it for you at once."

Mrs. Penmark remembered these things with painful clarity, and now, looking back, she also remembered that neither she nor her husband had been asked to the funeral, although the other neighbors had gone. She also recalled that, later on, when she'd met Edna in the elevator, and had spoken to her, the daughter, who had always been so pleasant and friendly, had turned her back and pretended not to hear. . . . For a time Rhoda had worn the ball each night when she went to bed; for a time she would rest against her pillow, her lips pursed, her eyes narrowed in an expression reminiscent of the old woman, and peer down into the shifting opals, as though she had not only taken the old woman's pendant, but her personality as well.

Upon impulse, Christine went quickly to her child's room. She saw the opal ball looped over one post of the little girl's bed, as though it were a charm. She lifted the ornament in her hand a moment; but she let it fall at once, as though it were somehow evil, as though it had burned her hand.

When Rhoda came back from the park, Christine said abruptly, even before the child had put her book away, "Were the things you told the Fern sisters about Claude Daigle the truth?"

"Yes, Mother. They were all the truth. You know I don't tell lies any more, after you said I mustn't."

Christine waited a moment, and then went on. "Did you have anything to do—anything at all, no matter how little it was—with Claude getting drowned?"

Rhoda stared at her, an expression of surprise on her face, and then said cautiously, "What makes you want to know that, Mother?"

"I want you to tell me the truth, no matter what it is. We can manage things some way, but if we're to do it, I must know the truth." She put her hand on the child's shoulder, and said impulsively, "I want you to look me in the eyes, and tell me. I must know the absolute truth."

The child gazed at her with bright, candid eyes, and said, "No, Mother. I didn't."

"You're not going back to the Fern School next year," said Mrs. Penmark presently. "They don't want you there any more."

An expression of wariness came over the child's face. She waited, but since her mother did not go on with the subject, she moved away slowly, and said, "Okay. Okay." She went immediately to her own room, sat at her table, and began working on her jigsaw puzzle.

Later Christine got out her typewriter and began a letter to her husband, a much longer one than she usually wrote him. She dated the letter June 16, 1952, and began: *My darling, my darling!* . . . She typed on and on, as though it were only thus she could rid herself of the things that troubled her. She gave him the details of the penmanship medal which Rhoda had not won, after all; she wrote of the Daigle boy's death; she told him of the Fern School's unwillingness to accept Rhoda for the coming term; she spoke of the death of the old lady in Baltimore.

She said, *I don't know why these things frighten me so. I was always considered the calm one. It was one of the things you said you admired in me when we met that first time at your aunt's apartment, with all those others trying to talk one another down. Do you remember that now? Do you remember the things you said to me the next evening when we went dancing together? I remember them, my darling! I remember them all! I remember the moment I first knew I loved you, and would love you forever. Don't smile at my silliness, but it was when you picked up your change, looked up sideways, and smiled at me.*

*That was such a happy evening. But I feel now as though I'd been caught up in some dreadful trap I'd not expected at all, one I can't escape from. I feel as though I have something to face which I haven't the strength to face. There are so many things, so many intangible things, I can't explain to you, or even put into logical, everyday thought for myself.*

*You must not jump to any conclusion based on the things I've told you in this long letter, because these things, as you can see, are susceptible of more than one interpretation. But I keep seeing old Mrs. Post after she fell while Rhoda was visiting her; and I keep seeing, in my mind's eye, at least, the bruises on the Daigle boy's forehead and hands. I do not know. I tell you, I simply do not know.*

*I wish you were here at this moment. Then you could hold me in*

*your arms and laugh at my silliness; you could laugh your soft, wonder-*
*ful laugh and rub your cheek against mine and tell me not to worry so.*
*And yet if I had some magical power to bring you back, I would not use*
*it. I swear to you, I would not use it, my dearest one.*

*My darling! My darling! I am deeply worried. What shall I do?*
*Write and tell me what I must do now. Write at once—I did not know I*
*was so vulnerable.*

She finished her letter, but long before she had done so, she
knew she would not send it, for she realized how important the
work he was doing was for her husband at this point in his career.
She felt its success or failure would be the turning point in his career in this new place, and, of course, the turning point in hers,
too, since her life was forever tied to his own. No! Kenneth must
go on with his work untroubled and unhindered, and she must
go on with hers as best she could. The problem of Rhoda was ba-
sically her problem, and she must solve it. She must manage
somehow.

She addressed the envelope, sealed it, and put it in the
drawer of her desk, the drawer she always kept locked, aligning
it evenly with the pistol she also kept there. She felt better afterward: perhaps she was making too much of imponderables.
Perhaps. . . .

# five

TOWARD THE END OF THE WEEK, Mrs. Breedlove telephoned
and said, "I'm truly ashamed of myself for neglecting Rhoda's
locket the way I have; but I must go to town this morning, and

this will be a good time to get it fixed. If you'll ask Rhoda for it, I'll pick it up on my way out."

Her daughter, Christine said, was playing under the Kunkels' big scuppernong arbor, but she was confident she could find the locket without help; Rhoda kept her valued possessions in a Swiss chocolate tin in her top dresser drawer, and the locket should be there, too.

The locket was where she thought it would be, and returning the box to its original place, Mrs. Penmark felt something flat and metallic under the oilcloth that covered the drawer. She outlined the object with her forefinger, wondering what it could be, and then, lifting the covering in sudden, intuitive panic, she found the lost penmanship medal.

For an instant, the occurrence had little meaning for her, her mind refusing to accept the implications of its discovery; it seemed merely part of a thing she'd read once in a book, a thing with neither value nor application for herself; then, as the inevitable significance of the discovery of the medal in this particular place came to her, she returned it to its place under the oilcloth, her palms pressed against her cheeks, and stood perplexed in the room. *Everything she told me about the medal is a lie*, she thought. *Everything. She had it all the time.*

She walked to the window and stood there, hearing the voices of her daughter and the Kunkel children raised in shrillness across the street. A sense of petulant sadness came over her, a feeling that she was being most unjustly treated, was being wrongfully punished for things she had not done. . . .

What was the matter with Rhoda, anyway? Why couldn't she behave like other girls of her age? What was the basis of her strange, unsocial conduct? She looked back, reviewing the little girl's life from its beginning, in an effort to see how she had gone wrong in training or affection, to find the mistakes she had made—for it was plain, now, that she had made many mistakes—eager to blame herself, in this moment of self-abasement, for any omission, any error in judgment, no matter how tiny, no matter how innocently done; but she could find nothing of any true importance.

She was still standing there by the window, undecided as to what she must do now, her hands opening and closing in little spasms of anxiety and doubt, when Monica rang the bell. At once she opened the door and gave Monica the locket. Monica was in one of her more jovial moods; she talked about the locket and the memories it had once held for her, as though she were still on the couch of Dr. Kettlebaum, and associated freely for him.

Christine smiled, listened, and nodded, but her mind took in little that was said. She thought: *Rhoda has been given love and security from the beginning. She was never neglected, and she was never spoiled. She was never unjustly treated. Kenneth and I always made it a point to see that she felt important to us, and wanted. I don't understand her mind or her character. I do not understand it.*

Mrs. Breedlove said, "My own monogram was never on the locket, but I think I'll have Rhoda's engraved on the reverse side, if you're agreeable."

*Whatever the trouble is,* thought Christine, nodding and saying absently, "Yes, yes, of course," and then half turning and resting her forehead against the panel of the door: *I don't believe environment had much to do with it. It must be something deeper than that.* She sighed, raised her head, and looked at Mrs. Breedlove once more, thinking: *It was something dark. Something dark and unexplainable.*

"Has Rhoda a middle initial?" asked Monica gaily. "It's odd, but I never thought to inquire before."

Christine came back to reality and said the child' full name was Rhoda Howe Penmark. She'd been named for Kenneth's mother, a formal woman of unbridled respectability. The elder Mrs. Penmark had opposed her son's marriage into the Bravo family with considerable heat. They were, she said, a family of international vagabonds who had never taken root anywhere; they were dissident Bohemians, or at least Richard Bravo, the father, seemed to be, if one could judge from his writings, and it was only fair to assume his family would be like him, forever taking issue with the fundamental and established order of things, the things that more stable people revered and perpetuated from generation to generation. She had predicted the direst consequences if her son persisted in "this mad folly"; she wanted to be put on record that she, at least, had seen clearly, and had done her duty—had warned him in advance, no matter how painful the issuance of the warning had been to her, no matter how deeply her forced disapprobation had hurt her mother's heart. Rhoda had been named for the jealous old lady as a sop to her vanity, in an effort to win her tolerance and good will—an effort which had never been entirely successful.

Monica took the locket, dropped it in her bag, and said, "Oh, that New *England* type. I know it so well, my dear."

When she had gone, Christine sat by her window that overlooked the park, her forefinger absently moving along the arm of the chair. She thought about her child, and wondered what course she must take now. Then, all at once, she had a sense of weary familiarity, as though she'd been over these things before, and had got nowhere, just as she would get nowhere this time, too. Again she felt self-pity. Her husband had never said so, but she knew the death of the old woman in Baltimore, and the subsequent expulsion of the child for theft from the progressive school, had been the true reasons he'd asked for a transfer from his position there, to this, in a way, lesser position, where he would be among complete strangers. . . . But when she had pitied herself enough, when she had exhausted the possibilities of how unjustly she was treated, when compared with happier women, women whose children were ordinary and predictable, her sense of proportion returned to her, and with it, hope and something of her normal good nature.

She would no longer jump to unsupported conclusions. Perhaps Rhoda had a truthful and logical explanation for having the penmanship medal. Perhaps she'd been too frightened to admit its possession, with the Fern sisters badgering her in a body, and asking her all those shaped, pointed questions. At least, she had not lied this time, except indirectly, of course, for nobody, so far as she now knew, had thought to ask the child if she had the medal herself, or knew where it was.

She washed her face in cold water, put on new lipstick, and sat for ten minutes to compose herself; then, crossing the street, she went to the Kunkels' back yard and told Rhoda to come with her. When they were home again, she got the medal from its hiding place and put it on the table before them. Rhoda's eyes opened wide in alarm, and then, glancing from side to side, she closed them warily.

"How did the penmanship medal happen to be in your dresser drawer?" said Christine. "Tell me the truth, Rhoda."

Rhoda took off one of her shoes, examined it slowly, and put it on again, but she did not answer at once. Then smiling a little, dancing away from her mother in a gesture which others had always found so charming, she said, to gain time, "When we move into our new house, can we have a scuppernong arbor, too? Can we? Can we, Mother?"

"Answer my question, Rhoda! But remember I'm not as innocent about what went on at the picnic as you think. Miss Octavia Fern told me a great deal when I went to see her. So please don't bother to make up a story for my benefit this time."

But the child remained silent, her mind working, waiting shrewdly for her mother to continue talking, and betray the answer she expected; but Christine, as though aware of her child's intention, and repelled by her calculated but clumsy efforts at evasion, only said, "How did Claude Daigle's medal get in your dresser drawer? It certainly didn't get there by itself. I'm waiting for your answer, Rhoda."

She got up from her chair and walked about the room, a sense of anger suddenly burning in her. The child should be thoroughly spanked, she felt. She'd never been spanked in her life, and perhaps that was the real trouble with her now. She should be thoroughly and efficiently spanked; she should be taught, without further delay, a lesson in kindness and consideration for other people. But her anger died quickly, and she knew she could never bring herself to hurt the child, no matter what she'd done. Perhaps Rhoda knew that, too. Perhaps it was really the strength of her polite, unyielding stubbornness.

"I don't know how the medal got there, Mother," said Rhoda, her eyes wide with innocence. "How should I know how the medal got there?"

"You know. You know quite well how it got there."

She seated herself again and, continuing in a softer voice, she said, "The first thing I want to know is this: did you go out on the wharf at any time—any time at all—during the picnic?"

"Yes, Mother," said the child hesitantly. "I went there once."

"Was it before or after you were bothering Claude?"

"I didn't bother Claude, Mother. What makes you think that?"

"When did you go out on the wharf, Rhoda?"

"It was real early. It was when we first got there."

"You knew you were forbidden to go on the wharf, didn't you? Why did you do it?"

"One of the big boys said there were little shells that grew on the pilings. I didn't believe that shells grew on wood, and I wanted to see if they did or not."

Christine nodded, and said, "I'm glad you admit being on the wharf, at least. Miss Fern told me one of the guards saw you coming off the wharf. He said it was much later than you claim, though. He said it wasn't long before lunchtime."

"He's wrong, though. I told Miss Fern that, too. It happened like I said it did." Then, as though feeling she'd won the initial point, she said, "The man hollered at me, and told me to come off, and I did what he said. I went back to the lawn, and that's where I saw Claude. But I wasn't bothering Claude. I was just talking to him."

"What did you say to Claude?"

"I said that if I didn't win the medal, I was glad he won it. So Claude said I was sure to win it next year, as the medal wasn't ever given twice to the same pupil."

Christine shook her head wearily. "Please! Please, Rhoda! This isn't a game. I want the truth."

"But it's all true, Mother," said Rhoda earnestly. "Every word I tell you is true."

Christine was silent for a short time, and then she said, "Miss Fern told me about one of the monitors who saw you try to take the medal off Claude's shirt. Did the girl really see what she said she did?"

"That big girl was Mary Beth Musgrove," said Rhoda. "She

told everybody she saw me; even Leroy Jessup knows she saw me." She paused, and then went on, her bright eyes opened wide, as though complete candor were now the only course open to her. "Claude and I were playing a game we made up. He said if I could catch him in ten minutes, and touch the medal with my hand—it was like prisoners' base, or something—he'd let me wear the medal for an hour. How can Mary Beth say I took the medal? I didn't."

"Mary Beth didn't say you took the medal. She said you grabbed at it, and tried to take it. She said Claude ran away down the beach when she called to you. Did you have the medal even then?"

"No, Mother. Not then."

She was becoming more sure of herself under the questioning, and convinced at last that her mother knew little, or nothing at all, she came to her, put her arms about her neck, and kissed her cheek with such ardor that her mother was now the passive, patient one.

At last Christine said, "How did you get the medal, Rhoda?"

"Oh, I got it later *on*."

"I want to know how you got possession of the medal, Rhoda."

"When Claude went back on his promise," said Rhoda, "I followed him up the beach. Then he stopped and said I could wear the medal all day if I gave him the fifty cents you gave me for spending money."

"Is that the truth, my darling? Is that really true?"

Rhoda said, a slight contempt in her voice at her easy victory, "Yes, Mother. That's just what happened. I gave him the fifty cents, and he let me wear the medal."

"But if you paid him to wear the medal, why didn't you tell

Miss Fern that when she questioned you? Why did you keep quiet about it all this time?"

The child began to whimper, to glance about her with a simulated apprehension. "Miss Fern doesn't like me at all. She doesn't, Mother! She really doesn't! I was afraid she'd think bad things about me if I told her I had the medal." She rushed to her mother, embraced her, and rested her head against her shoulder, cutting her eyes up expectantly, as though awaiting some cue.

"You knew how much Mrs. Daigle wanted the medal, didn't you? You knew she paid those men to go down in the water and look for it; we discussed that once before. You knew she held the funeral up, hoping the medal would be found in time, so that Claude could be buried with it. You knew all these things, didn't you, Rhoda?"

"Yes, Mother. I guess I did."

"If you knew how anxious she was to find the medal, why didn't you give it to her? If you were afraid to take it back, I would have done it for you."

The child said nothing; she merely made placating noises in her throat, and stroked her mother's neck softly. Christine waited, closed her eyes, and said, "Mrs. Daigle is heartbroken over Claude's death. It's almost destroyed her. I don't think she'll ever recover from it, at least not completely." She disengaged her child's arms, and holding her away from her, she said, "Do you understand what I'm talking about? Do you understand at all, Rhoda?"

"I suppose so, Mother. Well, I guess so, Mother."

But Christine sighed and thought: *She doesn't understand at all. She hasn't the least idea of what I mean.*

Rhoda shook her head, and said stubbornly, "It was silly to want to bury the medal pinned on Claude's coat. Claude was dead, wasn't he? Claude wouldn't know whether he had the medal pinned on him or not."

The child felt her mother's sudden, and, to her, inexplicable, disapproval; and then, as though to win back the ground she had lost, she kissed her mother's cheek with little hungry kisses. "Oh, I've got the *sweetest* mother!" she said. "I tell everybody I know I've got the sweetest mother in the world!"

But Christine pulled away from her daughter, and sat alone by the window, looking out at the tree-lined street; then Rhoda, feeling her tested approach, which had always worked so well in the past when she wanted her way, had mysteriously failed her this time, tilted her head sidewise and said, "If Claude's mother wants a little boy that bad, why doesn't she take one out of the Orphans' Home?"

In a feeling of sudden revulsion, Christine pushed the child from her, a thing she'd never done before, and said, "Please go away! Don't talk to me any more! We have nothing to say to each other."

Rhoda shrugged and said patiently, "Well, okay. Okay, Mother."

She sat at the piano and began working on the piece her teacher had given her the week before; she practiced with earnest concentration, her tongue sticking out between her teeth, and when she struck a wrong note, she sighed, shook her head in disapproval, and began the piece all over again.

Christine, not long afterward, went about preparing lunch. When she and her daughter had eaten, and she was putting away the last washed dish, she glanced out of the kitchen window and saw Leroy in the courtyard below. He smirked, showing his stained, irregular teeth, rolled his eyes in invitation, and turned away. He had been out the night before drinking beer with his wife, and he still had a slight hang-over. That trough-fed, pink, Christine Penmark, he thought. That dizzy blonde! That one didn't have enough sense to come in when it rained. That blonde was sure dumb. That dumb Christine let Rhoda put it over on her all the time.

He went into the coolness of the basement, remembering again the incident of the hose, and the rude things Mrs. Breedlove had said to him that day. He'd never got even with her for saying them things, but he would; just wait and see. . . .

Her garage door was open, and her car gone; she must be downtown somewhere spending money and gabbing. He bet she wasn't eating no lunch wrapped up in a paper bag; he bet she was eating at one of them real nice places, throwing her weight around, and going gab, gab, gab. His eyes wandered about the littered room, and he saw a big, discarded scraper standing in one corner. He laughed suddenly in pleasant anticipation of what he was going to do, wheeled out the scraper, and abandoned it in front of Mrs. Breedlove's garage. Then, as though that were not enough, he set his buckets near by, and draped his mops over the scraper, to give an air of informal credibility to the affair. He surveyed the work he had done, and when his artistic conscience was satisfied, he went back to the basement, finished his lunch, and sat there chuckling in anticipated pleasure of what Mrs. Breedlove's face was going to look like when she had to get out in the hot sun and move the obstruction before she could put her car up.

He had fixed up a makeshift bed for himself in the basement; he had piled papers and excelsior in one corner, behind an old broken sofa, a place where none of the tenants could see him easily if they happened to peep inside; and often, when he was feeling like he did right now, he would slip in there and take himself a little snooze without nobody being no wiser. He smoothed out the old quilt he had put over the papers and excelsior, stretched out, sighed voluptuously, and let his mind wander. He wondered what that dizzy blonde did for her fun, with her husband out of town so much. He'd like to have her with him right now, if anybody asked him. He'd show her some tricks, all right. He was just the one to do it, the way he was feeling right now. And when he got through with that dumb blonde, she'd write a letter to her husband and tell him to not never come back. He turned on his side, watching a fly walk across the ceiling.

That dizzy blonde was a good-looking woman, all right—she made lots of them movie queens look sick; but she was too dumb for him. She was too soft and foolish-like. You could tame that one and break her down fast; you could have that one eating out of your hand, and begging you for it all the time. That one was too much like his wife. . . . But that mean little Rhoda was something else. You couldn't put nothing over on that mean little girl. And when she grew up, she was going to be *something*. If a man tried to treat her sorry, just as likely as not she'd bounce a skillet off his head. He smiled with contentment, the voluptuousness of his fantasies flooding his senses, turned slowly on his bed, and was instantly asleep.

Mrs. Penmark sent Rhoda to the park to play, got out the material she'd selected for the child's school dresses, and started on the first one. She had it cut out and the material basted when Mrs. Breedlove stopped at her apartment on her way upstairs. She was tired from her trip to town, and plainly she was angry about something. She accepted the glass of iced tea Christine offered her, sipped it, and said, "I'm not going to endure Leroy another day. He gets more impossible all the time. If it weren't for his poor wife and children, I'd—"

She broke off, shrugged, and said, "But why go over these things again? You know him as well as I do. I'm not even going to discuss the matter!"

But she did, of course, and in the completest detail. When she had finished, she was in an excellent humor once more, and laughing a little, tossing her head wildly, she said, "But why delude myself any more, dear Christine? I enjoy screaming at Leroy, and I'm sure he knows it. There's a streak of fishwife in me, and Leroy is the only one I know who brings it out and ventilates it."

She took off her hat, tossed it on the sofa, and said suddenly, "Rhoda's locket! That's what I really stopped by for, not to tell you about Leroy Jessup."

She went on to explain that she'd taken the locket to Pageson's since she considered them the best jewelers in town, and talked with old Mr. Pageson himself, whom she'd known a long time. Mr. Pageson had listened to what she said, had agreed to what she'd suggested; but he'd also said she couldn't get the locket back for at least two weeks, if that soon, there being so much work in advance of hers. She had told Mr. Pageson in return that she'd really counted on getting the locket that same day, not two weeks later—in fact, she'd counted on getting it in about two hours at the outside; but Mr. Pageson had shaken his frail head and said it was entirely out of the question, a complete physical impossibility.

Christine smiled and said, "I can imagine what you said in reply to poor old Mr. Pageson."

"Oh, I doubt it!" she said with delight. "I doubt if even you, who knows me so intimately, dear Christine, can guess how I handled the man this time!" She thrust out her massive, tubular legs, and continued. "My approach was quite simple, and, if I do say so, inspired. I merely said in my most reasonable voice, 'You mustn't forget, dear Mr. Pageson, that I'm running the Community Chest again this year, and I can't wait for the locket because I must hurry home and make out my estimate of the donations we expect from various individuals and businesses. I'm glad I made the trip to your store, anyway, for I had no idea your business was doing so *well*. I'd already put you down for a thousand dollars in my mind, but of course, knowing what I do now, I'll be happy to revise the figure upward—oh, so definitely upward!'"

"Monica! Monica! Aren't you ashamed of yourself?"

"Not at all!" screamed Mrs. Breedlove. "Not in the slightest, my dear Christine! . . . 'I think about twenty-five *hundred* would be a fair donation from a going concern like this one,' I said; but of course I winked at him when I said it. He got the point, all right, and he said, 'You can put me down for any amount you like. I don't have to pay it, you know. There's no law that makes me contribute a penny to the Community Chest if I don't want to.'"

Mrs. Breedlove put down her glass and touched her eyes with the hem of her handkerchief. "'You think so, Mr. Pageson?' I asked. 'You really and truly think so?'"

"He said, 'I not only think so, I know so!' So then I had to tell him how we dealt with cases like his. We put them in our 'Difficult Extractions' folder, and then our volunteers really went to work. I told him, 'First we send down a bevy of last year's debutantes, girls who'll do anything in the name of charity. They'll be instructed to weep on your counter, and implore you to loosen up—preferably while the store is full of customers, of course. But if that doesn't work, I'll have to call in old Miss Minnie Pringle—an expert at imploring if I ever met one.' And when I mentioned Miss Minnie, I knew I had him on the ropes, my dear."

She broke off to add that since Christine had never had the

pleasure of meeting Miss Pringle, she had something to look forward to in the future. Miss Minnie had a voice as piercing as the
sharpest knife, as powerful and monotonous as a foghorn; she
had the sensitivity of a rhinoceros, the tenacity of a snapping
turtle. Minnie was actually the most terrifying old battle-ax in
town, even worse than Monica herself. . . .

"I knew I had old Mr. Pageson on the run," she continued; "but
to throw me off, he said, 'Minnie Pringle won't bother me at all. I
rather like the woman. We'll be glad to have her in the store any
time.'"

"So I reminded him that Minnie's approach would be to
stand just inside his front door and remind him, and of course his
customers, too, that although he had this flourishing business,
this little gold mine of wealth, he owed it not to his own efforts,
but to the tolerance of One On High. One On High had given
him this tidy, prospering business; but One On High was equally
prepared to smite him with lightning and blast him with thun-
der, to take it all away from him, in fact, if he didn't accept his
civic responsibilities and give the Community Chest its cut."

"Would you have done it?" asked Christine in astonishment.

"Of course not, my dear!" said Mrs. Breedlove. "If I did a
thing like that, Emory would drown me in the bathtub. I had no
idea of doing it. I was only kidding poor Mr. Pageson, but he
wasn't sure I was any more than you were. You see, I have a reputation of being an eccentric—a great advantage in dealing with
others, I assure you. People are afraid of eccentrics; they can
never be sure which way they'll jump, or what they'll do next.

"So, to end my tiresome story," said Mrs. Breedlove, "I
walked out of the store, saying over my shoulder, 'I've got some
errands, but I'll be back at twelve-thirty on the dot. I have every
confidence that the locket will be ready at that time.'"

Christine laughed and said, "Was the locket ready for you then?"

"Oh, my dear!" said Mrs. Breedlove. "Oh, my dear but naïve little Christine! Of course it was ready!" She opened her pocketbook and took out the locket. It had been cleaned. The clasp had been fixed. The stones had been changed. The letters R. H. P. were beautifully intertwined on the back. She gave the locket to Mrs. Penmark, and continued to talk in a delighted voice. After she'd got things her own way, her conscience troubled her for the way she'd blackmailed dear Mr. Pageson; then she remembered he liked coconut pies better than anything. But he was most particular about his coconut pies: he liked them made from fresh coconut, not from that tasteless, shriveled up stuff that came in boxes. He liked the milk of the coconut mixed in with the custard, with little morsels of fresh coconut distributed through the pie just before baking. He liked grated coconut on top of the pie, and the pie then browned in a quick, hot oven. He had told her all this a few years ago, and how Mrs. Pageson, before she died, had fixed pies for him exactly the way he liked them; but he'd not had a really good one since, for nobody in this generation of short cuts and easy solutions would go to all that trouble.

Mrs. Breedlove opened her shopping bag and took out a big, shaggy coconut. "I stopped off at Demetrios the Fruitman's," she said, "and picked out the nicest one he had. I'm going upstairs in a minute and make Mr. Pageson, that dear man, a coconut pie the way he likes them. He may not know it, but it will be far better than anything his wife ever made, because his wife, in spite of everything he says, was an indifferent cook, at best. Really, it will be the best pie he ever ate. I make the best pastry in town and I know it."

When Mrs. Breedlove had gone, Christine felt again the unhappiness she'd known earlier in the day. That evening, after dinner, she said to Rhoda, "I've been thinking of the medal all day. I'm going to return it to Mrs. Daigle, and I'm going to ask her forgiveness for your having stolen it."

"I didn't steal the medal, Mother. How can you say anything like that? Claude sold me the medal like I told you."

"I don't know how you got the medal," said Christine wearily. "But I know you didn't get it the way you said you did. But even if you did rent it from Claude, it was dishonest to keep it afterward."

The child looked at her steadily, her eyes filled with cold, shrewd calculation, a calculation she no longer tried to hide from her mother, since already Christine knew so much. "It's not Mrs. Daigle's medal," she said. "Mrs. Daigle didn't win it. It belongs to me more than it does to her."

Christine did not answer the child's argument. She merely said, "I won't be gone very long. I want you to stay here in the apartment until I get back. Do you understand?"

At first, she had considered taking the child with her, to give her an object lesson in the sorrows of others, but she decided against it as both embarrassing and useless, and, putting the medal in her purse, she went alone, telling nobody of her intention. Mr. Daigle received her at the door, but hesitantly now. There was a tense uneasiness about him, and he wavered in his intentions for a time, a time long enough for Mrs. Penmark to feel, and wonder about; and then, pressing his hands together, he asked her into the living-room. Abruptly he wheeled and went to tell his wife of her presence, and at once Christine heard Mrs. Daigle's metallic, hysterical voice in the room across the hall. "Why is she coming here again?" she said. "Did you think to ask her? Hasn't she caused us enough heart-break and sorrow without her coming here again to gloat over us? She came here to remind me that her child is well and happy, and that mine—" Her voice rose almost to a wail, and her husband said in a nervous voice, "Please, Hortense! Please! She can hear you."

"Then let her hear me!" said Mrs. Daigle. "Let her hear me! What difference does it make?" Then, in a softer voice, she went on wearily. "Tell her to go away. Tell her we don't care to see her, and she must go back home at once."

Mr. Daigle came back into the room. He said apologetically, "Hortense isn't herself these days. Perhaps you can understand. She resents anybody who's happier than she is—and God alone knows that's everybody who lives. She's been very unreasonable since Claude's death, and she's under a doctor's care. He came this afternoon again." Then, lowering his voice even more, he added, "We're worried about her."

Mrs. Penmark pressed his hand in understanding and moved toward the door, but at that moment Mrs. Daigle burst into the room. Her eyes were red and swollen, her hair hung in damp strings around her face, which seemed puffy and inflamed, as though she had been recently bitten by some poisonous insect. She took Christine in her arms and said, "Don't go now. Since you're here, you must stay." She wept noisily, her head pressed to her visitor's shoulder, and said, "I'm glad you could come. I enjoyed your last visit so much. I've often spoken of it to my husband. If you doubt me, ask him, and he'll tell you I have. It was pleasant of you to drop by again. I said I hoped Mrs. Penmark would drop in again."

Then, releasing her guest, she sat on the sofa and said, "Come sit beside me, Christine. May I call you Christine? I'm quite aware that you come from a higher level of society than I do. I'm sure you made a debut and all that, but perhaps you won't mind this once. I was a beauty-parlor operator you know. I always considered Christine such a gentle name. Hortense has such a fat sound, doesn't it? When I was a child, the other children used to sing a song they'd made up that went, 'My girl Hortense, hasn't got much sense. Let's write her name on the privy fence.'" She sighed, wiped her eyes and said, "You know how nasty children can be sometimes?"

"Hortense! Hortense!" said Mr. Daigle. Then, turning to Mrs. Penmark, he added, "Hortense isn't herself. She's under a doctor's care."

"You're so attractive, Christine. But, of course, blondes do fade quickly. You have such exquisite taste in clothes, but I'm sure you have a great deal of money to buy them with. When I was a young girl, I always hoped I'd look like you, but, of course, I never did." She giggled at some obscure memory of her own, and went on. "I went to see Miss Octavia Fern about little Claude's death, but she told me nothing I hadn't read in the papers, or heard over the radio. Oh, but she's a sly one—that Miss Octavia Fern! She'd made up her mind she wasn't going to tell me anything, and you can be sure she didn't. She knows more than she tells, I think. There's something funny about the whole thing, and I've said so over and over to Mr. Daigle. He married quite late you know, in his forties. But I wasn't exactly what the fellow calls a 'spring chicken' either."

"Please Hortense! Please! Let me take you back to bed where you can rest."

"There's something funny about the whole thing, Christine!" she said knowingly. Then, impulsively, she turned to Mrs. Penmark and said, "I heard that your little girl was the last one who saw him alive. Will you ask her about him and tell me what she says? Maybe she remembers some little thing. I don't care how small it is. Miss Octavia isn't going to tell me anything, and I've resigned myself to that."

"Miss Fern told you all she knows, Hortense. You must get that idea that she's your enemy out of your mind."

"Miss Fern despises me. She knows my father used to run a little fruit stand down on St. Cecelia Street, near the wharves." Then seeing that Christine was about to interrupt her, she put her damp palm against her visitor's lips and said amiably, "Oh, yes, she does. Don't try to apologize for her. I'm no fool. But if that isn't the reason, she despises me because I was a beauty-parlor operator before I married. She and her sisters used to come in the shop where I worked. You know something, Mrs. Penmark? Miss Burgess dyes her hair. She'd faint if she thought I told anybody that, but it's true. She dyes her hair, all right."

Christine put her arms about the suffering woman, closed her eyes, and thought: *Don't let me show my emotions now! Let me wait till I'm home where nobody can see me!*

Mr. Daigle lit a cigarette and walked aimlessly up and down in the room, straightening a vase, aligning a picture, brushing with his fingers the beadwork that hung like cobwebs from the dreadful lamps. "Hortense isn't herself, Mrs. Penmark," he said. "You must pardon her." Turning to his wife he said pleadingly, "If you'll go back to bed, Mrs. Penmark will sit by you and hold your hand for a while."

Mrs. Daigle, moving toward her bedroom, said, "Will you, really? Will you really, Christine?" Then humbly she said, "You can wear such simple things, and they look so well on you. I could never wear simple things. I never knew why. . . . I know all mothers say these things, and most people laugh at them, but he was such a sweet child. He was such a lovely, dear little boy. He said I was his sweetheart. He said he was going to marry me when he grew up. I used to laugh and say, 'You'll forget me long before then. You'll find a prettier girl when you grow up and you'll marry her.'" Her voice was mounting again, and as she went into her bedroom, with her husband and Mrs. Penmark supporting her, it got steadily louder.

"And you know what he said then, Christine? He said, 'No, I won't, because there's not another girl in the whole world as pretty and sweet as you are!' If you don't believe me, ask our cook. She was present at the time, and heard it all, and laughed with me when I laughed. There were those bruises on his hands, and that peculiar crescent-shaped place on his forehead that the undertaker covered up. He must have bled before he died. That's what my doctor, who saw him, said. He said he must have bled some, but the water had washed it all away." Then, turning and pressing her face into her pillow, she cried out wildly, "What became of the penmanship medal? Where is it now? I have a right to know, so please don't try to stop me! I'm the little boy's mother, and if I knew what happened to the penmanship medal he won, I'd have a good idea what happened to him! Why doesn't somebody find the medal and bring it to me? Then I'd know for sure."

She sat up on the side of her bed and said, "I don't know why you took it on yourself to come here unasked, Mrs. Penmark. But if you want to please me, you'll be gracious enough to leave."

"Hortense is not herself," said Mr. Daigle.

Mrs. Daigle, brushing her limp stringy hair out of her face, said, "I'm impossible! I'm completely impossible!"

"Hortense is under a doctor's care," said Mr. Daigle.

When Christine returned home, the medal still in her bag,

Rhoda was sitting quietly in the lamplight reading her book. She saw the disturbed unhappy expression on her mother's face, she felt her unexpressed censure, her hurt disapprobation. She narrowed her eyes thoughtfully, wondering what her mother had said to Mrs. Daigle, and what Mrs. Daigle, in turn, had said to her mother. She stood up, smiled, tilted her head back, and clapped her hands in a lovely little gesture she'd picked up somewhere. "If I give you a basket of kisses, what will you give me?" she asked.

But Christine did not answer, and Rhoda, in sudden panic, danced eagerly to her mother; she put her arms about her mother's waist and said, "What will you give me, Mother? What will you give me?"

Christine sat down suddenly, as though too weak to stand longer, and took her child in her arms. She pressed her cheek against her daughter's cheek, and said, "Oh, my darling! Oh, my darling!" but she did not answer the child's question.

# six

MRS. PENMARK AGAIN found it difficult to sleep; she kept hearing, in memory, Mrs. Daigle's affirmation of her son's devotion, in tones alternately too shrill and too hoarse; hearing her ponder, in a kind of compulsive despair, the baffling factors of the boy's death. She slept at last, drifting into a dream too frightening to be remembered; but when she woke next day, with the sun lying in a gentle pattern on the carpet, with the familiar noises of morning everywhere about her, she felt calmer. Then, as though something in the forgotten dream had revealed some forgotten wish of her own, she knew she wanted now, and had wanted all along, to visit Benedict, to see for herself the woods, the house, the bay, and the old wharf there.

At nine, she telephoned Miss Octavia Fern, and Miss Fern said she understood completely. She'd be glad to accompany her, to act as a guide for the occasion. She suggested they go next day, and they agreed that Mrs. Penmark would pick up the older woman at ten, at the school gate. Christine turned from the telephone, thinking: *Rhoda was never disobedient or lazy or insolent, like so many children. She's got so many good qualities. There's only this one thing about her, this quirk in her character.*

Later she sat beside her window waiting for the postman, hoping there'd be a letter for her from Kenneth. She saw the postman turn the corner on schedule; and her neighbor, Mrs. Forsythe, who plainly had been waiting for him, too, met him on the flagstones. "Have you heard anything more about your son who's missing in Korea?" she asked.

"No, ma'am. We haven't heard anything more. We can only hope."

"Waiting for news is such a sad thing, Mr. Creckmoss. You have all my sympathy. I've been praying for him since he was reported missing."

"I appreciate that. You're a real nice friend to have."

"It's hard to understand sometimes why there must be so much pain and cruelty in the world. But it's something we've all got to face."

The postman said there were two ways of meeting experience—you could expect pain or you could expect happiness. "Now, I'm going to look on the bright side until I know to the contrary," he said. "I'm going to look on the bright side, and keep saying everything's going to come out the way I want it to."

"That's certainly better than looking on the dark side."

"I remember the last world war, when I had to deliver those sad messages to people I knew real well. It was the hardest thing I ever had to do, but I kept saying to myself, 'Somebody's got to do it, and I guess it's me.' But I don't think I could do it now."

He walked away, and when Mrs. Forsythe was in her apartment again, Christine took from her mailbox the letter she had awaited. She read it eagerly. It recounted her husband's activities, the things he had done thus far, the things that still remained to be done. He missed Christine and Rhoda more than he could say. His one desire was to wind up his work as quickly as he could and return to them.

When she'd read the letter, when she'd extracted from it the last subtlety of meaning, she went to her bedroom and examined the photograph of her husband on her dressing-table, a photograph which showed him in naval uniform, the way he had been when she first knew him. His hair was dark and cropped close to his skull; his brown eyes looked out at the world with a sort of innocent eagerness—a quality she'd always found so moving, so entirely charming in him; and at that moment she had a desire to see him again, to hear his soft laughter, to feel his arms about her, that was almost unendurable. She reached out and touched his smooth, tanned cheek with her finger, her heart filling again with all the richness of the love they shared, her mind remembering once more those tender, absurd, secret joys they'd known together; and then, since she could not bring him back to her, she turned regretfully and began work on Rhoda's school dresses.

But she quickly found they no longer interested her, for her thoughts kept turning another way, and putting her typewriter on her desk, she wrote another long letter to her husband. She recounted the depth of her fears, which, as yet, had such ambiguous facts to sustain them, but which, nonetheless, persisted to trouble her. She spoke of finding the medal, and of Rhoda's evasive response to her questions. She described her second visit to the Daigles. She spoke of the postman whose son was missing in Korea. In future, she would resolutely heed his words— she would react as he did to circumstances that could not be altered; she would put doubt behind her; she would anticipate happiness, not sorrow. She wrote, *I'm saving these letters that I cannot send, my darling. When you are back with me, and my fears have all proved foolish, perhaps we can read them over together. Then you can hold me in your arms and laugh at my weak, unreasonable fears, can ridicule in your dear, gentle voice my overheated imagination. . . .*

She wrote on and on, saying that, in her distress, she felt herself turning for comfort to some force stronger than herself. She had never been religious in the accepted sense of the word, but she'd always believed in the power that had once shaped the universe, and guided it now. She chose to think of that power as benign. She saw so clearly now that the thing which had repelled her in the past, and had kept her from the expected orthodoxy, had been the efforts of institutions to visualize God in human images, to define him with man's definition of himself, to catch his power in obsessive rituals, to confuse the laws with laws that man devised for his own safety. . . .

She wrote: *Do I sound too much like Monica now? Are you surprised to know these thoughts are in my mind, and have been there for a long time? I'm not really the conventional, passive person I've schooled myself to be all these years. I learned the things others see in me from my mother. You see, my father, in spite of his charm, his bril-*

*liance and kindness, could be most unpredictable at times. He had periods of doubt and nervous depression, and it was then he turned to my mother, and later to me, for serenity and faith in himself once more. Giving him what he lacked, what he must have to be what he became, was my mother's greatest joy, her true reason for existence, she once told me. I learned something of her serenity, perhaps because I, too, loved her so greatly. Do not be mistaken in me, my darling. Do not be misled. My emotions deep down are disturbed and powerful. They are stirred up now, and I must struggle to get them under control once more.*

*I miss you so badly. I long for you so deeply at this moment. When you get this letter, drop everything, no matter how important it seems now, and come back to me. Laugh at me. Tell me my doubts have no basis in fact. Take me in your arms again. But come back to me! My darling, come back to me! Please come back to me quickly!*

When she'd finished the letter, she put it in the locked drawer of her desk. She went and stood by her window for a time, her hands pressed against her cheek; and then, her heart lighter, she went about her ordinary affairs. Later, she sat down to read the morning paper. On the front page was a long account of a murder case which was being tried at the time, a case which the paper had featured, since some of the principals in it were locally known. Usually, she did not read these things, having no interest in them, but now she read the story in all its detail. It concerned a man named Hobart L. Ponder who was accused of killing his wife for her insurance.

She had hardly finished the long account when Mrs. Breedlove stopped by for a chat. She came into the room, put a book down on the table, and said, "You're looking a little pale and tired, my dear. You seem distrait. What is it that troubles you?"

Mrs. Penmark said she'd been reading the Ponder case—perhaps that was it; and Mrs. Breedlove, as though the name were one to put her tongue in rapid motion, said she'd known Hobart Ponder's mother at one time. She'd had two sons—Hobart, the elder, now on trial for murder, and his brother Charles. Bad luck seemed to have trailed Hobart from the beginning. When he was about seven or eight years old, he'd accidentally locked Charles in an old icebox and had forgotten him.

Christine said, "What is the book you brought? Is it for Rhoda?"

"It's an illustrated copy of *Robinson Crusoe*. Emory had it as a boy. He thought Rhoda might be interested in it."

But she was not to be diverted from her history of the Ponders, and she went on to say that Hobart's maternal grandmother, who'd lived with her daughter after she married Mr. Ponder, had been mysteriously murdered with one of young Hobart's golf clubs when the boy was about fourteen.

Christine said, "I loved *Robinson Crusoe* as a child. I'm sure Rhoda will, too."

"Then, when Hobart was twenty," said Mrs. Breedlove implacably, "his father hanged himself in the garage. It was all most vague, and nobody seems to have understood the truth of it, even now. Then his mother died suddenly, too. An attack of acute indigestion, they said. And now this dreadful thing about his wife and the shotgun!" She sighed, and continued shrewdly, "But why are you reading murder cases all of a sudden?"

The next morning, Mrs. Penmark left her daughter with Mrs. Forsythe, saying she'd pick her up as soon as she returned from her visit to Benedict. Rhoda had her copy of *Robinson Crusoe* with her, and she went to the small marble balcony that jutted out in a sort of plump half-moon from the side of the Forsythe apartment. She sat down to read, but almost at once she heard Leroy laughing and talking guardedly to himself. She bent over the balcony, and saw him at work on the sweet olive bush below.

He did not look up, but he knew he had her attention, and he said out of the side of his mouth, "There she sits on Mrs. Forsythe's little gallery, reading her book and looking cute and innocent. Looking like butter wouldn't melt on her tongue. She can fool some people with that innocent look she can put on and take off when she wants to, but she can't fool me. Not me! Not even a little bit, she can't!"

The child stared down at him with no expression at all, and then, as though his presence bored her, she turned back to her book.

Leroy laughed and said softly, "She don't want to talk to nobody smart. She likes to talk to people she can fool, like her mamma and Mrs. Breedlove and Mr. Emory."

Rhoda closed her book on her forefinger, and said, "Go trim your bush. You talk silly all the time."

His eyes met the coldness in her own, and raising his head, tilting his neck back, he pressed his shears against his dirty coveralls, and said, as though they were playing the balcony scene in some ancient play, "I been way behind the times heretofore, but now I got your number, miss! I been hearing things about you that ain't nice. I been hearing you beat up that poor little Claude in the woods, and that all three of the Fern sisters had to pull you off him. They tell me it took that many to pull you off him. I heard you run him off the wharf, he was so scared. That's another thing I heard."

Rhoda put down her book, gave him her full attention, and said, "If you tell lies like that, you won't go to heaven when you die."

"I heard plenty," said Leroy. "I listen to people talk, and hear what they say. I'm not like you who's gabbing all the time and won't let nobody get a word in edgeways. I listen all the time. That's the way I learn things. That's why I'm smart and you're so dumb."

"People tell lies all the time," said Rhoda. "I think you tell them more than anybody else."

Leroy swung his shears outward in a wide, impassioned gesture. "I know what you done to that boy when you got him out on the wharf. I know. You can fool other people, but you can't fool me, because I'm not dumb. I got your number, miss. You better treat me pretty from now on."

"What did I do, if you know so much?"

Leroy made a downward, dramatic movement with his shears, and said, "You picked up a stick and hit him with it, that's what you done! You hit him because he wouldn't give you that medal like you told him to I thought I'd seen some mean little girls in my time, but you're the meanest."

Rhoda rested her arms on the marble of the balcony, and said, "You tell lies. Everybody knows it. Nobody believes anything you say."

"You want to know what you done after you hit that boy? Okay, I'll tell you what you done then. You jerked that medal off his shirt. Then you rolled that sweet little boy off the wharf, among them pilings." He laughed silently to himself, thinking: *I got her listening to me now. I got her real worried.*

Rhoda stared down at him, her clear, luminous brown eyes stretched wide in innocent surprise. "I'd be afraid to tell lies like that," she said primly. "I'd be afraid I wouldn't go to heaven."

"Don't bother to give me that innocent look, Miss Rhoda. I ain't no dope like them others. I ain't—"

But at that moment Mrs. Forsythe came onto the balcony, and Leroy dropped suddenly to his knees and began pruning the sweet olive bush. "Who were you talking to, Rhoda?" asked the old lady. She looked about mildly, but seeing nobody, she said, "I was sure I heard voices out here."

"I was reading out loud to myself," said Rhoda. She picked up her book, opened it, and said, "I like to read out loud. It sounds better to read out loud."

Below them, Leroy crouched against the side of the building, laughing with pleasure at his cleverness. That mean little girl talking about *him* lying! That little girl could out-lie anybody in town without half trying! His fantasy about Rhoda and the stick was real smart. He didn't believe it for a minute himself! He wasn't dumb enough to believe a little eight-year-old girl would have the nerve to do a thing like that. But it was real clever, anyway. Not everybody could think up a story like that on the spur of the moment. And then, when Mrs. Forsythe's voice ceased, and he heard the screen door shut, he rose cautiously and said in a whisper, "You know I'm telling the God's truth. You know I've done figured out what happened."

Rhoda leaned forward on the marble balustrade and said, "Everything you say is a lie. You tell lies all the time, Leroy. Everybody knows you tell lies."

"It ain't me that tells lies all the time," said Leroy. "It's you that tells lies all the time."

And then, as though to close this little balcony scene of hate, Rhoda took her book inside, and Leroy pruned at the branches of the sweet olive with pleasure, as though it were the child, and not the shrub, he snipped.

Mrs. Penmark parked at the Fern School gate, and Miss Octavia, spying her through the blinds, came down the walk to meet her. They rode for a time in silence, or discussing things in which neither had the least interest; and then, as they approached Benedict, and came down the long avenue of live oaks and azaleas, Miss Fern said, "You must examine our oleanders while you're here. They're very old. My grandfather planted them originally as a hedge to screen the place from the road, but now they're like trees. They're in full bloom at this season, as you see."

Then, as the two women got out of the car, Miss Fern said she'd phoned the caretakers at Benedict the evening before, and lunch would be ready at noon. It would be a simple one: crab omelettes, buttermilk biscuits, a green salad of some sort, and iced coffee. She did hope Mrs. Penmark like crabs. "They are so plentiful at this time of year," she said. "All you need do is scoop them up in the shallow water near the beach. Once, when I was a little girl like Rhoda, my father had the idea of building a pen out into the water, so we could put crabs there and fatten them up to eat when they weren't plentiful at all; but it was as impractical as most of my father's ideas. You see, the crabs, when they were penned together, ate one another before we could eat them."

They walked about the grounds, examining everything. They stood on the bridge that spanned Little Lost River, and looked at their shallow reflections in the black, sluggish water; then, hearing the luncheon bell, they came back to the house. Afterward, Christine said she'd like to go to the wharf alone, if Miss Fern would permit it; and Miss Fern nodded graciously and said, "Of course. Of course. I'll join you there later, if that's agreeable. I want to take some cuttings from the flame-colored oleander for a friend in town who's always loved that color. It's a sort of botanical sport, and I've never seen that exact shade anywhere else. We have lots of time. I've no plans at all for the afternoon."

Christine went to the end of the wharf, and stood there in indecision; then, knowing why she wanted to visit this place alone, she opened her bag, took out the penmanship medal, and dropped it among the pilings. In a way, she was as guilty as Rhoda, she thought. She flinched a little, seeing how furtive, how dishonest, she had become, how greatly her character was disintegrating under the force of her anxiety and guilt. But this seemed the best way to dispose of the medal now, for she had known, after her visit to the Daigles, she could never return it to them. Then, as though to justify her action, she said softly to herself, "Rhoda is my own flesh and blood. It's my duty to see that she isn't harmed."

She went into the summerhouse, a rickety structure which hurricanes had almost demolished, and stood there in uncertainty, trying to arrange her thoughts logically. Perhaps her worries were justified, perhaps not. But how could she know? How could she be entirely certain? Doubt was a dreadful and destroying thing, she thought. It would be better to know surely, no matter what the answer was. She sat down and raised her hands in a gesture of impotent helplessness.

Miss Fern joined her, a basket of the cuttings she had taken resting on one arm. They sat in silence, watching the level bay, with only gray mullet breaking the silence as they jumped in long, graceful arcs over the sandspit that ran out from shore. Then, at length, Miss Fern said, "Smooth those lines out of your brow. You're so much prettier when you're smiling. Believe me, there's nothing in the world worth a frown, much less a tear."

Christine said, "Will you tell me what you think happened that day at the picnic? I'm nervous and worried, as you see."

Miss Fern said in surprise, "Why, I thought you knew." Then, lifting her cuttings and arranging them one by one in the basket, she said it was her belief that the boy, to escape Rhoda's persistence, had hidden on the wharf, perhaps in the summerhouse where they now were. But Rhoda had found him, and when he saw her approaching, he became confused and backed away from her into the water.

Christine said. "Yes. Yes, I can imagine that."

Miss Fern continued, saying that Claude, despite his seeming frailness, was a good swimmer, and, of course, Rhoda knew that. Once in the water, she had every reason to expect him to swim to shore. How could she have known the pilings were at that exact spot? Children were quite strange, she felt. We should not judge them by the standards we use in judging adults. Children are often so insecure and helpless. Perhaps the thought in Rhoda's mind at the moment of the boy's falling into the water was that he'd ruin his new suit, and she'd get a scolding for causing it. The guard's calling to her at about that time had made her even more panicky, perhaps, and she ran ashore. Perhaps she stood behind those crepe myrtles to watch; but when Claude didn't swim ashore at once, she probably thought, with the odd logic of childhood, that he'd hidden under the wharf to frighten her. So she did nothing at first; and of course later on, when it was too late to do anything, she was afraid to admit what had happened.

She put down her basket, shaded her eyes, and looked at the blue, rippling bay. She said, "I think the worst thing we have to face, since you want me to be frank with you, is this: Rhoda, in an emergency, deserted under fire like a frightened soldier. But then so many soldiers, so many older and wiser people than herself, have run away at their first barrage."

They got up and moved down the wharf, and impulsively Miss Fern rested her hand on Christine's forearm. "I am not your enemy," she said. "You must not think of me that way again. If you need me, you must come to me at once."

"I have been so distressed about the boy's death," said Christine. "So anxious, and so guilty, too."

Miss Fern said she could understand Mrs. Penmark's feelings very well; but insofar as guilt was concerned, she was hardly in position to give advice to others, since she, herself, had been raddled with irrational guilts all her life. It was all so foolish, so illogical, to feel that way, for guilt, when you examined it dispassionately, could be seen to be only a painful form of pride.

But it was only natural to expect that we all have our particular guilts, since our development, our very place in the world we live in, is based on that premise. We are taught from the beginning that the human impulses we have are shameful and degrading, that man himself is entirely vile, that his very birth is the end result of a furtive sin to be wailed over and atoned somehow. She thought it rather ingenuous of those who were shocked when the bishops and preachers and cardinals the Communists took broke down so easily under stress and confessed every evil action, every ill-defined sin their captors put into their mouths: they had been conditioned to an acceptance of their individual guilts from the cradle onward. The surprising thing, in her opinion, was not that they confessed to monstrous impossibilities so soon, but that they held out as long as they did.

Christine said, "I don't know. I'm not really intellectual."

They got into the automobile, and Miss Fern, continuing her theme, said that unless man was able to comprehend infinity, that baffling anomaly of a universe without dimensions, he could not comprehend the nature of God. She thought the efforts of mortals like ourselves to catalogue, to limit, to attribute our own moral precepts to Him, or even to define His nature, were both foolish and presumptuous.

Christine thought: *I'm going to accept what Rhoda told me. I'm going to give her the benefit of every doubt. There's no reason to think the death of the old lady in Baltimore, and the death of the little Daigle boy are connected. There's nothing else I can do but trust her, unless I want to worry myself sick.*

Miss Fern continued to speak softly, breaking off her discourse occasionally to point out an unusual tree, or some historical landmark with which she was familiar. She said, "How can we know that our own concepts of good and evil concern God in the slightest? How can we be so sure He'd even understand our tests and definitions? Certainly there's nothing in nature, in the cruel habits of animals, that should lead us to think He does."

Christine said, "Perhaps so. I don't know."

"Monica Breedlove once referred to me humorously—it was in a speech for one of her drives—as 'that simple, romantic Whistler's Mother among school ma'ams.'" She laughed disdainfully, steadied her basket on the seat beside her, and said, "Actually, it's the other way round. Monica thinks man's mind can be changed through lying on a couch and talking endlessly to another man who is often as lost as the patient. Really, Monica is far more trusting and romantic than I."

After lunch, Rhoda asked permission to sit in the park, and Mrs. Forsythe said she could. She took her book and went to her usual place under the pomegranate tree. She had hardly turned to the correct page when Leroy, who could never leave her alone very long, came into the park and pretended to sweep the path behind her. He swept the same spot over and over, and at last he said, "There you sit reading a book and trying to look cute. Maybe you're thinking about how you hit that little boy with a stick. Is that what you're thinking about right now? Is that what makes you look so pleased and happy?"

Rhoda, in the tone that a bored but tolerant adult might use, said, "Finish sweeping the walk and get away from me. I don't want to listen to you. You talk silly all the time."

Leroy put down his broom for a moment and examined the pomegranate tree, snickering and nodding his head. He picked off a dead branch and held it in his hand; then, coming in front of the child, weighing the branch in his palm, he said innocently, "Is this about the size stick you hit him with?"

"Sweep your path. Either that, or talk to somebody else."

"After you rolled little Claude in the bay, he tried to pull himself up on the wharf again; but you hit him on the back of his hands that time until he had to turn loose, and drown; but before he done that, you fetched him another good lick on the temple, and that was the lick that bled so free."

Rhoda looked about her for a bookmark, as she did not want to damage her property by turning down a leaf. Before her, on the path, was a small, soft pigeon feather; she picked it up, blew on it to rid it of dust, and marked her place with it. Then, putting the book on the bench beside her, she stared calmly at him.

"You make out like you don't know what I'm talking about," said Leroy in delight, "but you know what I'm talking about, all right. You ain't dumb like them others—I got to admit that, no matter how mean you are. You know what time it is, just like I know what time it is. You ain't no dope—that I must say—and that's why you didn't leave that bloody stick where people could pick it up. Oh, no! You got better sense than that. You took that stick with you when you ran off the wharf, and when you were among the trees, with nobody to see you, you went down to the beach and washed off that bloody stick good. Then you threw it in the woods where nobody could find it."

"I think you're a very silly man."

"I may be silly, but I'm not silly like you are," said Leroy. He was enjoying the scene more and more. That mean little girl was letting on like she wasn't interested, but she was interested, all right! She was scared, deep down, but she wouldn't admit it. "You're the silly one, not me," he continued, "because you were silly enough to think you could wash off blood, and you can't."

"Why can't you wash off blood?"

"Because you can't, that's why. You can wash and wash, but it won't come off, leastways, not all of it will come off. Everybody knows that but you. You'd know it, too, if you didn't talk so much, and not listen to what people who know about things say."

He began sweeping the path vigorously. "Now, I'll tell you what I'm going to do, unless you start treating me nice," he said. "I'm going to call up the police, and tell them to start looking for that stick in the woods; and they'll find it, too. They got what they call 'stick bloodhounds' to help them look; and these stick bloodhounds can find any stick there is, provided it's got blood on it. And when them stick bloodhounds bring in that stick you washed off so careful, thinking nobody could tell, if that stick looked clean to you, they're going to sprinkle some kind of powder on it, and that poor little boy's blood will show up to accuse you of what you done. It'll show up a pretty blue color, like a robin's egg. And then them policemen—"

He turned away quickly, for he saw Mrs. Penmark come into the park, seeking her daughter, and walk toward them. She felt the tension at once and said to Leroy, "What have you been saying to her this time? What have you done to annoy her?"

Leroy said, leaning against his broom, "Why, Mrs. Penmark, I wasn't saying nothing out of the way to her. We were just talking a little."

"What did he say to you?" asked Christine.

Rhoda got up from the bench, picked up her book, and said, "Leroy said I ought to run about and play more. He said I was going to make myself nearsighted if I kept on reading all the time."

But Mrs. Penmark had seen the cold, angry look in her daughter's eyes, and she saw now the smirking expression of triumph which came over Leroy's face at the child's words. Again she felt anger rising in her, but controlling her voice and hands, she said, "I don't want you to speak to Rhoda again under any circumstances. Do you understand?"

Leroy opened his eyes in a hurt, simulated astonishment, and said, "I didn't say nothing out of the way to the little girl. You heard what she told you."

"Just the same, you're not to speak to her again. If you worry her again, or any of the other children, for that matter, I'm going to report you to the police. Is that entirely clear?"

She took her daughter's hand, and together they walked around the lily pond toward the gate. When they reached it, as Christine tugged at the heavy handle, Rhoda turned and gave

Leroy a hard, thoughtful, appraising glance. She made one of the conventional answers of childhood, an answer both wise and very deep: "What you say about me, you're really saying about yourself."

That night after supper, Leroy took off his shoes, laughed, and told his wife of the affair. His own three children were sitting on a bench under the althea bush, stringing four-o'clock flowers on grass, their bare, tough toes digging into the packed earth. When he'd finished, Thelma lowered her voice, so that the children could not hear her, and said, "I done told you to leave that girl alone, Leroy. You're going to get yourself in bad trouble. You're going to keep messing with that child until you get yourself in a big jam."

"I just like to tease that mean little girl. I couldn't get nowhere with her before, but I got her listening to me now."

"You're heading for trouble, is all I can say."

"I'm not going to get in no trouble. That little Rhoda is a cute one. She don't run away crying and blabbing. That little Rhoda's mean, all right, but she's cute, too." He sat quietly, smiling, nodding, and digesting his dinner.

There was a curious smell about the place, a vague moldiness which could not be traced to its source, as though the beds had been rained on and had dried out in the shade. Thelma went into the house and got herself a can of beer. When she returned, she said, "Rhoda may not tell on you, but somebody's going to hear you, like Mrs. Penmark almost heard you today. Then there's going to be trouble. Suppose she does hear you, and calls the police like she said. The police'll take you down to the station house and kick your teeth in."

Leroy stretched, laughed indulgently, and said, "What do you think I am, anyway? A dope?"

# seven

AFTERWARD CHRISTINE FELT RELIEF, as though Miss Fern's certainty had dissipated her own doubts, and during the next days she went about her duties of preparing meals, sewing, and looking out for her child and her house. She went to an afternoon wedding with Mrs. Breedlove where both wept a little behind their handkerchiefs; she shopped for an old-fashioned, hard hair mattress that Kenneth wanted for his bed; she went to a dance given by the treasurer of her husband's company for his nieces from New Orleans. She was determined to deny her fears, to forget her uncertainties, and she did so as long as she kept herself busy, or was with others; but at night, with Rhoda asleep and the house so quiet that vibration and sound were magnified in her mind, her doubts came back to trouble her.

She awoke one morning thinking if she did not take herself in hand, did not make a greater effort at self-control, she'd soon become as overwrought as Mrs. Daigle. It occurred to her then that if she questioned Rhoda's normality, if there were true grounds for her feeling that the child had criminal traits, she should no longer avoid the issue; it was her duty, if her fears were grounded in fact, to educate herself, to read and study the things she'd avoided in the past—to accept any reality that faced her, no matter how unpleasant, with courage and resourcefulness; to remedy the situation if possible; if not, to make the best compromise she could with facts. It was only through knowledge that she could help her child, could guide her with both understanding and intelligence to more acceptable attitudes, toward more conventional goals.

Her mind turned automatically to Reginald Tasker, to the talks they'd had together. She wanted to telephone him instantly, to ask his guidance; but already doubt had undermined her good sense a little, and she felt fearful at doing so, as though he would guess the true motive of her interest; then, although she despised her guilty deviousness, she decided to handle the matter another way. She'd give a cocktail party and ask him to it, along with other guests in whom she was not momentarily interested at all; she'd make an opportunity to be alone with him, and she'd ask him with misleading casualness, as though the matter had just occurred to her, to advise her in her reading. Certainly under those circumstances he would attribute no motive to her except the idleness of her mind; but if he did, she'd be forced into another untruth. She'd tell him she was thinking of trying her hand at a novel, now that Kenneth was away and time hung so heavily on her hands.

She gave her party on the last day of June. She arranged that Rhoda stay with Mrs. Forsythe across the hall; but Rhoda wanted to come in for a little while to meet her mother's guests. Christine consented, and when the guests were all there, Mrs. Forsythe brought in the child. Rhoda was dressed in white lawn embroidered in yellow, a frock her mother had made her a few days before. She wore white shoes and yellow socks, and her hangman braids were looped back with little yellow bows. The guests were enchanted with her. She smiled her hesitant, charming smile; she curtseyed in the manner Mrs. Forsythe had recently taught her; she listened with solemn intensity when she was complimented, her eyes wide and innocent of guile; she was polite, dignified, and serious, and when Mrs. Forsythe said they must leave, she nodded gravely and, making the soft sound a contented and pampered animal makes, she ran to her mother and embraced her with calculated spontaneity; and then smiling again, looking down in modesty, her shallow dimple plain for all to see, she held Mrs. Forsythe's hand, pressed close to her thigh for protection, and left with her.

When the child had gone, and her guests no longer needed her attention, Christine went to Reginald and said that since that time at Monica's when he'd told the story of Nurse Dennison, she'd found herself more and more interested in his field; she'd even read the accounts of the Ponder trial. Then, touching his arm, her head tilted to one side and lowered in gracious surrender of her mind to his, she said she'd never be reading such shocking things if he'd not first introduced her to them— and wasn't he ashamed of himself for going about town corrupting old married ladies? Reginald said he wasn't in the least ashamed. On the contrary, it was one of the things he'd boast about in his old age, or use in an expanded and flattering version in his memoirs.

Behind them on the balcony, his voice coming through with shrill clarity, an intellectual young man said, "A great novelist with something to say has no concern with style or oddity of presentation. Now, take a man like Tolstoy. I've just read *Anna* again. Tolstoy had no fear of the obvious. He wallowed in platitudes. That's why his work has survived."

Christine said, "The last time we talked about crimes, it was about the crimes children commit. You said, although I found it hard to believe, that it wasn't rare for children to commit major crimes. You said the ones destined to become famous in their field almost always began young. Were you serious, or were you taking advantage of my innocence?"

"Well, I never thought of Tolstoy as dealing in platitudes. Dickens, yes. But hardly Tolstoy."

Reginald said he'd been serious, indeed. There was a type of criminal he was particularly interested in. The type was his specialty, and for a long time now he'd been clipping and saving reports of cases, and making notes for a sustained study of the type. In this sort of criminal, which seemed different from all others, there seemed to be as many women as men, which was unusual to begin with. His type, if they weren't too stupid or too unlucky, ended up as murderers on a grand scale. They never killed for those reasons that so often sway warm but foolish humans. They never killed for passion, since they seemed incapable of feeling it, or jealousy, or thwarted love, or even revenge. There seemed to be no element of sexual cruelty in them. They killed for two reasons only—for profit, since they all had an unconquerable desire for possessions, and for the elimination of danger when their safety was threatened.

"I'm very interested," said Christine. "Will you let me look at your material? I'll take very good care of it."

Mrs. Breedlove, a Martini in her hand, moved through the crowd and came closer to them. She stood listening in a sort of dramatic astonishment, then impulsively she said, "But dear Christine, what's come over you? Why have you done such an about-face?"

Christine smiled self-consciously and said, "I doubt if there is a reason."

Mrs. Breedlove shook her head in patient denial, sat between them, and said, "There's a reason, dear Christine; there's a sound psychological reason for everything we do, if we can only find it." Then, with seeming inappropriateness, she said. "When I was in analysis with Doctor Kettlebaum, I used to go early, having such a positive transference to the poor man. There was an attractive young Englishman who preceded me, and we met in the waiting-room quite often. Sometimes when Doctor Kettlebaum was tied up on the phone between patients, and was late in calling me, we talked together. This young man—I've forgotten his name years ago, which is symptomatic, too, as you'll soon see—once told me that he considered me unusually attractive; except for one detail, I'd be his ideal, he said. His temperament was an odd one, you see. He said he adored only one-legged women, and I so plainly had two."

Reginald whistled between his teeth and said, "Boy, is that a new slant."

Monica continued. "So I said to him, 'I'll admit you're very handsome. I'll even go further, and say you've got the nicest eyelashes I ever saw on a man—but if you think I'm going to cut off a leg to please you, superior though you may be, you're dreadfully mistaken, my dear!'"

Reginald and Christine laughed at the same instant; and Mrs. Breedlove, herself giggling in memory, continued. "And so this young man with odd tastes stared at me in that composed manner the British have perfected, and said, 'I didn't expect it, I assure you.'"

"But where did he find one-legged women?" asked Christine.

"My dear," said Monica. "My dear, our minds are so in accord; now that's precisely what I asked him, too; but he looked at me in the completest astonishment, and said, '*Find* them? My dear lady, the problem is, how do you *avoid* them! London is full of one-legged women, as you've surely noticed. You see them everywhere you go.'"

There was silence, and then Christine said, "Is the moral meant for me? Is it that the eye finds what the mind is seeking?"

"But of course!" said Mrs. Breedlove. She went on to say that she'd always considered Mrs. Penmark's unwillingness to accept sordid or criminal data as symptomatic. In other words, she regarded it as a positive wish concealed under a negative reaction. It meant, really, that for a time she'd been emotionally unable to examine with a necessary detachment her drives toward hate and destruction; but now, with her anxieties so plainly abated, she was able to do so at last. On the whole, she was pleased with Christine's sudden preoccupation with crime, with her new, more wholesome attitudes. It indicated a wider tolerance, a greater maturity than she'd had before.

She turned and looked searchingly at her friend, and, in confusion, Christine gave the explanation she'd prepared in advance, the explanation she was later to use so often in justification of her actions. There'd always been a desire at the back of her mind to write a novel, although she doubted that she could really pull it off. Nevertheless, the things she'd heard from Reginald were so fresh, so off the beaten path—or so they seemed to her—that she'd been tempted to use them in this autobiographical book she was turning over in her mind—a book to be reinforced and supported by the details of actual cases. She stopped with sudden wariness, thinking: *Why did I say an* autobiographical *book? That's strange, I think.*

She waited for Mrs. Breedlove to catch her up on the slip, but since she did not, she got up and said she must go now and see to her other guests. It was then that Reginald offered to lend Mrs. Penmark the case material he'd collected. He'd digested many of the cases, and had sorted them roughly into categories. His own book, if he ever got round to doing it, would be factual, so there'd be no conflict between them. He asked if she'd decided on a plot for her novel, if she'd worked out as yet any of its details. She said she had not; she knew only in a general way that the novel would be about a mass murderess and her disastrous effect not only on her victims by violence, but on those who survived her. It wasn't much to go on, she knew; but it was all she'd worked out so far.

The following morning Mrs. Forsythe suggested, as a special treat, that she and Rhoda go to the corner and have an ice-cream soda together. She was a thin, tall woman in her late sixties with wide, flat hips and sloping shoulders. She had been a great beauty in her time—the perfect Gibson Girl, Mrs. Breedlove said—and she still wore her streaked, fair hair in a variant form of the pompadour of her triumphant days, a smaller, less imposing, more rounded pompadour with a tight, solid knot at its center, so that the effect now was that of a cushion held in place by a paper weight. She and the child came out of the door together, and Rhoda saw Leroy waiting for her near the sidewalk. All at once he thought of a new way to tease her, a variant method of showing his enamored hatred of the child. The idea seemed both subtle and witty to him. He went to the basement and took a dead rat from the cage where it had been since morning. He tied a bow about the rat's neck, and put it in one of the Christmas gift boxes he'd saved. Then, wrapping the box in colored paper, and tying it with Christmas ribbon, he had it ready when the child returned.

He winked knowingly when Mrs. Forsythe's back was turned, and made a suggestive gesture toward the back of the building, but the child ignored him; she remained standing on the flagstones, as though she awaited some more explicit explanation, and as the old lady went up the steps, paused, and fumbled in her untidy handbag for her keys, Leroy came closer, and hummed softly, as though he were serenading the little girl, "I got a real nice present! Yes, I got a real nice present! I got a present I been saving all for you!"

Rhoda nodded, and he went to the basement, standing inside the door where he couldn't be seen. Rhoda joined him quickly, and he said in a whisper which was unnecessary, since there was nobody near to hear him, "I figure you and me ought to be real good friends. So I got you a present to make up for the mean things I already said to you. When I seen this present I'm talking about, I thought right away of you. I said, 'That present sure makes me think of Rhoda Penmark.'"

"What is it, Leroy? What did you get me?"

"Open it. Just open the box and see."

The child opened the box. She lifted her head and stared at Leroy with a peculiar faraway look in her eyes. Leroy laughed and sat down on his bench, overcome with the wittiness of his gesture; but he laughed guardedly, as though he and the child were involved together in a conspiracy which must never be revealed.

"You know what your present puts me in mind of?" he asked when he could get his breath again. "It puts me in mind of Claude lying dead in his coffin." He waited for the child's response, but since there was none, he went on. "I thought first of getting you some sweet-smelling flowers, but I didn't have time to go to the graveyard and steal some off Claude's little grave."

Rhoda got up, but Leroy, catching at her hand to detain her, said, "Tell me one thing, now that we're good friends again. Did you find the bloody stick you washed off so good? If you didn't, you sure better hurry up and find it. I might get mad with you again and tell the policemen to go look for it."

That afternoon Reginald called at the Penmark apartment to

leave the cases he'd promised. Clipped to each case was a digest of its particular contents, and often his own comments, too. When he'd gone, when Rhoda was in the park reading, Christine took up one of the folders and read three cases marked: *Young. Simple situation. Offenders not too bright. Caught early.*

Raymond Walsh, a sixteen-year-old boy, shot his even younger friend to death for a few dollars. Beulah Hunnicutt and Norma Jean Brooks, both young girls, killed a farmer who had befriended them for the two dollars he had in his pocket. Milton Drury murdered his mother and set her on fire for the money she carried on her person.

There was a note in Reginald's handwriting attached to the folder that contained, as he said, these simple, and in a sense relatively wholesome cases. They'd all acted with the greatest stupidity; they'd all been caught young—perhaps at the beginning of their careers. Greed, he felt, was the driving power behind them all, the common denominator of their kind. None had any conception of human morality; none was able to understand loyalty, affection, gratitude or love; they were all cold, pitiless, and entirely selfish. Perhaps the general type could be seen more clearly in these simple kindergarten cases than in the more elaborate cases to be dealt with later on.

Mrs. Penmark sighed, lit a cigarette, and put the folder down, leaving the other cases in it unread. She went to her window, knelt on the seat there, and looked for a long time at the green untroubled street, and trees shimmering in the hot sun of July; then, coming back to her chair, she read again. These were cases concerned with more experienced practitioners, people who were perhaps more intelligent than the first group, but not too much so. At least, they'd been lucky for a time, and they were perfecting their various techniques when caught.

Tillie Klimek of Illinois poisoned five husbands for their insurance; Houston Roberts of Mississippi murdered his two wives and one of his grandchildren for the profit involved in their deaths. He tried to murder a second grandchild, but she recovered, and he was caught. Daisy de Melker of South Africa was a poisoner for gain on a major scale. She was executed at last for the murder of her son whom she'd insured for five hundred dollars.

Mrs. Penmark put the cases away in her desk, went to her back window, and called her daughter in to lunch. Rhoda walked slowly out of the park, but as she passed the basement door, Leroy stuck his head out and said, "When the policemen find that stick and make it turn blue, they going to put you in the electric chair. They going to fry you out real slow. You ever seen your mamma cook bacon and watch it swivel up? That's what you're going to look like in that electric chair. You going to turn brown, and you going to swivel up all over."

"The electric chair is too big for me," said Rhoda. "I wouldn't fit in it."

"That's what you think," said Leroy laughingly. "Now, let me tell you something. They got a special chair for mean little girls like you. They got a little pink chair that's just your size. I seen it plenty times, miss. It's painted a real pretty pink, and it looks nice, but of course it don't look so nice to the little girl that's frying up like a pork chop inside it."

"What you said about making a stick turn blue was something you made up. You're not going to heaven if you keep on telling stories the way you do. You're going to the bad place when you die, that's where you're going, Leroy."

"Go on in the house, and eat your lunch. Your mamma told you not to talk to me no more, and she told me not to talk to you, either. So I'm not going to talk to you no more. But you better find that stick, is all I can say. I could tell you a lot of things you want to find out, but your mamma said not to talk to you no more. Go on in the house and quit bothering me."

When she had gone, Leroy lay on his improvised bed thinking of his cleverness. He knew how to manage that one now; he sure had that mean little girl worried, and worried *good*. It wouldn't be long before she'd jump and fidget when he spoke to her. Just wait and see if she didn't.

Rhoda came into her apartment and ate her lunch; then, after she'd practiced her piano lesson, she said casually to her mother, "Is it the truth that when blood has been washed off anything a policeman can still tell it was there if he puts powder on the place? Will the place really turn blue?"

"Who's been talking to you about such things? Leroy?"

"No, Mother, it wasn't him. You told me not to talk to Leroy. It was some men I heard talking about it when they passed the park gate."

Mrs. Penmark said she didn't know about the bloodstains, although she'd call Uncle Reginald, who was an authority on these matters, if Rhoda really wanted to know; but Rhoda, in sudden alarm, shook her head from side to side, and said, "No." It was then Christine went back to her kitchen, to finish the luncheon dishes there; but her suspicions were now aroused, and she wondered why the child had asked her strange question, for she knew now, and had known for a long time, that Rhoda asked nothing idly, for the pleasure of hearing her own voice, as other children did.

Later she saw Rhoda go to her bedroom and come out with a parcel wrapped in paper; then, after looking cautiously about her, to see that she was unobserved, she opened the door to the

back hall, and shut it noiselessly behind her. Mrs. Penmark
cracked her kitchen door, which also opened on the back hall,
and watched her daughter with both curiosity and fear; and
when she saw the child approach the incinerator chute, she hurried down the hall in pursuit, caught her daughter by the arm,
blocked the incinerator with her back, and said, "What have you
got in that package? Give it to me, Rhoda! Give it to me at once!"

"I haven't got anything in it, Mother."

"There's something in it you wanted to burn. Give it to me!"

She took the parcel from the sullen child; she guided her back
to the apartment door; but Rhoda pulled away from her in unpredictable panic, and suddenly began biting and kicking like
some insane, trapped animal. In her surprise, as the child's sharp
teeth sank into her wrist, Mrs. Penmark dropped the parcel, and
Rhoda snatched it and ran down the hall. She had her hand on
the lid of the chute when her mother caught her; and again
Christine wrested the package from the struggling child.

Rhoda stood quietly when she knew she was defeated, and
she stared at her mother with such cold, unforgiving hatred that
Christine's hand automatically lifted and pressed against her
heart, as though the scene were unendurable to her; then, making little primitive, animal sounds, the child flew at her mother
again, as though she'd lost control of her senses. But this time
Mrs. Penmark seized the little girl and shook her by her shoulders, her bangs rising and falling, her thin, immature neck swaying back and forth. She shoved the child before her, entered her
living-room, and opened the parcel; and there, just as she'd
known it would be, were the cleated shoes that Rhoda had worn
to the picnic, but had not worn since.

Christine said, "I know now why you were so interested in
blood. You hit Claude with your shoe, didn't you?" She was sur-

prised at the calmness of her voice, how impersonally she was able to act at this moment, in the face of such dreadful knowledge. "You hit him with the shoe, didn't you?" she repeated. "Tell me! Tell me the truth!"

Rhoda did not answer immediately. She glanced warily at Christine, her mind busy even then with plans to bend her mother once more to her will, to win her approval and loyalty again.

"I know now, so there's no sense in lying any more," said Mrs. Penmark. "You hit him with the shoe; that's how those half-moon marks got on his forehead and hands."

Rhoda moved off slowly, an expression of patient bafflement in her eyes; then, throwing herself on the sofa, she buried her face in a pillow and wept plaintively, peering up at her mother through her laced fingers. But the performance was not at all convincing, and Christine looked back at her child with a new, dispassionate interest, and thought: *She's an amateur so far; but she's improving day by day. She's perfecting her act. In a few years, her act won't seem corny at all. It'll be most convincing then, I'm sure.*

"Answer me!" she said in sudden anger. "Answer me!"

The child, seeing she was not impressing her mother, got up from the sofa, walked leisurely to Christine, and stood before her. "I hit him with the shoe," she said calmly. "I had to hit him with the shoe, Mother. What else could I do?"

Mrs. Penmark's anger mounted, and in the desperation of her panic, she slapped the child so hard across her face that she staggered backward and fell into one of the big, overstuffed chairs, her legs stiff and straight before her. Christine pressed her palms against her forehead, feeling sick and frightened. She sat down to compose herself, and when her anger had vanished, and there was left only a feeling of nausea in her stomach, a sense of unreality in her mind, she said wearily, "Do you understand that you murdered the boy?"

"It was his fault," said Rhoda patiently. "It was all Claude's fault, not mine. If he'd given me the medal like I told him to, I wouldn't have hit him." She began to cry, pressing her forehead against the arm of the chair. "It was Claude's fault," she said; "it was his fault."

Christine closed her eyes and said, "Tell me what happened. I want the truth this time. I know you killed him, so there's no sense in lying again. Start from the beginning and tell me how it happened."

Rhoda threw herself into her mother's arms and said, "I won't do it again, Mother! I won't ever do it again!"

Christine wiped the child's eyes, brushed down her bangs, and said quietly, "I'm waiting for your answer. Tell me. I must know now."

"He wouldn't give me the medal like I told him to, that's all. . . . So then he ran away from me and hid on the wharf, but I found him there, and told him I'd hit him with my shoe if he didn't give me the medal. He shook his head and said, 'No'; so I hit him the first time, and then he took off the medal and gave it to me, like I asked him to."

"What happened then?"

"Well, he tried to run away, so I hit him with the shoe again. He kept crying and making a noise, and I was afraid somebody would hear him. So I hit him again, Mother. I hit him harder this time, and he fell in the water."

Christine closed her eyes and said, "Oh, my God! Oh, my God!"

The little girl was crying harder now, her mouth twisted with her apprehension. "I didn't take the medal. Claude gave me the medal when I asked for it. But after he gave it to me, he said he was going to tell Miss Octavia I took it from him, and then she'd make me give it back. That's why I hit him after the first time."

Mrs. Penmark thought, *What must I say? What must I do now?*

Suddenly the child wiped away her tears, embraced her mother, and said coquettishly, "Oh, I've got the prettiest mother! I've got the nicest mother! That's what I tell everybody. I say, 'I've got the sweetest—'"

"How did the bruises get on the back of his hands, Rhoda?"

"He tried to pull himself back on the wharf, after he fell in the water. But I wouldn't have hit him any more, except that he kept saying he was going to tell on me. So I hit him on the hands to make him turn loose of the wharf. But he wouldn't turn loose right away, no matter how hard I hit him, Mother; so I had to hit him on the head some more, and on the hands some more, too. I hit him the hardest of all that time; and that's how I got blood on my shoe. So finally he closed his eyes and turned loose of the wharf like I told him to. But it was all his fault, Mother. He shouldn't have said he was going to tell on me, should he?"

Then, remembering what Leroy had told her, the child cried again, but in fright this time, gasping out between her sobs, "Are they going to put me in that little chair and turn on the electricity?" She came closer to her mother and said, "It wasn't my fault Claude got drowned. It was his fault."

Christine walked about the room in aimless panic, her hands pressed against her cheeks. The child clung to her mother's waist and said, trembling with sudden terror, "You won't let them put me in that chair, will you? . . . Mother! Mother! You won't let them hurt me, will you?"

Christine stopped suddenly, turned to the frightened child, and said, "Nobody will hurt you. I don't know what must be done now, but I promise you nobody will hurt you."

In relief, the child wiped her eyes. She smiled in her old manner, her dimple showing effectively. She went through all her charming antics for her mother; and she said at length in her small, ingenuous voice, "If I give you a basket of kisses, what will you give me?"

"Please!" said Christine. "Please!"

"Give me the answer, Mother! If I give you a basket of kisses, what will you—"

"Go into your room and read," said Mrs. Penmark harshly. Then, in a weary voice, she added, "I want to think. I must decide what's best to be done."

But even as she spoke, she knew she was unable, in that moment of stress, either to make the decisions now inevitable for her new, required attitudes toward her child, or to formulate the plans necessary to put into motion such decisions, even if made. Her mind no longer moved in the straight line of rational thought; it turned like a rotating wheel in rapid, intense circles of emotion which she seemed unable to escape, the things the child had confessed repeating themselves over and over in a neat, inaudible pattern in her ear.

She had wanted to assuage her doubts, to know the truth—and now she did know. What she'd dreaded in fantasy so long, she faced at last in unalterable reality. And now that she did know, she comforted herself, even in this moment of turmoil, with the certainty that no matter how dreadful the truth had been, at least she could no longer torture herself with half-knowledge, or lash at her mind with doubt.

After a time she came into her child's room and said, "Why

don't you go into the park and play? I want to be alone. I must think what's best to be done for all of us."

She added, as Rhoda nodded, smiled, and approached the door, "You must promise me you won't tell anybody else what you've told me. It's very important. Do you understand? Do you—" But seeing the tolerant, contemptuous look in her daughter's eyes, she suddenly felt inexperienced and a little gauche. Her voice wavered and ceased, for she knew her warning only betrayed the depth of her own amateurish ineptness, that there was no chance whatever that Rhoda would needlessly reveal what she'd done. Then, wearily, while the child stood in amusement before her, though outwardly submissive, as she always was, she added, "How did you manage it with the old lady in Baltimore? I know so much now, another thing won't matter greatly." And Rhoda, sure of her triumph, smiled and said meekly, "I shoved her, Mother. I shoved her a little."

When her child had gone, she went to her bathroom, her purpose not clear in her mind; she stood there in indecision, but seeing her reflection in the mirror, she pointed her finger at her image and laughed shrilly. Then, resting her head against the glass, her arms hanging limply at her sides, she knew she must live with her secret as best she could; she must optimistically hope for the best.

She wanted more than anything to discuss her daughter with another, but she knew she could not, certainly not at the present time. It would be difficult even to tell Kenneth, as, of course, she inevitably must. Then, when the desire to confide was too strong for her to bear longer, she made a sort of left-hand, compromise confession to Reginald Tasker, a confession she was sure he'd fail to interpret at its true worth. She telephoned him and said she'd been working steadily on the structure of her novel. She'd decided the book would revolve around a criminal child, a child not unlike what any of the murderesses she'd been reading about had once been.

"How about the mother? Is she going to be criminal, too?"

"No. The mother will be commonplace, and rather stodgy."

"There's your conflict," said Reggie. "When you figure out what you're going to do with it, let me know, won't you?"

They chatted for a time about people they both knew, and when they'd finished, Christine sat again by the window, her hands resting in her lap. The wild spinning in her head had lessened now, and she forced her mind to consider the courses open to her in dealing with her daughter's future. The first thing to consider was the child's sanity; was Rhoda actually insane and, as such, not responsible for what she'd done? If she were insane, didn't she belong in some place where she could be treated, and perhaps cured—where she'd be prevented, at least, from doing further harm to people? But almost at once she shook her head in denial. Rhoda was not insane, and anyone who knew her at all, knew that well. But even if she were, even if she and Kenneth agreed later on that that was the best thing to do with her, how did you arrange such matters? Would Kenneth's family have to know? She shook her head helplessly. She did not know how these things were done.

She got up suddenly and walked about her apartment, arranging and rearranging her belongings without conscious thought, as though her actions were merely the outward mechanics of an inward turbulence she could not so easily arrange. She told herself she'd read no more of the criminal cases; they would only serve now to enhance her anxieties, to deepen her depression; and then, moving with the detached precision of a walking toy, she began eagerly to read again, as if knowing, somewhere in her being, the cases would point out to her, sooner or later, things she wanted to learn; would reveal to her at last some secret knowledge of her own life—knowledge which, she felt now, she could no longer reasonably avoid.

She read cases concerned with the work of the more celebrated women mass murderers, all of whom had been interested only in the profit in it for them. There was Mrs. Archer-Gilligan, owner of a home for the aged, who took her guests on a lump-sum, life basis and who took the proper precautions to see that she did not go into the red; there was Belle Gunness of Indiana who, after striking her admirers with a hatchet, was said to have chopped them up into a sort of silage and thriftily fed them to her pigs; there was Miss Bertha Hill, who lived in a village called "Pleasant Valley"; there was Christine Wilson, the English girl, who used colchicum with such enthusiasm that the doctors of her day thought a new, unknown epidemic had broken out in England; there were Mrs. Hahn, Mrs. Brennan, and Miss Jane Toppan; there was Susi Olah who, almost unaided, practically wiped out the male population of two Hungarian villages.

There was a series of cases involving the male mass murderers, but she read only one of them: Albert Guay, the Quebec jeweler, blew up a plane and the people in it, to collect the trip insurance he'd placed on the life of his wife, one of the passengers. There was a note attached to the Guay case. In Reginald's opinion, he'd leaped, with his twenty-three victims, into the ranks of the distinguished mass murderers not through merit but through accident. Compared with such outstanding artists as Alfred Cline, James P. Watson, or the Incomparable Bessie Denker, he'd been fumbling and foolish indeed.

Mrs. Penmark laid aside the folders, stood beside her window that overlooked the park, and said in a puzzled voice, "Bessie Denker. Bessie Denker—Where have I heard that name before?" She toyed with the cord of the Venetian blind, and after a moment her lips, as though functioning without the prompting of thought, shaped the words, "Bessie Denker! August Denker! Emma Denker! . . . And there was an old lady we called Cousin Ada Gustafson."

In sudden panic, she called Rhoda in from the park; and when the child stood before her, she said harshly, "Take the shoes and put them in the incinerator!"

The child moved away to obey her, and Christine called out in a shrill, agonized voice, "Hurry! Hurry, Rhoda! Put them in the incinerator! Burn them quickly!"

She stood beside her door, watching while the little girl went down the hall, lowered the chute, and dropped the bloodstained shoes into the furnace below.

# eight

LATER THAT AFTERNOON Mrs. Breedlove entered the Penmark apartment in her usual aggressive, effervescent manner. She'd been shopping, and she sank down into the first chair she saw, saying, "I bought both of us a little present. It's something I've wanted for a long time, but could never find before. I knew you'd want one, too, because your kitchen is just like mine."

It was a soap dish to be fastened above a kitchen sink. "You don't have to drill holes in the tiles to put it up," she said. "It fastens to the tiles by suction." She exhibited the suction cups, and continued. "You coat the inside with castor oil, of all things, and slap it on the tiles with a firm, quick motion. It sticks like it was nailed there."

But Mrs. Penmark was still under the shock of what she'd recently heard from her child, and she listened to Monica in a withdrawn silence, smiling vaguely, nodding her head at regular intervals, and hearing little her guest said.

Mrs. Breedlove fanned herself and went on. "The arrogance of salespeople never ceases to astonish me. When I bought the dishes, the salesman said, 'I'd better show you how to put it up, madam.' And so I said, 'My dear man, I can read a bit, I assure you; and the directions are plainly printed on the card.' And then he smirked in that superior way men affect, particularly when there are other men around listening, and said, 'The ladies aren't much good when it comes to mechanical things. My wife can't even screw in a light bulb and keep it straight.' And so I said, 'I daresay I can fix anything you or any other man can fix, and what's more, it wouldn't surprise me if I couldn't fix a lot of things you can't fix.'"

She talked on and on in a pleased, hearty voice, repeating the things she'd said to the salesman, and the things he'd said to her. Mrs. Penmark smiled in agreement, and sat with her hands so inert in her lap that already they seemed to have lost some of their realistic, everyday power. Mrs. Breedlove's story came to her vaguely, not as a thing in itself, but only as a background for her own thoughts, for her mind was still on the problem of Rhoda, and what to do with her now. . . . Should she go to the police and confess the things her child had done? Was that the best solution? Of course, it wasn't likely a child so young would be arrested and tried for murder; but certainly they'd take her away and put her in an institution. *They used to call them reform schools*, she thought, nodding again, and smiling reassuringly in Monica's direction, *but I'm not sure if they still call them that.*

"Now, when I was a young girl," said Monica with determined good nature, "I had an older brother who died later of scarlet fever. He was named for my father: Michael Lanier Wages, and he was very bright. I remember people saying, when I was small and so timid I'd run off and hide if a stranger so much as spoke to me, 'How lucky it is, Mrs. Wages, that if one of the children had to be stupid, it was the girl. It doesn't matter how dull a girl is. She can always find herself a good provider, and make out all right; in fact, it's probably an advantage for her to be a little stupid; but a boy's got to be smart if he expects to get any place in the world.'"

She paused and glanced at Christine, and Mrs. Penmark, who had heard little that she said, smiled obediently, and said, "Yes, indeed, Monica. That's so very true, isn't it?" She looked down again, thinking that if she confessed, and the authorities took Rhoda away and put her in some semi-penal institution, there would inevitably be publicity, and stories in the papers. Perhaps the situation would be considered unusual enough for printing everywhere, in newspapers all over the country. . . . She frowned, seeing in her mind's eye the headlines that inevitably announced the story: *Bravo Granddaughter Double Murderer*, or: *Tot Kills Two*. Once she had put the machinery in motion, there'd be no way of avoiding the usual publicity. Monica and Emory and the Fern sisters—everybody in town, in fact— would know, and pity herself and Kenneth, a thought that she found unendurable. Her husband's career would be brought to an end once more; they'd be forced to leave this place, to find another haven for themselves. Were they, then, to be forever on the run, to have no peace for themselves? Must they always be the victims of their child's avarice? . . .

Mrs. Breedlove paused uncertainly, and then said, "My mother, who didn't have any backbone at all—she was like all the women of her day, I suppose—who agreed with everything others suggested, particularly if that other person were a man, said, 'Yes, it's certainly an asset for a boy to be brainy.' And then the visitor said, 'All a girl needs to get by is to be pretty. It's important for girls to be pretty.' And when the visitor said that, I made up my mind I wasn't going to be pretty, even if it turned out that way naturally, which, of course, it didn't."

She giggled, tossed her pebble over her shoulder, and looked anxiously at Mrs. Penmark, whose face was set automatically in a smile of placating falseness. She was not even aware for a moment that Mrs. Breedlove regarded her with such searching interest, for she was thinking that the exposure of her child's crimes would not only destroy herself and Kenneth, it would inevitably bring destruction to Kenneth's mother and unmarried sisters, too. They were all conventional and prudish, with no understanding of others who differed from themselves, with no forgiveness in their hearts. They'd never be able to accept the reality of a criminal Penmark; they'd blame her for the child's abnormality. She could endure that, although the knowledge would be bitter; but her husband's situation would be even more difficult than her own. He was tied to the stodginess of his family in ways he neither realized nor admitted. His family had disliked her from the beginning; they'd made no secret of their resentment at his marriage. Would he not, then, after the acceptance of their joint tragedy, look at her with more appraising eyes, would he not wonder if his mother and sisters had not been right in their objections, after all? . . . She sighed again, shaking her head in helplessness.

"And so I said to myself," continued Mrs. Breedlove, "'I'm going to be as smart as any man alive, and on his terms, too,'" She moved restively, and went on. "I said to myself, 'What do men think they are, anyway? Going around like the Lords of Creation! I'll show them where to get off,' I said."

Christine nodded in absent-minded agreement. The more she considered matters as they were, the less she could see how any benefit could be had from the child's exposure at this time. Even if she were committed to a reform school, what would be accomplished, in the long run, by such an act? If what she'd heard about such institutions were true, the school no doubt would only serve as the final background of the child's corruption, if, indeed, there was a final corruption for her to achieve. . . . Then, looking up, feeling that something was expected of her, she smiled again, made an unintelligible sound with her lips, and said at length, "Yes. Yes, I'm sure that's true, Monica."

Mrs. Breedlove talked for a minute more, her voice getting less and less decisive; and then, coming to the end of her involved reactions to the perfection of men, she raised her eyes and stared searchingly at Mrs. Penmark; and seeing that her friend no longer made even a pretense of listening to her, she said with humorous petulance, "What's the matter with you today? You look pale and distraught. You're definitely worried about something. Who's been hurting your feelings, dear Christine? Who's been treating you badly?"

She moved in her chair, and thrust her legs straight before her, her knees tilted outward and outlined under her summer dress, the rims of her shoes resting at an ungraceful angle on the rug. Then, speaking in the high, artificial voice one uses in pla-cating a difficult child, she said, with real concern in her voice, "I'm going to be quite frank with you, dear Christine. Emory and I are concerned about you these days. We were discussing you last night at dinner, and we came to the conclusion you've not been yourself of late. Won't you tell me what's troubling you? Won't you let me help?"

Christine laughed disarmingly, and protested in a voice which she knew fooled nobody, "It's nothing, Monica. I haven't been sleeping well lately. Perhaps it's the heat. I'm not as used to it as you and Emory, you must remember. I'm just not feeling up to par. Please don't worry about me."

"You haven't been quite the same since the day of the Fern picnic," said Monica. "Emory said that last night. At first I didn't agree with him, but when I look back, I think it's true." She waited, and then added cheerfully, "Oh, well, if you don't want to tell me, you don't want to tell me." She got up to leave, saying, "Take your time, my dear. I'm sure you'll tell me when the right moment comes."

Christine said, "There's nothing to tell. Nothing at all."

She talked gaily for a time, as though in denial of Mrs. Breedlove's words that she'd changed; but all the time she was smiling and asking questions, she kept shaking her head in-wardly and saying to herself, "You're wrong. I'll never tell you or anybody else about Rhoda. How could I possibly tell anyone else such things?"

Mrs. Penmark remained awake that night for a long time, turning nervously from side to side; but toward morning she fell into unquiet sleep, into a troubled dream. She was alone in a white city where nobody lived, although the city was full of peo-ple. A menacing sky stretched over her, a sky with strange, slipper-shaped clouds lying motionless at the horizon. She went about peering into the small houses where people lived, and yet did not live, and said, "I am lost. Will somebody show me the way out of this cold place?" And then the city was full of people. She walked through them as easily as they walked through her. They would not speak to her, or acknowledge her existence, and she said, "I am one of them, but they do not know it yet."

She was tired and depressed, and she stood weeping before one of the houses which she knew to be her own. Then she began to run, knowing at last that she was nothing, that she was only an insubstantial ghost like the others, until she reached a little hill beyond the city, and resting there on top of the hill, trembling with fear, she saw a house shaped like a shoe, with the name *Christine Denker* written across its face in Rhoda's neat hand, collapse into nothingness, with only gray dust rising and settling slowly to show where the house had been. She was close to waking at that moment, and she said, "She will destroy us all. I did not escape either. She will destroy us all, in time."

She awoke with her hands trembling, her nightgown wet with sweat. She got up, lit a cigarette, and stood in the dark smoking it. Then, suddenly, cocks were crowing in the back yards of the poor, unpainted shacks a few blocks away, and she knew it was close to dawn. She went to her window and looked at the sky turning pink and pearl-gray above the bayous, and the intricate pattern of rivers and bays to the east. She wept suddenly, her palms on the wide ledge of red brick outside her window, and the dew that had collected there broke under her hands like blisters. Then, coming into her living-room, she turned on her reading lamp, the light from the globe dispelling the unreal half-light of dawn.

She closed the door to her daughter's room, so that the typewriter would not disturb her, and then, sitting at her desk, she wrote again to her husband, one of the detailed, impassioned letters she had no intention of sending him. In it, she confessed her anxiety and despair; she had insisted on knowing the truth, and now that she knew it, she could not see how this matter with Rhoda was to end; the only comfort she could take in her knowledge was the fact that she could no longer shatter her mind with doubt. But at this moment, she said, she wished that she did not know, that she could go on believing, in spite of her average common sense, in the off-chance of her child's innocence.

The problem that she and Kenneth now faced—a problem she knew in its entirety, but he, as yet, did not know—was one so difficult that it seemed impossible of satisfactory solution. What was to be their duty in future both to their child, and to the society in which they lived?

She wrote: *If you were only with me, my darling. If you were only here at my side to sustain me, to advise me what to do. But you are not here, and I must manage as best I can until your return. I must try to believe that Rhoda is too young to understand the things she's done, and yet other children no older than she is understand these things very well. Do you think, as I try to think, that she's learned her lesson, and that she'll never do such things again? I'm determined to think of the things I now know as little as possible. I must go on hoping that matters will somehow work themselves out in the end.*

*I am almost lost, my darling. What shall I do now? Come back to me quickly! I want you with me now. I need you so badly. Come back to me! For God's sake, come back to me quickly! I'm not nearly so brave as I pretend to be.*

When her letter was finished, she put it with the others in her locked drawer. It was now light outside, with the sun well risen, and she made coffee for herself, and sat drinking it, a strange, contemplative look on her face, while her mind moved restlessly in its unbroken circle of thought. . . . She was foolish and rather presumptuous to assume that she alone must make the necessary decisions concerning her child, as though only her opinions had value. . . . No, that was not true; responsibility for the child was a joint one that she shared equally with Kenneth; and when his work was wound up, and he was with her again, they'd talk the matter over in calmness; they'd draw strength from each other; they'd decide together what they must do.

But the fact remained, no matter what the child had done, that she was their own flesh and blood, and plainly it was their duty to protect her against the cruelty of the world. She did not know how Kenneth would feel when he, too, knew beyond doubt the things Rhoda had done; but insofar as she was concerned, she was going to protect her child as best she could. Of course, she'd look out for the welfare of others, too; she'd constantly watch her child to see that she harmed nobody else. But perhaps she was distressing herself needlessly in going over and over these matters; perhaps such a thing would not happen again, now that she knew what Rhoda had done, and Rhoda was aware that she knew. But no matter what the little girl was now, or became in future, she was going to protect her. That much was certain. It was her duty to protect her child. What kind of monster would she be if she betrayed and destroyed her own child? The idea was unthinkable, and shaking her head in despair, she spilled coffee in her saucer, and cried out involuntarily, "What else can I do? My God, what else can I do but protect her?"

She took her cup to the kitchen and put it on the drain board; she returned to her chair and took up the cases again, although they both repelled and frightened her. She told herself that she did not really want to read them, but now that she'd begun them, she felt a compulsive need to continue. She told herself in justification of her continued reading that she'd lived in ignorance long enough; perhaps if she'd faced reality sooner, she might have understood Rhoda better, and at a much earlier time; but even then, somewhere in her mind, she knew her facile explanations to herself were only partly true, that they were not even the most important truth, for she read the cases now, in spite of the fact that she told herself she did not want to learn more, with a reluctant eagerness, as though knowing that one of them, if she persisted in her efforts, would reveal not only the true enigma of her daughter's mind, but would clarify much that was hidden in herself, as well. Then, sighing a little, she began to read, to search diligently for the particular case she looked for, the case she had not as yet encountered.

The alarm, which she'd set for eight, went off at that moment in her bedroom, and, waking her daughter, she went about her preparations for breakfast. From her kitchen window, she saw Leroy coming to work. When he reached the garage doors, he yawned, scratched himself, snickered, and looked up at Rhoda's window. He stood under the window and whispered, "Rhoda! Little Rhoda, you up yet?"

Mrs. Penmark drew back into the room, so that he could not see her, and then Leroy, looking cautiously from side to side, said softly, "Rhoda! Rhoda! Tell me one thing—you found what you been looking for yet?" The child gave no sign of his presence under her window, and he turned away, laughing his muted, triumphant laugh. He said, "If you haven't found it so far, you better look harder. One thing's sure. I better not find it first." He spoke in a high whisper, one finger raised coyly to his lips; and then, resting against the steps, his eyes still fixed on the child's window, he said "Z-z-z-z! Z-z-z-z! You know what that means, now don't you? If you don't know, you sure better find out." He laughed again, and continued, "Z-z-z-z! Z-z-z-z!" He turned toward his basement room, adding, "I know you're listening to me back of that curtain. I know you heard everything I said to you."

When the child came into the breakfast room, Christine said, "I heard you and Leroy talking together. What did he mean by that peculiar sound he kept making?"

"You didn't hear us talking *together*," said the child primly. "You heard Leroy talking to me. I don't talk to Leroy."

"What did he mean by that hissing noise he made?"

"I don't know what he meant. Leroy's a silly man. I don't listen to Leroy more than half the time."

She sat at the table and unfolded her napkin, her face rested and untroubled, sleep still in her eyes. Then she yawned, covered her mouth daintily with her palm, and picked up her spoon. Christine, looking at her, thought, *She has no capacity for either remorse or guilt. She's entirely untroubled.* And afterward, when Rhoda was in the park, Mrs. Penmark went on with the cases. She paused from time to time to speculate on the odd mind of the criminal, to discover the lesson each taught for her own guidance. She wondered what force had caused these unusual people to become what they were. Was it the result of faulty training? Was it bad environment? Or was it some inborn, predestined thing which could at best be modified only a little?

These speculations so occupied her mind that later in the morning she telephoned Reginald Tasker for his opinion. Reginald said that for years he'd read, collected, annotated and digested cases of the type in which they were now both interested, and it seemed to him that environment had little to do with its persistent appearance, although, conceivably, environment might modify its outward aspects. The simplest way to understand the type was to regard them as the normal human beings of fifty thousand years ago, before man began his task of civilizing himself, or built his code of axioms into the moral codes that govern us all.

In other words, most of us were able somehow, under the molding force of precept and example, to develop the strange thing we call conscience, to acquire a reasonably acceptable moral character; but others did not have this ability at all, no matter what benign influences they were subjected to. They were not even able to love another except in the crudest manifestations of the flesh. They had a mental understanding of the shadings of right and wrong, but none of them had the same moral understanding of these things. They were the true, inborn criminals that can neither be changed nor modified. . . .

When she turned from the telephone, Mrs. Penmark took up the folders and read again. She read on and on, but at last she came to a case marked in Reginald's hand, *The Unparalleled Bessie Denker.* She held the folder limply in her hands, frowned, and shook her head in puzzlement at the insistent familiarity of the name. The story was by Madison Cravatte, whose name was familiar to her by this time, and who wrote with that special sort of tittering wit so typical of his specialty.

He began: *Now, if I were commanded to pick my favorite murderess from the army of her talented sisters, it would not be the bleached Eva Coo, whose name was so soft, and whose heart was so hard; it would not be that simpering chocolate drinker, Miss Madeleine Smith, whom the British so wildly adore. It wouldn't be our equally loved Lizzie Borden, who is now immortalized in doggerel, and who is said to have perfected her technique with the hatchet through chopping off the heads of her pet kittens; it wouldn't be the handsome Lyda Southard, a*

*lady who's never received the plaudits due her from an unbelieving pub-*
*lic; it wouldn't be saintly Anna Hahn who, in addition to a free use of*
*arsenic, sleeping pills, and strychnine, introduced a new lethal agent*
*into American letters: croton oil, of all things, my dears!*

*No, it would be none of these artistes in the art of murder, talented*
*though they were. My choice for first place would be the unrivaled Bes-*
*sie Denker, queen of them all: Bessie Denker who had a built-in icebox*
*for a heart, a steel rod for a spine, an instrument as accurate and imper-*
*sonal as a comptometer for a brain. I make no secret of my admiration*
*for this endearing lady. Bessie Denker was tops in my book. We're going*
*steady now. Bessie Denker is my sweetheart, and I don't care who*
*knows it.*

At this point Mrs. Penmark made a gesture of distaste, put
aside the folders, and went about her usual tasks. That afternoon, feeling a need to clear her mind, she took Rhoda to a
movie. She sat in the darkened theater, trying to concentrate on
the shallow story, but she could not. Afterward she and the little
girl went to a pastry shop for ice cream and cakes. She did not
look at the cases again until that night when Rhoda was asleep;
then, turning quickly to the Denker case once more, she continued to read its dreadful details.

She learned that Bessie Denker had been born Bessie Schober
in 1882, on a farm in Iowa, the eldest child of Heinz and Mamie
(Gustafson) Schober. She had had a brother and sister, both
younger than herself. The little boy died from an accidental dose
of arsenic which Bessie had, in her seven-year-old innocence,
spread on his bread and butter, mistaking it for sugar. The little
girl, while helping her sister draw a bucket of water, somehow
fell in the well and was drowned. Years later, when Mrs. Denker
was charged with other crimes, and on trial for her life, it was
said by neighbors who remembered the family, at that time,

thanks to Bessie's energy and determination, entirely extinct, that her Grandfather Gustafson had been shot one Sunday afternoon as he nodded in his rocking chair on the back porch. Nobody had ever known how it happened, or who had done it. Certainly, at that time, nobody has suspected quiet, wide-eyed little Bessie Schober who had been alone with him, and who was only eleven years old in those days.

Mr. Cravatte apologized for his inadequate presentation of these early, speculative affairs that concerned his ideal; but if the reader wanted a more detailed picture, a truly profound study of the early years of Bessie Schober Denker, he referred them to the remarkable series of articles by the late Richard Bravo, who had reported Mrs. Denker's trial, and who had studied her life in the minutest detail; who was, in fact, the acknowledged authority on her early antics.

Mrs. Penmark's hands were sweating; they shook as she put aside the folder and lighted a cigarette. She wondered why her father had never spoken of the Denker case, if he were the recognized authority on certain aspects of it, as he'd spoken of other affairs of his time in which he'd played a journalistic part. Or had he spoken of it, and had she, being uninterested, merely heard and forgotten? If the latter were true, she could understand why the names Denker and Schober and Gustafson seemed so familiar to her now, as though she'd known them all in some distant time in the past, why she could at this moment, even before she'd read the facts, anticipate some of the things that were to happen later on. She did not know. And suddenly she did not want to know. She felt that she'd been unwise in reading these cases of calculation and cold greed. Really, they served no purpose. The whole idea had been a mistake. She'd read no more.

But, against her will, she kept remembering the Denker case, and saying to herself, "There was a boy called Sonny, I think. Was his real name Ludwig, do you suppose? There was another boy, older than Emma, named Peter. . . . Yes, I'm sure his name was Peter. And there was another girl, the youngest of the Denker children, but I can't remember what her name was now, although I certainly knew it at one time."

She went to her mirror and stared at herself in astonishment, thinking, *Have I lost my senses? How could I have ever known such people?* Then she told herself she'd read no more. She meant it this time. She'd return the files to Reginald the next morning. She would dismiss from her mind those implications that struggled so strongly to be recognized. She glanced at her clock, and seeing it was after midnight, she went to bed, although again she was restless and could not sleep. She said to herself, "How can Bessie Denker concern me? I don't want to know anything more about her. I have my own problems to solve."

# nine

ON JULY TENTH, Mrs. Breedlove and her brother Emory Wages closed their apartment in town and went each year to the Seagull Inn for the days that remained in that month, and for the entire month of August. Usually, before departure, Monica gave a big buffet supper at the country club, as though to console her friends for the loss of her society over such an extended period. This time she planned her supper for the Fourth of July, since an elaborate display of fireworks was scheduled at the club that par-

ticular year, a display which, she felt, she and her guests might as
well take advantage of and enjoy. She'd been making plans for
the party since middle June. She'd discussed matters exhaustively with Mrs. Penmark, debating with her the appropriate
drinks to be served, the proper dishes to be ordered from her ca-
terers this year.

She was a little surprised, therefore, when, on the morning of
the Fourth, Christine telephoned to say she couldn't come, after
all, she wasn't well, as Monica knew. Then, too, Rhoda was
something of a problem. Mrs. Forsythe had been so kind in the
past about looking after her, that she couldn't possibly ask her to
do it again. . . . Of course, she could call in a regular baby sitter,
but for reasons of her own, which she wouldn't go into at the
moment, she didn't want to do that, either.

Mrs. Breedlove laughed at the suggestion of a baby sitter for
Rhoda, a child so poised, so calmly mature in outlook. The idea
seemed faintly absurd. If anything, it should probably be the
other way round! She said, "Don't worry about Jessie Forsythe.
She adores Rhoda. She'll jump at the chance of having her to
herself for a few hours. She told me just the other day she enjoyed talking to Rhoda more than anybody she knew. I wanted
to say, 'But don't you find her a little advanced for you, Jessie
dear?' but of course I didn't. Her own grandchildren can't abide
the poor woman, and they make fun of her to her face. But of
course Rhoda, being such a little lady, has more tact and consideration for older people."

"Perhaps so. Perhaps you're right, Monica."

"The truth of the matter," said Mrs. Breedlove cheerfully, "is
that you're brooding too much. You're neglecting your social obligations so much lately that even Emory, who notices nothing at
all as a rule, remarked on it. Now, you must disregard your little

depression of the moment and come to the party, even if you don't feel up to it. You're sure to be the belle of the ball, as you always are, with the settled married men yearning at you, and wishing their horrible wives looked more like you. Just leave everything to me, dear Christine; all you have to do is look your prettiest. I've got to be at the club early to see about the decorations, but Emory has been instructed to pick you up around six."

At the party, Mrs. Penmark sighted Reginald at once, and pushed her way through to him. They sat on the terrace together beside the open French doors, and he asked her how she was getting on with the case histories. She said she'd got into the Denker case a little way; she'd read a few pages of it, but it disturbed her so she'd had to put it aside. She paused, shook her head in puzzlement, and said, "Did you ever go to a strange place, or meet a strange person, or even hear a conversation for the first time with the feeling that everything that was happening then had happened before?"

"Yes, fairly often. There's a name for it, but I've forgotten what it is."

"Well, as silly as it sounds, I have the feeling about Bessie Denker. I don't understand it."

"You've probably read the case before, and just forgot it."

Christine said after a moment, "I was surprised to find my father's name mentioned in the case. I didn't know he'd ever met these people."

"Maybe that's why the case seems familiar to you. He probably talked about it when you were a kid."

"I don't think so. It's something else, I'm sure."

Reginald said enthusiastically that Bravo's reports of the trial had been far more than the accurate reporting of journalism;

they'd been little chiseled essays, really; and already they'd become classics of their kind. Her father had set a standard in the
Denker case which other reporters had imitated, but never
equaled.

"I'm always finding out things about him I didn't know before."

Reginald nodded in agreement, finished his cocktail, and
said, "How far did you get into the Denker case before you put it
aside?" And when she told him, he said he'd save her the trouble
of reading the earlier aspects of the case, some of which were
entirely incredible, by telling them to her.

He took another cocktail, closed his eyes for concentration,
and said in his light, rather rapid voice, that Bessie's father, old
Heinz Schober, had died oddly in an accident which had involved
a threshing machine, an accident never adequately explained.
Later on—years later—Mrs. Denker's admirers had seen significance in the fact that Bessie was working beside her father at the
time, but if she was involved in his death, such an involvement
was never established. At any rate, the old man had left his
widow comfortably fixed. Bessie was about twenty years old in
those days and eager to embark in earnest on a career already
auspiciously, if haphazardly, begun. But she felt she could do better in a city, and already her thoughts turned toward Omaha,
Nebraska.

But she remained on the farm for a time, to look out for her
mother, who'd suffered from indigestion since her husband's
death; then, when her mother died on schedule, and Bessie had
the farm and the insurance money for her own, she sold out and
moved away. In Omaha she married a man named Vladimir
Kurowsky, a man of considerable substance. At the insistence of
his bride, he had himself heavily insured. He left his widow of

less than a year to her grief and quickly earned possessions. So the Widow Kurowsky cashed in her policies, sold her property, and moved to Kansas City. Not long afterward she met and married a young farmer named August Denker. He came of a well-to-do family, although his particular branch of it had little. When Mrs. Denker closed her Kansas City residence, and embarked with her new husband for his farm, she began the major phase of her career, the phase that was later to both delight and astound her contemporaries.

Reginald lighted a cigarette for both himself and his listener, and then went on to say that Richard Bravo had done a remarkable study of August Denker, whom he considered the class victim, the preordained one who turns up over and over in the career of the mass murderer—the one who, through his natural trust and the innocence of his outlook, makes possible the murderer's triumphs over such extended periods of time. He had seen a photograph of August Denker, taken about the time of his marriage to his incredible wife. He was blond, with delicate, almost feminine, features; and his eyes had looked out at the world with innocence and candor. He was quite handsome in a negative sort of way. He played the violin, but not very well, it was said. . . .

Mrs. Penmark pressed her hands against her eyes, shook her head, and said under her breath, "No. No, it wasn't the violin. I'm sure it wasn't. It was a wind instrument of some sort—at least it was something you *blew* into. . . . I think it was a cornet."

A group came onto the terrace and stood chatting near by, and Reginald was silent until they passed out of earshot; then he talked once more of Mrs. Denker and the remarkable things she'd accomplished. At the time she married August Denker, she'd already worked out a master plan for the annihilation of his family, and for a long time everything went according to schedule.

Christine interrupted him after a moment. "How did she get away with it so long?" she asked. "Wasn't anybody suspicious, with all those deaths?"

In Reginald's opinion, the fact that Bessie Denker had escaped detection so long wasn't nearly so implausible as Mrs. Penmark seemed to think. In the first place, good people are rarely suspicious. They cannot imagine others doing the things they themselves are incapable of doing; usually they accept the undramatic solution as the correct one, and let matters rest there. Then, too, the normal are inclined to visualize the multiple killer as one who's as monstrous in appearance as he is in mind, which is about as far from the truth as one could well get. He paused and then said that these monsters of real life usually looked and behaved in a more normal manner than their actually normal brothers and sisters; they presented a more convincing picture of virtue than virtue presented of itself—just as the wax rosebud or the plastic peach seemed more perfect to the eye, more what the mind thought a rosebud or a peach should be, than the imperfect original from which it had been modeled.

He stretched delicately and went on to say that Bessie Denker must have been one of the truly talented actresses of her time with her church-going, her visiting around with other members of her husband's family, her tireless baking of pies and cakes for church bazaars, and her little thoughtful errands of mercy for those less fortunate than herself.

He talked on and on, but Mrs. Penmark, growing restive, interrupted him to ask, "Who was Ada Gustafson? What part did she play in Mrs. Denker's affairs?"

Reginald flicked cigarette ash onto the grass, laughed, and

said, "Oh, *that* one!" Then almost at once he went on to explain that Ada Gustafson had been a poor relation of Mrs. Denker, an eccentric spinster who'd come late into the picture, after most of the Denker members had been accomplished, in fact, and who was usually referred to in the record of Bessie's trial as "Old Ada Gustafson." She had been a woman in her late sixties at that time, but she was still spry and strong; and having no place else to go for the remaining days of her life, she had sought asylum with her distant cousin, Mrs. Denker; and once taken in, she had earned her keep by cooking, scrubbing, nursing Bessie's four children, or even working in the fields with August and the men. She was shrewd and observant with, perhaps, more than a touch of Bessie's own temperament in her; and she was to be Bessie's stumbling block at last, the Nemesis of her defeat. She had observed everything that went on at the farm with a cynical lifting of eyelids, a wry pouting of her old lips. For a long time she said nothing, but she fell into the habit of following Cousin Bessie about with her eyes, nodding thoughtfully, as though collating and winnowing the impression she'd already formed of her. It was for the murder of Cousin Ada Gustafson, and not for one of the Denker murders which would have been more difficult to prove, that Mrs. Denker was tried and eventually executed.

Christine listened in silence to the long description, thinking: *I remember Cousin Ada dimly. None of us liked her at home. She had a dog named Spot. He used to snap at Emmy and Sonny, and at me, too, but we made friends with him. But he'd never make friends with Peter, I remember.*

Suddenly she moved forward in her chair, put her glass down, and locked her fingers together; there was a sense of inescapable knowledge that she could no longer deny, a feeling of approaching doom which she sought to avoid, but knew now that she could not. She half-turned in her chair, looked steadily at the hedges beyond the green lawns, and said in a voice which was almost inaudible, "What was the name of the youngest of the Denker children?"

Reginald said cheerfully, "Why, her name was Christine, the same as your own. And apparently she was just as pretty as you are, too. She was blond like her father, and she had his fine features. Your own father met her and was greatly taken by her. His essay on her plight was one of his finest. It's still reprinted occasionally today."

Suddenly Mrs. Penmark got up, swayed against her chair, and said she was not feeling well. She thought she'd better go home immediately. Reginald said he'd drive her there, but she insisted it would be simpler to call a taxi. She went at once to Mrs. Breedlove, to explain her sudden indisposition, and the latter said in a provoked voice, "What's the matter with you these days? You aren't like yourself at all. Your face is drawn and quite white, my dear. There's a distinct twitching over your eye."

Christine, unable at that moment to answer, trembled and turned away; but Mrs. Breedlove caught her by the arm and said in a concerned voice, "If you must go home, then you must go. But don't bother with a taxi. Edith Marcusson just arrived—you remember Edith, of course?—and her chauffeur is still turning in the driveway."

She went outside, halted the chauffeur, gave him instructions, and then said, "When you get home, you must lie down and be quiet. When this thing is over, I'll look in on you."

Christine nodded and turned away, saying to herself, "I know who I am now. I can't delude myself any longer." She leaned back on the seat and pressed her cheek against the upholstery of the car, knowing herself to be on the verge of nervous tears, but once in her own apartment, with her familiar things about her, something of her panic left her; and a little later she knocked on the Forsythe door to call for her child.

Mrs. Forsythe said, "Oh, what a pity! Rhoda and I had planned a little buffet of our own, and we're just setting the table. We're going to turn on the radio while we dine, and have music from the Arbor Room. Can't you let her stay a little longer? I promise to take the very best care of her."

Her cushionlike pompadour, which she so carefully buttressed and shored up with hairpins and little amber combs, had strained away from its moorings, and the tight, rocklike knot that anchored the mass tilted with its rounded cushion in the direction of her left ear. She sighed and righted her hair, her big, violet eyes wide and imploring.

"It will be such a disappointment if Rhoda leaves now," she said earnestly. "Such a disappointment to all concerned."

Mrs. Penmark said the child could stay. She went back to her own living-room, and then, as though impelled by forces stronger than her anxiety and distaste, her determination to think no more of her mother's dreadful life, she began to read the Denker case at the point where Reginald's telling of the story had ended.

According to Madison Cravatte, the Denker relationships had been as complex as those in a three-volume Victorian novel. You needed charts and blueprints and a cast of characters at the front of the book to keep them all straight. But little Bessie Schober, after her marriage into the family, hadn't grudged the time she'd spent studying them for her own deadly purpose. She had analyzed the personalities and characters of her new relations with a most flattering care. She had studied closely the degrees of relationship they bore one another, the closeness of their blood ties to Grandfather Carl Denker, who controlled the money, with the same concentrated attention that a chess player brings to the moves in his championship game. . . . And if he might be permitted to carry his somewhat trite figure of the chess champion further, her moves to divert the flow of the Denker money from other branches of the family, and to direct it inevitably in her husband's direction, were as shrewd, as calculated, as coldly brilliant in her game of murder for profit as any champion's were in his less violent field.

This she had conscientiously done by poison, the ax, the rifle, the shotgun, the simulated suicides by hanging and drowning; and while it would take far too long to go into these family tragedies in the detail they deserved, he would say that at the end of ten years Bessie had accomplished her goal in twenty-three moves of such boldness, such brilliance of strategy, such remarkable rightness of detail, that she'd become the particular darling of the intellectual murder fan. But if the interested reader wanted more information, to study both this remarkable woman, and the details of each of the varied Denker deaths exhaustively, then he referred him to Jonathan Mundy's volume on Bessie Denker in the *Great American Criminals* series.

It was getting darker in the apartment, and Christine went to the table and turned on her reading light; but she stopped to look at the western sky, glowing with muted colors. Birds, flying high, made a thin line across the soft, waning colors; the live oaks lifted rhythmically under the evening winds from the Gulf, showing arches of horizon that were cloudless, polished, and deep blue. She stood quietly a moment, and then she walked nervously through her house, turning on lights without sense, and as capriciously turning them off again.

She came back to the case at length, to read its ending: *At the*

*time of Bessie Denker's trial the only member of the Denker family re-*
*maining alive was the little girl Christine, about whom so much has*
*been written. What happened eventually to this tragic child who some-*
*how managed to escape her mother's "master plan" is not known, al-*
*though it is generally believed she was taken for adoption by some*
*respectable family. But one cannot help wondering what her life has*
*been like since. Where is she now? Is she married, with children of her*
*own? Has she forgotten the horrors she must have known in her early*
*childhood? Did she ever really know, or understand what her mother*
*had done? One can only wonder at the fate of this tragic, frightened lit-*
*tle girl who somehow escaped her mother's fury. The chances are we*
*will never know now what became of her. Her new identity has been*
*well guarded indeed.*

Christine dropped the folder in confusion, lay on her bed and
pressed her face into her pillows. She wept and said, "Here I am,
if you want to know. Here I am." And then, after a moment, "I
didn't escape after all. . . . Why did you think I escaped?"

Again Mrs. Penmark could not sleep. She lay on her bed staring
up at the white ceiling, faintly luminous in the dark, her eyes
fixed on the elaborate decoration of fruits and flowers which
originally had been the centerpiece of a chandelier. Outside, she
could hear trees rustling as the breeze lifted their branches and
moved them gently about. There was the smell of crushed camphor leaves near by; and farther away, and sickeningly sweet odor
of the night-blooming jasmine bushes on the Kunkels' lawn;
then, when she could no longer bear the silence, nor the
thoughts that went through her mind in a repetitive pattern, she
got up, went to her rear balcony, and looked up. There was a light
on in Mrs. Breedlove's study, and in desperation she went to her
telephone and dialed Monica's number.

Mrs. Breedlove said, "I'm so glad you called, dear Christine. I wanted to get in touch with you when Emory and I came back from the party, but it was after eleven, and I was sure you'd already retired. But you know how guests are, I'm sure. They never go home, once they get high."

Then in a softer voice, as though just remembering that her brother was asleep, she lowered her voice, and said, "I was sorry you couldn't stay to the end. Now, take care of yourself. We mustn't let you get sick. None of us could endure that, dear Christine." She paused a moment, and then, as though she'd glanced at her watch in the interval, she said, "Why don't you run up for a little visit? It's only half past one, and I'm not in the least sleepy. We'll make a pot of coffee—I'll put the water on now—and sit in the kitchen like a couple of old peasant widows."

She met her guest at the door, a warning finger to her lips. She was wearing a flowered kimono, and her face was smeared wildly with cold cream, her hair rolled up in kid curlers. She laughed cautiously, and said, "I've always had a passion for the fat little curl, although the fat little curl is plainly not for me. Laugh heartily, if you'd like to, my dear. I'm not at all concerned when others find me ridiculous."

Christine nodded and smiled as best she could, thinking: *I should have left well enough alone. I shouldn't have gone prying into the past to find out what my secret was. My foster parents were so wise in never telling me. They were right in shielding me from a past I could neither change nor help. But I couldn't let matters remain as they were. I had to go seeking and prying. And now I know.*

When the coffee had dripped, Mrs. Breedlove served it, and they sat together under the harsh kitchen light overhead. Monica talked in detail of her buffet party, apologizing occasionally for the muddiness of her thoughts, the clumsiness of her phrasing; then suddenly the tenor of her thoughts changed, and touching Christine's cheek, she said, "There's something troubling you. Won't you tell me what it is? I think you know by this time you can trust me all the way."

Christine shook her head, sighed, and looked down helplessly. "I can't. I can't tell you. Not even you, Monica." She went to the icebox, took out a carton of cream, and poured it into Monica's pewter creamer, thinking, *How can I blame Rhoda for the things she's done? I carried the bad seed that made her what she is. If anybody is guilty, I'm the guilty one, not Rhoda.* She suddenly felt both humble and guilty, thinking how she'd wronged the child, even if she'd done so unwittingly. "I'm the guilty one," she said again to herself. "I was the carrier of the bad seed."

Mrs. Breedlove waited awhile and then said that if Christine wouldn't tell her the trouble, she must guess at it. "Tell me this," she added. "Have you and Kenneth come to the parting of the ways?" She laughed at her own fancy, and went on. "Has he found a little Spanish girl in Chile, and given you the brush-off, with nothing to remember him by except a curt note of explanation?"

"It's nothing like that, Monica. I wish I were as sure of everything as I am of Kenneth."

Mrs. Breedlove waited, sipping her coffee, and then said, "The only other thing I can think of is health. Are you afraid you have some disease—something like cancer, for example? If you suspect that, we must face it with courage. We must do everything that can be done, and there *is* so much that can be done these days; and whatever there is that can be done, we'll do it."

"I'm perfectly healthy, as far as I know."

Mrs. Breedlove put down her cup. "I'm not going to bully you any more, Christine. I'm only going to say I love you truly and deeply, my dear—as though you were my own, in fact. Emory feels the same way about you; but I needn't tell you that, for you know it already."

Christine nodded and rested her forehead on the table. Monica stood above her, put her hand on her shoulder and said in the soft, serious voice she rarely used, "You know you can trust me. You know you can trust me." Then Christine got up blindly, put her arms about the old woman, and wept without restraint. Mrs. Breedlove said, making soft, sympathetic noises with her lips, "Dear, dear, Christine! You'll feel better now. Perhaps you can manage to get some sleep." Then, in her customary voice she added, "Doctor Ewing left a bottle of sleeping pills for me a week or so ago when I was a little upset, too. I didn't use them. I'm going to get them for you now. There's no sense in your not sleeping."

She returned with the bottle; but when Christine was in her own apartment, she opened the locked drawer of her desk and put the bottle in with the pistol and the letters she had not sent her husband.

# ten

SHE SLEPT AFTER A LONG TIME; and when she did, she became involved in a terrifying dream. There was a woman with a hatchet in her hand who moved up from the road. She paused at the farmhouse, and searched it; and when she did not find what she looked for, she went toward the barn, holding the hatchet behind her for concealment, and called out in a sweet, patient voice, "Christine! Where are you, Christine? Don't be afraid of me. Do you think your mother would harm you?"

But Christine, hidden in the tall grass, would not answer; and when she looked up again, the barn was full of windows, and each window framed the face of one of her mother's victims. There was one window vacant, and she heard her mother saying, "Christine! Christine, take your place with the others!" Then the others at the windows chanted in chorus, "You'll never find Christine. Her present identity is well concealed."

The faceless woman said, "I'll find her, no matter where she is. I'm the Incomparable Bessie Denker. I'm the one whose master plan worked so well."

Then, plainly, she saw her mother's placid, conventional face, and, trembling, she pressed herself closer to the earth, while the people at the windows turned to one another in concern and said, "The Incomparable Bessie Denker wants Christine this time. Christine, take your place with the others. Has anybody seen Christine? Christine is the one who escaped."

Mrs. Penmark, turning nervously on her pillow, struggled upward to reality, her wet hands pressed together. She sat up in bed and smoothed out her pillow. She lay trembling for a time, her teeth chattering in an irregular rhythm, as though she were cold. She tried to sleep again, and at length she did. When she woke, it was morning. It was raining, with a wind that threw the rain over the tops of the trees and through the patterns of their tossing branches. The trees in the park looked drenched and desolate as they bent before the wind, shivered, and righted themselves once more. The gutters were overflowing, and water ran down to the courtyard with a quarrelsome sound so close to speech that you felt, if you listened more attentively, you could surely know its meaning.

She closed her windows and mopped where the rain had blown into the house; then going to the kitchen to fix breakfast for her child, she saw Leroy, wrapped in an old plastic raincoat, his wet shoes squashing as he walked, carrying out ashes from the basement. She stood irresolutely beside her window, as though already she'd forgotten her purpose, hearing the banging of the cans as Leroy set them in the alley for the garbageman to pick up at nine. He came back to the courtyard, and bent down to clear a flooded, leaf-stopped drain; and though she could not hear his mumbling voice, she could almost know the words he said by the petulant motion of his lips.

When Rhoda had eaten her breakfast, had folded her napkin and put it away in the sideboard drawer, she asked permission to visit Mrs. Forsythe. The old lady, she said, had promised to teach her to crochet; and now that it was raining, and she must stay inside in any event, she thought it a good time for her first lesson. Mrs. Penmark frowned in indecision. Now that she knew the horror of Rhoda's inheritance, could chart with a reasonable certainty what her career would be, she wondered if she were morally justified in allowing her to be alone with anyone; perhaps, she should no longer let her out of her sight, should even warn others of her criminality; but knowing how difficult these hysterical things were of accomplishment, she looked down helplessly, and renewed her intention of making no decision until her husband returned. She said, "If I let you go, you must promise not to do anything to Mrs. Forsythe. Do you understand me?"

"No, Mother. I don't know what you're talking about."

"Please, Rhoda! Let's not have any more charm or acting. We understand each other very well. Let's be natural with each other from now on. You know quite well what I'm talking about."

Rhoda giggled, nodded her head, and said in a matter-of-fact voice, "I know what you mean. But I won't do anything to her." And then, pressing her hands together, rolling her eyes roguishly, she added, "Aunt Jessie hasn't got anything I want."

When her child had gone, when her routine tasks of the morning were partly done, the implications that had lain so strongly in Mrs. Penmark's mind since she knew, at last, who she was, broke through strongly. She paused while polishing her rosewood console table, and turned away frowning; a moment later she could not remember what had brought her to her bedroom in the first place. She put down her chamois cloth, and stood in confusion beside her bed, her hands making futile gestures in the air.

The discovery of her true identity had clarified much which had once seemed so baffling in her child. She could see now that Rhoda was not responsible for the things she'd done. She, not Rhoda, was the guilty one, for it was she who had passed on the inheritance from Bessie Denker to the little girl, the inheritance that had lain dormant for a generation, but had bloomed once more to destroy. Knowing these things, how could she blame her child? How hold her accountable? . . . The more her poor, distraught mind dwelt on these matters, the plainer her guilt seemed to her, and she kept saying to herself, "I'm so ashamed. I'm so ashamed."

She sat down at length, despair flooding her mind; then, in a final effort to ease herself from the guilty knowledge she knew would destroy her, she wondered if the circumstance of grandmother and grandchild being alike in their criminality was anything more than coincidence, an accidental fact like any other—one with no implications behind it. Perhaps, in taking her guilt for granted, she assumed too much. Perhaps she was not the inevitable link between Bessie Denker and her child; was blameless, after all. She felt that if anybody knew about these matters, Reginald Tasker would know; but for a long time she debated with herself the wisdom of calling him, fearing he would not consider her question an abstract one as she hoped, that he would connect it quickly with the problem she faced, would thus know the secret she was determined to guard from everyone.

She came to the conclusion that he would probably not suspect the true purpose behind her question. He knew a little of the reality that faced her, but not enough. She alone knew all the parts of the puzzle—the death of the old lady in Baltimore, the death of the Daigle boy at the picnic, the horror of the child's inheritance—those parts which, like an elementary jigsaw puzzle, a puzzle with less necessary pieces than the ones Rhoda loved to assemble, implacably revealed the whole.

She walked about in perturbation, unable to make up her mind, and at last Reginald solved the problem for her. At noon he telephoned to ask if she were now feeling better. At once he said, "Did you get a chance to finish the Denker case? We were just getting hot when you had to go."

"Yes, I finished it."

"That Bessie Denker was really something, wasn't she?"

"Yes. Yes, she certainly was."

He talked on and on; but when he paused for a moment's concentration, she asked her question quickly, more bluntly than she'd planned. He said it wasn't a point he'd particularly considered, but, after all, he didn't see why *not!* The thing that made these people what they were wasn't a positive quality, but a negative one. It was a *lack* of something in them from the beginning, not something they'd *acquired*. Now, color blindness and baldness and hemophilia were all caused by a lack of something or other, and nobody denied that they were transmitted. Feeble-minded-ness was a lack of something, too; and certainly it was passed along from generation to generation. . . .

She had asked him for reassurance, but she had not received it, and she said in a small desperate voice, "But what do psychiatrists think?"

Reginald laughed at her simplicity. To answer her question, he said, he'd first have to ask a few questions of his own: What did *what* psychiatrist think? And what year did he think it in? . . . He'd recently read the testimony in the old Thaw case, and it might interest her to learn that six psychiatrists, among the most learned of their day, testified to one thing for the prosecution, while six others, equally distinguished in the psychiatric field, testified to the opposite for the defense.

When she hung up, Mrs. Penmark walked about her apartment, feeling as though she'd surely collapse; and it seemed to her then that the essential and terrifying pattern of her life was now plain. But this thought was too dreadful for her to face at once, and sitting beside her window, watching the trees bending under the force of wind and rain, she said in a thin, frightened voice, "Oh, please! Oh, please!" . . . Then, overwhelmed with guilt so powerful that it was not bearable, she walked about the room in nervous panic, her damp hands pressed together, as though imploring some remote implacable power to give her peace once more, to deny for her the truth she could herself no longer deny.

She wrote her husband another of her long passionate letters. . . . In a way, she'd married him under false pretenses, she said. She told him who her mother was, and how she'd made the discovery. Richard Bravo had been closely associated with the Denker case. It wasn't difficult to understand now

how he and his wife had come to know her—the one who had
survived—and later to take her for their own; but she kept
wondering why they'd done it. *Perhaps they'd hoped to rescue me,
for they were both most kind and gentle people; to save me from the
things I'd seen and knew about even at that age. They very nearly succeeded, but not quite.*

She wrote: *I've been thinking, since I've discovered the truth about
myself, of your mother's objections to our marriage. She was right to be
suspicious of me—only the reasons she gave for her suspicions were
wrong. She must have known by instinct there was something dreadfully wrong about me, that I would bring you only ruin and despair.
And that is what I will bring you, my darling. I see it now with such a
frightening clarity.*

*But if your mother was instinctively right in opposing your marriage
to me, I was instinctively right in telling you nothing of the things I've
found out about Rhoda since you went away. I wonder now if I can ever
bring myself to tell you those things. I do not think so. You see how shameful that would be for me, don't you? How humiliating? I must think
things through clearly, or as clearly as I can, and I must live my life with
Rhoda with some sort of courage which I do not possess at the moment. I
must do the best I can.*

*I feel now more strongly than ever that the problem of Rhoda is not
the joint one I considered it. The problem is mine, and I must solve it
alone. I alone am responsible. It was I who carried the bad seed that
made her what she is, not you. When you return and know these
things, for I know, of course, I must tell you somehow, sometime, and
accept their implications as I have already done, I think you should
abandon Rhoda and me. You are still young, and you must marry
again and have the children you are entitled to, children who will be
healthy and average without this hateful taint that is in my daughter
and me.*

Before she'd finished her letter, the summer storm had passed and the hot July sun was shining again. It beat against the dripping camphor trees, their wet leaves reflecting the light in a brilliance so blinding that the unshaded eye could not endure it. She lowered the blinds and tilted the slats, hearing the last of the rain swishing down the drain pipes and sighing in the gutters. It was Saturday, and presently she saw Emory park under the wet, reflecting trees and come up the walk, followed by his sister Monica. They saw Christine beside the window and waved in their usual, genial manner; and when they'd passed out of sight, Monica said gravely, "I don't know what's come over Christine lately. I'm concerned about her, and I may as well confess it. Christine was always so careful about her person, but I don't think she's had her hair or nails done in a month. She's beginning to look gaunt and seedy. She's not eating properly, I know. She says she is, but I'm convinced she's not."

"Look!" said Emory in an amiable voice. "Look, Monica, why don't you quit prying into Christine's personal affairs? Why don't you mind your own business for a change?"

That afternoon, Mrs. Penmark bundled up the cases Reginald had lent her and returned them to him. She had not meant to go in; she'd planned to leave them at the door when his houseboy answered the bell, but Reginald saw her and came out to welcome her. He insisted she come in and have a cocktail with him, but she said she'd rather have tea, and the houseboy went to fix it. Reginald asked how she was getting along with her novel. Had she worked on her characters in detail? Did she have her plot pretty well in hand?

Christine said the book would be about a child who repeats the criminal pattern of her grandmother's career, and Reginald said, "That explains it. I wondered this morning why you were interested in the heredity-versus-environment theme."

"Yes," she said. "Yes."

"How about the child's mother? Is she tarred with the same brush, as the saying goes?"

"No, I don't think so. I see the mother as an ordinary woman without too much sense; the sort you meet everywhere. She's helpless, and pretty vulnerable. She's rather a dull, stodgy woman, I'm afraid."

"It'll be nice for contrast," he said. He sipped his cocktail, and said, "Tell me this: is the stodgy mother sure about her child, or does she only suspect? I mean, has she anything to go on, where her child is concerned?"

"She has something to go on. She has a great deal to go on."

"Does the conventional mother know about the criminal grandmother?"

"She didn't at first, but she finds out. It explains to her so many things in her own daughter."

Reginald nodded and said after a moment, "It sounds all right. But remember one thing: try to keep the tensions high." Then, as she got up to go, he added, "The old biddies at Monica's party were interested in your abrupt departure; and if you want to know their verdict, they all think you're 'expecting.'"

The idea sent Mrs. Penmark into wild, hysterical laughter. She laughed so long that Reginald became a little alarmed, and, handing her a cocktail, he said, "Drink this down, Christine. You need a drink after all."

When Mrs. Penmark was home once more, Rhoda practiced her piano for an hour, and toward nightfall she sat under the lamp memorizing her Sunday school lesson for next day. When she was letter-perfect, she asked her mother to question her, and

Christine did so, thinking, *Rhoda has some strange affinity for the cruelties of the Old Testament. There's something as terrible and primitive about her, as there is about them.*

The child got out the butterfly-starred cards she'd earned on a new prize, and showed them to her mother. She said, "I'm sure to have a perfect lesson tomorrow, too; and that'll make four cards; and all I'll need then is eight more. It won't be long before I get another prize. I hope it's not another book."

Mrs. Penmark was ill next day. She felt faint and dizzy, and after she'd sent her child to Sunday school, she rested her head in her cupped palm, caught up in such a feeling of unreality that for a time she felt she'd never be able to get up again. But Mrs. Breedlove came down later for her usual Sunday morning visit, and hearing her voice in the hall as she chatted with Mrs. Forsythe, Christine went to the door, determined to ignore her fears. Monica, still concerned about her friend, entered with a resolute cheerfulness. She had rehearsed one of her anecdotes on her way down the stairs, and seating herself solidly, she began talking about a woman she knew, a woman whose tackiness was a source of laughter among her friends.

She said, "Poor Consuela came to my buffet supper, and I'd particularly wanted you to meet her, but she didn't show up until later—after you'd gone, as a matter of fact."

Christine nodded and smiled as best she could, and Mrs. Breedlove went on. "Everybody pities Consuela for her lack of style. Martha David mentioned it this morning when she called to discuss the party with me, but I said, 'Oh, no. Oh, no indeed. Consuela is nobody's victim, believe me. There's something in Consuela that makes her want to wear what she does. It isn't ignorance, and heaven knows it isn't a lack of money to buy the right things with. It isn't that she takes what the shopkeepers fob off on her as you suggested. Oh, no. Never, my dear. It's all a part of a very well defined design.'"

Mrs. Penmark looked about her in desperation, suddenly sick of her friend's unending, aggressive cheerfulness. She stirred in her chair, and then looked down at her hands.

Mrs. Breedlove said, "'If Consuela bought the first things shopkeepers tossed at her, the effect would be quite different,' I said. 'Now, in the first place, no stores carry that sort of stuff these days—not even those little cheap stores down by the wharves. Not even the mail-order houses carry high-button shoes, colored veils, and those five-gored skirts. To find them at all, she must search for them with ardor. Oh, you may depend on it that Consuela has dedicated her life to the search for her wardrobe oddities with the same passion a diver brings to his search for the flawless pearl.'"

Christine got up suddenly, feeling as though she'd faint, and lay down on the living-room couch. Monica sat beside her, greatly concerned. "I'm not going to argue the point with you, Christine," she said. "I'm going to call my doctor and have him take a look at you. If you're sick, and it's plain you are sick, something must be done."

She was already dialing as she talked, and the doctor said he'd come at once. He did so, and Mrs. Breedlove met him in the foyer for one of the whispered, preliminary conversations that doctors endure. He found nothing physically wrong with Mrs. Penmark. He advised her not to worry so much; he told her to eat more than she'd been eating, even if she had to force herself to do it. He left a prescription for sleeping tablets for her insomnia. When he'd gone, Christine resolutely got out of bed, determined to think no more of the things that troubled her; and in the days that followed, she managed as best she could in a routine so strict, so filled with trivial activities, that she had no time to brood over her problems.

She developed an abnormal tenderness for her child. She followed her about with her eyes, placating her, apologizing to her, serving her in humility, as though imploring forgiveness for the inheritance she'd given her. They shared a bond of horror that bound them together, that tied them to a common past, a community of guilt that could never be changed through thought or word. They were fixed together by the life of Bessie Denker. There was no going behind that fact. There was no escape for either of them.

Sometimes, when they were together in the apartment, as though Mrs. Penmark had worked out some wishful illusion which could never be true in reality, and knew, but denied the fact, she would put her arms about the little girl, and draw her to her in a gesture of expiation, as though love itself were strong enough to change the child into the creature she desired her to be—the simple, affectionate child who loved her, too; and as her sick affection increased, she would descend on her without warning, to passionately kiss her forehead or cheek, to embrace her with longing. At such times, Rhoda would endure the caress in astonished silence, smooth down her bangs, straighten her frock, and back away. She avoided her mother as best she could. She read, she practiced the piano, she studied her Sunday school texts, she pursued her lessons in needlecraft, she sat idly under the pomegranate tree and thought her particular thoughts.

Once, in desperation, Mrs. Penmark said to the retreating child, "Don't you love me at all? Don't you have any affection for anyone? Are you entirely cold?"

And Rhoda, moving implacably toward the door, not knowing what was expected of her, laughed charmingly, tilted her neck in the gesture she knew older people found irresistible, and said, "You're silly! I think you're silly!"

As the date of her departure came nearer, Mrs. Breedlove wondered if she were justified in going at all—in leaving dear Christine, who was oddly upset, and not at all well, alone. She sought to solve the problem through having Christine and Rhoda come with her to the inn. She was sure, with her influence, she could arrange reservations, even at this late day; but Christine refused. She begged her friend not to worry about her. She'd be perfectly all right. If anything did happen, she'd call Monica at once.

"Oh, very well, if you insist on being stubborn," said Monica in an exasperated voice. Then, more softly, "But at least you'll call me if you *need* me. That I insist on. You know where I'll be. It isn't far."

She was leaving the next day, and Christine helped her with her preparations. When everything was ready, Monica parked her car in the driveway, and she and Christine returned to the apartment to see that the gas was turned off, that there were no dripping taps, that the windows were secured. From her back balcony she called to Leroy, telling him to bring her bags down and stow them away in the trunk of her car. He did so, and Rhoda followed him down the back steps. When they were in the courtyard, he winked at the child and said in a voice so soft that the women above could not hear him, "You better ask Mrs. Breedlove to look for that little bloody stick while she's at the bay. I done told you over and over you better find that stick before I do, but you won't take stock in what I say."

"There's not any stick to find."

Leroy laughed, held his head to one side, and said in the sly, intense voice of courtship, "Z-z-z-z! Z-z-z-z! You know what that noise means, now don't you, Miss Rhoda Penmark?"

"I know you're a silly man. That's all I know."

"That's the way mean children sound when they're frying up in that little blue chair."

"You said it was a pink chair before."

"They got two chairs. You'd know that by this time if you didn't talk so much, and not listen to what other folks try to tell you. They got a blue chair for mean little boys, and a pink chair for mean little girls." He put his hands on his hips, swayed voluptuously from side to side. "You don't know much, do you? I used to say you was smart, but I don't say so any more. Now I think you're real dumb."

The two women came down the steps, and as the car pulled away from the curb, and Christine turned up the path toward the front of the house, Leroy laughed silently, put his forefinger against his nose, and said, "Z-z-z-z! Z-z-z-z! You know what that noise means as well as I do. You know, all right. But if you don't know right now, you'll find out soon enough."

Mrs. Penmark, without turning her head, called her daughter, and Rhoda joined her on the walk. Leroy stood watching them as they walked away. That corn-fed Christine wasn't looking so well these days, he thought. She sure had got thin and tired-looking. Her skin was sort of stretched-like and pale, too. And then there were them circles under her eyes. That one looked ten years older than she did a month ago. He wondered what the cause was. . . . That trough-fed Christine must be suffering from what they used to call "battle fatigue" in the last war. No, that one wasn't suffering from no battle fatigue; that one was suffering from *bed* fatigue!

The cleverness of his thoughts so overpowered him that he

sat on the back steps and laughed silently, glancing from side to side. Somebody was putting it to her, all right! Somebody must be climbing up that back porch when everybody was asleep, and giving her plenty of it. And that Christine just stood there in a nightgown, if she wore even that, to let him in. He wondered who it could be. It couldn't be Mr. Emory Wages—he was too old. He couldn't climb a porch, anyway. It couldn't be that little Reggie Tasker who wrote them crime pieces. That one would jump out of the window if a woman made a pass at him. He thought a long time, trying to figure it out, but all he could see was a vague figure without a name, somebody who looked re-markably like himself.

"That one's not suffering from *battle* fatigue," he repeated. "That one's suffering from *bed* fatigue!"

He laughed again, his head bobbing up and down in approval of both his wit and his discernment.

# eleven

ONE SOURCE OF THE TOWN'S PRIDE was the Amanda B. Trellis Memorial Library, a building of brick and stone that covered al-most a city block. Its site was once the site of Old Yellow Fever Cemetery, but the graves had been leveled, and the ancient bones of the victims moved. A garden had been created behind the library itself, and there the crumbling walls which had shielded the graves from the curious eye, shielded the garden as well. There were pathways through the shrubbery; there were summerhouses fitted out with rustic benches and tables; there were pergolas smothered in jasmine and coral vine.

A few of the gravestones, with their authentic dates and affir-
mations of a quainter morality than our own, had been left as they
were, as though they, too, were shrubs of a sort; as though they
could put the earnest reader into that mood of sadness, that sense
of the transience of life, which is the reason of the philosopher's
reading.

Often in the morning, after the postman had come, and
Christine knew whether or not she'd get a letter from her husband that day, she'd go to the library and dig more deeply into
the appalling life of Bessie Denker. She found that a specialized
literature of legend had grown about her mother's name. She
was better known for the evil she'd created than the most compassionate people of her day were known for the good deeds
they'd done; and as she read on and on, she made notes in a
blankbook she carried, a book which lent credence to the story
she'd told the librarian who helped her in her researches: that she
was making notes now for a novel she hoped to write later.

Usually when she went to the library she left Rhoda with Mrs.
Forsythe, but occasionally she took the child with her. At such
times, Rhoda would sit, not beside her mother, but near by, and
read one of the books she'd taken from the shelves for her own
amusement, or continue the needlework she and her teacher
found so fascinating, while Mrs. Penmark rested in the summerhouse and read the Bravo articles on the Denker case. The sense
of guilty tenderness she felt for the child had worn itself out. She
regarded her daughter now with uncomprehending, chilly distaste. They rarely spoke when they were alone, an arrangement
which seemed more satisfactory to Rhoda than any she'd had
with her mother in the past.

On the days she remained at home, Mrs. Penmark would re-
cline by her window while Rhoda visited across the hall, or went
to the park to play. She'd instructed the child to sit always on the

bench under the pomegranate tree, where she could keep an eye on her; and Rhoda, understanding Christine's purpose, considering it both just and sensible—more sensible by far than her old attitudes of affection and blind trust—obeyed with a sort of cynical, approving resignation.

Sometimes, when she went to the library, and knew Rhoda would lunch with Mrs. Forsythe, Christine took lunch with her, which she ate at one of the rustic tables under the pergola; and once, an assistant librarian, a dowdy woman with a claret stain on her cheek, a mark she treated with the greatest contempt and made no effort to hide, came to the garden to eat her own lunch. She sat across from Mrs. Penmark, and said, "I don't think I introduced myself before. Well, anyway, I'm Natalie Glass, and I've been wondering how your book is coming along. Your first, isn't it? Have you started writing on it, or are you still at the research stage?"

"I'm turning the idea over in my mind. Probably nothing will come of it. It's too early to know."

Miss Glass unscrewed the top of her Thermos bottle, bit into her sandwich, and said in a muffled voice, "What's it about?"

Christine outlined the plot of her own predicament, just as she'd done with Reginald Tasker, while Miss Glass nodded, nibbled her sandwich, and caught the falling crumbs in her outstretched palm. She said, shrugging her square shoulders, "Oh, well, you can tone it down in the writing." Then, a moment later: "How 'bout the child's father? Does he know what his wife's ancestry was? Does he suspect the child, too?" Then, touching her tongue to the tips of her fingers, she said, "If you need anything we haven't got, let me know. Maybe I can get it for you."

"The father doesn't know about his wife's background. Remember, she didn't know it either until relatively late—long after they'd been married. He knows the child is odd, but he doesn't know enough to alarm him."

There was silence while Miss Glass sipped her coffee and digested in her mind the things she'd heard. Then abruptly she asked, "How you going to end it?"

"I don't know. I don't see the ending clearly."

"I don't see a happy ending, not with that setup."

"It can't be a happy ending. No. I see that, too."

Miss Glass paused with her coffee cup half raised to her mouth, narrowed her eyes, and bent forward as though somebody inside the library had called her name; then, sure that nobody had, she said, "The only way to end the book is for the mother to shoot the child before she grows up and *really* goes to work on the neighbors."

"Oh, no!" said Christine quickly. "Oh, no!"

Miss Glass seemed surprised at her vehemence. She said, "I don't see what else the mother can do. That one's really got a package of trouble on her hands if you ask me."

"Oh, no! She couldn't possibly do anything to harm her child. It wouldn't be in keeping with her character. She's a weak woman who just drifts along. She lacks the power to make decisions."

"You can let her 'rise to the occasion' as you writers put it."

"Oh, no. My heroine, if you can call her that, couldn't survive a thing of that sort. She wouldn't have the strength. It's impossible."

"But you've considered that ending, haven't you?"

"Yes," said Christine. "I've considered it over and over. But it's not possible."

"Well, I guess you're right," said Miss Glass. "When I think of it, killing the child seems more the beginning of a novel than the ending of one—unless you're figuring on something the size of

*Gone With the Wind.* If your heroine killed her child, she'd have to go on living with her guilt; she'd have to face her husband, and all sorts of complications are possible there. She'd have to make a thousand new adjustments, she'd have to start a new life—assuming of course that the cops didn't find out first, and hang her."

Christine said, "I don't know. I don't know—But I must decide soon. Something must be done soon."

Miss Glass gathered up the paper and the crusts of her sandwich; she thrust the empty Thermos under her arm and started back to her work; then, pausing, she said, "Your idea interests me. I'm going to think about it when I get home."

With her reading, her housework, her supervision of her child, her long, regular letters to her husband, Mrs. Penmark achieved a sort of lethargic resignation at last. Monica telephoned at intervals to see that she was all right, and one evening she said in excitement that there'd been a cancellation at her hotel. She knew that the management of other peoples' affairs was one of her more repulsive qualities—heaven knows she ought to, Emory told her often enough—but she'd been thinking of Christine and Rhoda so much, she'd missed them so greatly, that she'd taken the liberty of picking up the reservation, in their name. She hoped Christine would pardon her presumptuousness, but as a special favor to herself and Emory, wouldn't she make the effort—wouldn't she come to the inn for ten days? Then, not waiting for Mrs. Penmark's decision, she went on. "Everything's been arranged. Emory'll pick you up tomorrow about six, after he finishes up at the shop. Now, dear Christine, come with him! If you don't feel up to packing, say so; and I'll drive over in the morning and pack for you."

Mrs. Penmark said she could manage by herself, and the following afternoon she and Rhoda were ready. She enjoyed her stay at the hotel. In the mornings she lay with Rhoda on the beach, or wandered with her in the woods beyond. In the evening she played canasta with Emory, or contract with Monica and her friends. Rhoda behaved perfectly; the guests at the inn made much over her. She smiled, she curtseyed, she deferred to her elders, she showed her shallow dimple. . . . When Mrs. Penmark and her daughter returned to town on the first day of August, she felt that many of her tensions had left her. She began to hope again, to trust in the future.

On the next afternoon, when they were settled again to the familiar routine they'd known before, Rhoda went to the park to crochet under the pomegranate tree; and after a time Leroy approached her. He said, "I know why you begged your mamma into taking you to the bay. You wanted to go there to look for that stick. Now tell me one thing, just between you and I—did you find that stick?"

Without raising her eyes, giving no outward sign she was speaking to him, Rhoda said, "She's by the window watching me. If you want to talk to me, stand by the bridal-wreath bush. She can't see you there."

He moved to the place she mentioned, snickering and saying, "Z-z-z-z!" to himself. He started to repeat the sound, since it had for him unlimited possibilities of wit; and then in sudden revelation, as though seeing the importance at last of facts which had always been at the back of his mind, he rubbed his cheek, and said, "What happened to that heavy pair of shoes you used to wear? I'm talking about them shoes that went tap-tap-tap on the walk. You wore them shoes to the picnic that day, but I don't believe you've worn them since."

"You're silly. I never had a pair of shoes like that."

"You had a pair of shoes like that, all right! They went tap-tap-tap when you walked. I remember how they used to sound. I didn't like the way they sounded. I said to myself that day of the picnic when you went down the front walk, 'I don't like that tap-tap-tapping, and I'm going to wet them shoes.' That's the reason I turned the hose on them."

"They hurt my feet. So I gave those shoes away."

Leroy said, "You know one thing? You didn't hit that boy with no stick. You hit him with them shoes, that's what you hit him with. There never was no stick, and that's why you didn't worry about it. Ain't I right this time?"

"You're silly. That's all I can say."

"You didn't hit him with no stick. You hit him with your shoe. You didn't have to hunt no stick to hit him with. You had that shoe with them iron cleats handy to hit him with."

"Don't talk to me any more. You're a silly man."

"I'm not silly. It's you that's silly. You're so dumb you thought I meant it when I said you hit him with a stick; but all I was doing then was trying to make you say, 'No, Leroy. I didn't hit him with no stick. I hit him with my shoe that's got them iron cleats on the heel.' I said stick at first just to worry you. But I knew all the time what it was you hit him with."

Rhoda sat perfectly still, her mouth opened a little, her hands automatically practicing the stitch she was learning. She said, "You tell stories all the time. When you die, you're going to the bad place."

Leroy knelt, in an effort to simulate industry in the event anyone passed and saw him, at the base of the bridal-wreath bush, and examined its foliage. He said, "Now let me tell you something else about them shoes. While you and your mamma was over at that hotel skylarking and carrying on, I found me a key to your front door. And you want to know what I done when I found me that key? I went in your apartment and started looking, that's what I done! That's the way I found them shoes and took them away with me. I got them shoes hid out safe right now. I got them hid out where nobody'll ever find them but me. You sure better treat me pretty from now on. You better mind me, and do what I tell you to do. If you keep on acting uppity, I'm going to hand them shoes over to the policemen, and tell them what to look for on them. I'm going to say, 'Little Claude Daigle's blood's on them shoes. Now you go ahead and find it.'"

Rhoda said contemptuously, "You tell lies all the time. You haven't got those shoes. I put those shoes in the incinerator and burned them up. I'd be afraid to tell lies the way you do."

Leroy laughed his silent laugh, waited a moment, and then said, "You mean you *thought* you burned up them shoes. Now, I'm not saying you didn't burn them a little, but you didn't burn all of them up like you wanted to."

A strange, waiting look came into the child's eyes. She put her needlework on the bench beside her. She stared at the man with a frightening stillness. "Yes?" she said. "Yes?"

"Now, listen to this," said Leroy, "and then figure out which is the silly one—you, or me." He snickered in triumph and continued. "I was in the basement resting, and I heard something come rattling down the pipe. So I said to myself, 'What's that rattling down the pipe? It sure sounds like a pair of shoes with cleats in the heels,' I said. So I opened the incinerator door quick, and there they lay on top of the coals, only smoking the least little bit. Oh, they was scorched some; I'll admit they were scorched. But there was plenty left to turn blue and show where blood was. There's plenty left to put you in the electric chair."

He threw back his head, and in triumph laughed his shrill, foolish laugh, watching the child out of the corners of his eyes.

Rhoda got up thoughtfully and went to the lily pond, standing there with one foot on the rim of the basin; and then, convinced this time that Leroy told the truth, she said calmly, "Give me those shoes back!"

"Oh, no! Not me, Miss Rhoda Penmark! I got them shoes hid out where nobody but me can find them. I'm keeping them shoes to make you act better from here on."

He went into the courtyard. The situation had become too delightful for him to endure. He sat down on the back steps, rocking from side to side. The child followed him. She said patiently, "You'd better give me those shoes. They're mine. Give them back to me."

Leroy said, "I'm not giving those shoes back to nobody, see?" He gasped with delight, holding his face in his hands. Then, something in the child's fixed, cold stare caused his laughter to die away. He looked down uneasily at his own shoes and said, "I'm keeping them shoes until—" His voice broke off suddenly. He no longer wanted to play this game with the little girl. He got up from his seat and walked away nervously.

"Give me those shoes back. Give me my shoes back."

She followed him wherever he went, repeating her demand; and then he turned and said, "Now listen, Rhoda, I just been fooling around and teasing you about them shoes. I got my work to do. Why don't you go on about your business and leave me alone?"

He walked faster, but she caught at his sleeve, pulling him up short. "You'd better give me my shoes back," she said.

He turned in exasperation and said, "Quit talking loud. Everybody can hear what you're saying."

The child said, "Give me my shoes. You've got them hid, but you better find them and give them back to me."

"Listen, Rhoda! I haven't got nobody's shoes. I was just teasing you. Don't you know when anybody is teasing you?"

He went in the direction of the park again, but the child followed him insistently, saying softly, "Give me my shoes. Give them back." He picked up his broom where he'd left it leaning on the lily pond, and said plaintively, "Why don't you let me alone? What makes you keep bothering me?" But she would not leave him. She kept tugging at his sleeve and repeating her demand until Leroy said, "I was just fooling at first about you killing that boy; but now I believe you did. I believe you really did kill him with your shoe." He moved away once more, and once more she followed him; and then Leroy, as though he were about to stamp his foot in exasperation, said shrilly, "Go inside and practice your piano lesson! I haven't got nobody's shoe, I keep telling you!"

He went to the front of the house, where he was sure she would not follow him. He stood under the camphor tree alone, saying to himself in amazement, "I really believe she killed that little boy!" Then suddenly he said to himself, "I don't want to have nothing more to do with her. If she speaks to me again, I'm not even going to answer back." He'd thought at first how interesting the story of the retrieved shoes would be for Thelma that night when he got home; but now he knew he'd never tell it to her or anyone else.

He was afraid of the child. He came to work next day determined to avoid her; to his relief, she did not come into the park that morning; but looking up from time to time, he saw her at her window. All that morning, he was conscious that she followed his movements with her eyes, her head turning from side to side; and once, looking up quickly, their glances met. He turned uneasily away, aware of the unconcealed fury, the cold, calculating anger in the little girl's face. At twelve he ate his lunch on the bench beside the lily pond; at half past twelve he went to the basement room for his customary nap.

Not long afterward the ice-cream man, trundling his bell-decked cart, came into the street and drew up beside the park gate to sell his wares to the neighborhood children. A flock gathered quickly around him, leaving the park and the court-yard deserted for a time. Rhoda, seeing him there, asked her mother for money to buy an ice-cream stick, and Mrs. Penmark gave it to her. She started for the stairs, and then, as though having made up her mind at last, she turned and went into the kitchen; and Christine watched what she did there. She saw Rhoda take three big kitchen matches from the box above the stove. She held them a moment in her hand, as though debating a point, and then, deciding three matches were too many, she returned one of them to the box. She went slowly down the back stairs, bought her ice-cream stick, and sat on the steps near the basement to enjoy it, eating the stick with little mincing bites, listening with approval to Leroy's snores in the room beyond her.

Mrs. Penmark had moved to the kitchen window to watch, wondering what the child intended doing with the matches she'd taken; she did not have long to wonder, for Rhoda, looking cautiously from side to side to see that no eye observed her, went, her face bland and innocent again, to the basement door. She paused at the door and struck one match on the cement wall, shielding the flame with her palm. She disappeared for a moment from her mother's sight as she went on tiptoes into the basement room. When there, she stooped quickly and touched the match to the excelsior and piled papers of Leroy's makeshift bed. She came out of the basement quietly, closing the door behind her. She slipped the flimsy bolt that held the door shut when wind blew, and banged it about; then, sitting again in her original place, she nibbled her ice-cream stick, the burned match still held in her disengaged hand.

The thing had happened with such casual efficiency, with such sureness of purpose, that Mrs. Penmark—although part of her mind must certainly have known—had not been able to accept in actuality the event that had happened before her eyes. She stood as though paralyzed beside her concealing curtain; and at the instant she began to scream, she heard Leroy's fainter, answering screams coming like echoes from the other side of the basement door. Smoke rolled out of the barred windows on either side of the door. He threw his weight against the door, but for a time the bold held. Then his face appeared at one of the windows. He saw Rhoda enjoying her ice-cream stick. He said in a desperate, coaxing voice, "Unlock the door, Rhoda! I'm not mad at you!"

The child laughed charmingly, and shook her head from side to side.

He knew then, in those dreadful moments before death, precisely what had happened to him. He screamed again, a long, wailing note of despair, and said, "I haven't got them shoes! I was only teasing you a little! I don't know nothing about them shoes!"

Rhoda bent her head rhythmically to her ice-cream stick with delicate, miserly bites, her eyes interested and lifted upward. "You know," she said gently. "You know where they are."

Leroy threw his weight against the door time and time again; and at last the bolt gave way. He ran out into the courtyard. His clothing had burned away, and clung to his blackened body in long, fiery rags. Even his shoestrings were burning, even his hair was ablaze. He screamed, "I wasn't going to tell on you! I don't know nothing about nothing you done!"

Rhoda's pink darting tongue touched her treat for a final time; then lifting her head, pressing her palms together, she laughed the lovely, tinkling laugh of childhood and said, "You're silly."

She got up from the steps, straightened her frock, and put both stick and waxed paper in the garbage can under the stairs. She stood there smiling and nodding her head, as though in genial approval of a scene planned to divert her, as Leroy ran in flames toward the lily pond. But when his hand was on the knob of the gate, he shuddered and swayed backward; then, still clutching the gate, he sagged down to the cement, released his grip, and died there.

Mrs. Penmark turned from her window, saying to herself, "I'm not going to faint. This is an emergency. It's necessary for me to keep calm."

She went toward her bedroom with the intention of lying down a moment, but she did not reach her bed. Against her will, her knees buckled beneath her, and there was the terrible singing of blood in her ears. She lost consciousness for a time, and then, although she never knew how it happened, she was going down the back stairs, holding onto the railing for support, calling in a frantic voice, "Rhoda! Rhoda! Rhoda!"

The courtyard was full of people—people from the apartment house itself, neighbors from across the street, and strangers who had been passing, and had seen the flames from the basement. She went at once to the park fence, and stood beside her daughter, looking down at the dead man at her feet. . . .

There was somebody screaming somewhere, and she kept wondering who it could be. She turned to the people who watched her and said in a lost, chiding voice, "Quit screaming, please! Screaming doesn't help!" She closed her eyes and leaned against the fence; and then she knew the person screaming was herself.

Already men had formed a bucket line, and were passing water from one hand to another, or dragging, piece by piece, the burning junk from the cement of the basement to the cement of the courtyard. Then the fire engines were there; then the ambulance that took Leroy's body away. . . . Next, she was lying on the grass inside the park, and somebody bathed her face with water from the lily pond that Leroy had never reached. Mrs. Kunkel from across the street was standing over her and saying impatiently, "Stop that screaming! Stop it! Stop it!"

"You must try to control yourself," said Mrs. Forsythe.

Christine said, "I saw it! I saw it this time! I saw him as he came out of the basement! I saw him die at the gate!"

"You must control yourself," said Mrs. Forsythe. "You must make an effort to control yourself." She pressed cool water once more to her friend's face and continued. "You must take Rhoda as an example. Rhoda isn't upset at all. She's behaving like a seasoned little trouper."

Then, in sudden resolution, as though summoning the last of her strength, Christine stood up, and, supported by Mrs. Forsythe and a man she'd never seen before, she went to her own apartment, and lay flat on her bed. She turned on her side, thinking this time it was surely her fault. She might, with some justice, have found excuses for herself before, but not this time. She said under her breath, "This time I knew what would happen, or I should have known. And I should have stopped it. I should have done something about Rhoda weeks ago. Something must be done quickly now."

Mrs. Forsythe went to the kitchen to take ice from the trays; and Rhoda came into the room and stared contemptuously at her mother. She said casually, in a whisper that hardly carried to Christine's ears. "He knew about the shoes. He was going to tell on me."

Mrs. Forsythe came back with an improvised ice pack for Mrs. Penmark and said, "He must have been smoking in the basement again, which he'd been told not to do. They think he went to sleep with a lighted cigarette in his hand. Several of us predicted it would happen some day. Oh, I feel such sympathy for his wife and family. I doubt if his wife has enough to bury him decently. It was such a sad accident, really." She went to the window and adjusted the blinds so that light fell on the wall in small, precise slats that moved and shifted design when the trees moved, with the effect of sunlight shimmering on water. She said, "I'm going to take Rhoda to my apartment, where she won't disturb you. You must get some sleep if you can. You'll feel better after a nice sleep. But you must quit worrying so, or you'll make yourself ill. Just leave everything to me. Just sleep."

She slept after a time, a deep, dreamless sleep such as she'd not had for a long time; and when she woke, she felt a stolid quietness which was, in its way, more frightening than the wildness of her turmoil had been. It was as though she'd reached at last the windless center of the hurricane that had destroyed her. . . . Calmly she bathed her face, brushed her hair, put on new lipstick, and called for her child.

Later that afternoon, the telephone rang. It was Mrs. Breedlove. She had heard about the fire and Leroy's death, and she wanted to know at first hand what had happened. Christine told her what she knew—there was no damage to the apartment house; there was little damage to the basement itself; it was thought Leroy had gone to sleep with a lighted cigarette in his hand. Monica said in an earnest voice, "I'm pleased to see you're taking it so sensibly. To tell the truth, I was afraid you'd be upset and nervous again. I really called to see how you were getting along. I wouldn't blame you if you were upset, my dear. After all, it was a most terrible tragedy." Then, repeating the little anecdote she'd thought up for the occasion, she laughed for the first time, and hung up her phone.

When it was dusk, Mrs. Penmark called a taxi and went to Leroy's house on General Jackson Street. The place was filled with people, and she went only as far as the door; she could not bring herself to go inside. The widow, being summoned, came out to see who her visitor was, and sat with her under the blossoming althea tree near the porch. Christine identified herself and said, "I want you to give him the kind of funeral you want to give him. Don't worry about expenses. I'll take care of all the bills." Thelma stared at her in astonishment, and Christine went on. "You know who I am. Have the undertaker and the others telephone me. I'll tell them what I've told you." Then, getting up, she went to the waiting taxicab.

She awoke next morning with an obsessive desire to read the volume devoted to her mother in the *Great American Criminals* series. She drove to the library, took out the book, and returned with it to her apartment. She sat beside her window, reading again the things she already knew, but in greater detail this time.

When August Denker came into the property his wife had won for him, a change came over him, and he ceased to be the unquestioning, good-natured husband. He took on an air of sudden importance; he began giving orders to others; and, what was worst of all from Mrs. Denker's standpoint, he seemed bent on dissipating the estate through his impractical plans for its increase. She had not planned to remove him so soon, but seeing her lifework threatened, she departed for the first time from the cunning conservatism of her master plan and gave him his arsenic in buttermilk.

Her plan had now worked out to its final detail; the dreams of her girlhood had all come true; she was in possession of the Denker money at last. She settled back to enjoy the fruits of her labor, to play the role of the bereaved but courageous widow. It was doubtful that she ever regretted the things she'd done, or thought with remorse of her acts. She probably regarded herself not as a criminal but as a cunning little businesswoman who traveled in an unusual line of merchandise, whose foresight and skill lifted her above the fates of those less gifted than herself. . . .

But even as she rocked so contentedly in her tidy house, the first baying of the first hound was heard at the edge of the swamp; for Cousin Ada Gustafson, the silent, suspicious one, began to go about the countryside and speak her suspicions aloud: "August hadn't died of no congestive chill, like the doctor said, and nobody could tell her different. Cousin Bessie put something in August's buttermilk just as sure as God made little apples! . . . And Grandfather Denker dying like he did—so sudden, and all—sounded real funny, too. Why, that old man had been strong as a bull. . . . Then, too, there were those stories they used to tell about Bessie back home when she was a girl. It seemed real funny to her that things didn't start happening to folks until Cousin Bessie got *interested* in them."

At first the neighbors listened to the old woman with amusement and disbelief; then Ada went to the sheriff one afternoon and told her story. "Let's dig up August!" she said. "Let's dig up August and see!"

Then the county asked permission to exhume August Denker's body; and when Bessie weepingly refused to have her husband serve as the playing field of Cousin Ada's spite, the officials got a court order and dug up the body anyway; and for the first time in her life, perhaps, Mrs. Denker felt blind, unreasoning panic. She lost all the ordinary good sense that had served her so long. She devised a plan for her protection so foolish that it seemed incredible: she told everyone that August and Grandfather Denker had been poisoned, all right, but she wasn't the one who'd done it. Cousin Ada had committed these crimes, she said, and probably others, too. She'd suspected her from the first, but she'd kept quiet in fear of her own life, and in fear of the lives of her children, too. Cousin Ada had threatened time after time to kill her and the children, and burn the house down, too. If anything happened to her and the children, she wanted them to remember what she'd told them about Cousin Ada, and act as witnesses against her later on. . . .

That night she killed Ada Gustafson and all her children except the youngest, Christine. Apparently, she'd first stunned Old Ada with the blunt side of her hatchet, and then with a cleaver she'd severed the old woman's head. When these things were accomplished, she'd dressed the old woman in her own clothes, even putting her wedding ring on Ada's finger. For her escape, she dressed herself in a suit of her husband's clothes, and then, going out of her door for the last time, she'd paused long enough to set fire to the place. She'd hoped, although the hope proved to be a forlorn one, that the authorities would mistake the body of the old woman for her own, would assume that she, Ada Gustafson, had committed the crime, had been the murderer all along.

She had wrapped Old Ada's head in a newspaper parcel, and taking the bundle with her, she made her escape from the flaming farmhouse; but her disguise mislead nobody. They caught up with her the next morning as she sat in the waiting-room of the Union Station of Kansas City. The circular parcel was resting in her lap, and when the police cut the string and opened it, Miss Gustafson's head rolled off the seat and halfway across the tiles of the waiting-room floor.

Why the youngest child had been spared was anybody's guess. There was a story which still cropped up occasionally that Ada Gustafson had loved Christine more than the others, and fearing what might happen, she'd sent her to a neighboring farmhouse for the night; but there were no facts to support the story. Richard Bravo was of the opinion that Christine had been spared because the mother considered her too young to understand what had happened, or to testify against her later. Alice Olcott Flowers believed Bessie Denker expected, with the narcissistic arrogance of her kind, to outwit her pursuers and make good her escape. She'd probably want to start all over again some place, and she'd saved Christine for that future just as she might have conserved any other asset. After all, the child was an insurable piece of property that could be realized on later for working capital. . . .

Mrs. Penmark closed her eyes and said, "No. It didn't happen that way. They're all wrong. . . . I wasn't asleep when she hit Sonny with the hatchet; I saw her do it, and I ran out and hid back of the barn in the weeds. It was dark there, and she couldn't find me. When she'd killed the others, she came to look for me. She called me and called me. She said she wouldn't hurt me if I came to her. But I'd watched through the window while she killed the others, and I wouldn't answer her."

# twelve

MRS. PENMARK FELL INTO THE HABIT, immediately after breakfast, of dressing herself and the child and riding aimlessly about the countryside. On these trips they rarely spoke, as though, understanding each other so completely now, there was no longer reason for communication. Sometimes, when she did not feel like driving her car, Mrs. Penmark and Rhoda took bus rides that had no definite destination. To see them, sitting in separate seats, one would not have thought they were together, except that the child turned from time to time to watch her mother, as though waiting the signal that would reveal to her the thing they were to do next.

In the center of the town, there was a square filled with azalea bushes, camellias, and live oaks. There was a big iron fountain with four graduated basins beneath to catch the cascading water from the top of the structure, to hold it a moment, and to pass it at last to the circular moat below. There was always a breeze at that place, and sometimes she'd take the child to the square, knowing they'd not be likely to meet anyone but strangers in such a public place. They'd sit on the iron benches, while Christine looked vacantly about her, and Rhoda, on a separate bench, would go on with her needlework.

The park was the haven of the rootless stranger who had no other place to go; but one afternoon Christine looked up and saw Miss Octavia Fern approaching. The old lady stopped in doubt, then nodded, as if still not sure of herself. She said, "You're Christine Penmark, aren't you?"

"Yes. Yes, of course, Miss Fern."

"I thought you must be, but I wasn't too positive. Then I saw Rhoda sitting across the walk and, of course, I knew."

Christine smiled gently, but she neither answered, nor asked the old lady to sit down.

"I remember our morning at Benedict so well, with so much pleasure," said Miss Fern after a moment. "It was a charming day, really. The oleander cuttings rooted easily, and I transplanted two of them to our back garden just the other day."

Mrs. Penmark nodded in recognition that she heard, and Miss Fern went on. "I'd hoped you'd find time to visit me, but I know how occupied you must be these days." She paused again, feeling as though she addressed a stranger, as though she'd ineptly trespassed on the privacy of others, as though her presence in the park were a thing to be explained and condoned. She said hurriedly, "I rarely come through the square; but Burgess is waiting for me down the street, and this was a short cut."

She moved away, caught Rhoda's eye, and waved; but the child ignored her with a placid disinterest. Miss Fern stood in uncertainty, as though undecided what to do next, how to get herself in motion once more. She gave the impression that she was about to sit on the bench beside Mrs. Penmark; and then, as though the impulse were canceled at the instant the movement was contemplated, she fumbled in her handbag needlessly, as though searching for a card to give a stranger, and said, "We must have our visit sometime soon. . . . But I mustn't keep Burgess waiting. She fidgets so when she's kept waiting."

Late one afternoon, after she'd returned with Rhoda from the square, Mrs. Penmark's doorbell rang, and she went to answer it. She found Hortense Daigle in the hall. Mrs. Daigle came into the living-room, embraced Christine, and said, "I've been wanting to return your visit for such a long time; but I've been in mourning. But I said to Mr. Daigle this morning, 'What do you suppose Christine thinks of me? I must go see her today without fail.'"

She was a little drunk, and Mrs. Penmark placed a chair for her. She sat down, and seeing Rhoda reading beside the window, she said, "So this is your little girl? What's your name? Claude spoke of you so often, and in such high terms. You were one of his dearest friends, I'm sure. He said you were so bright in school."

"My name is Rhoda Penmark."

"Come let me look at you, Rhoda. . . . Now, how about giving your Aunt Hortense a big kiss? You were with Claude when he had his accident, weren't you, dear? You're the little girl who was so sure she was going to win the penmanship medal, and worked so hard. But you didn't win it after all, did you, darling? Claude won the medal, didn't he? Now, tell me this   would you say he won it fair and square, or that he cheated? These things are so important, now that he's dead. I've called Miss Octavia Fern on the telephone a dozen times, but she just gives me the brush-off. She—"

Christine disengaged her child from the hot, damp arms of the visitor, saying, "It's time for you to visit Mrs. Forsythe. She's looking forward to seeing you. You mustn't disappoint her."

Mrs. Daigle straightened in her chair. "Go by all means. I mustn't keep you from your social duties, I'm sure. Even my husband tells me I'm tiresome. Why don't you come out in the open and say so?"

Rhoda gave the woman a shrewd, amused look, smoothed down her bangs, and went through the door. Mrs. Daigle said, "Have you got anything to drink in the house? Anything at all.

I'm not the fussy type. I prefer bourbon and water, but anything will do." Mrs. Penmark went to the kitchen and began taking out ice cubes. She put a bottle of bourbon and one glass on a tray, and Hortense, following her into the kitchen said, "Aren't you going to join me, Christine? An old gentleman, a friend of Mr. Daigle's, has some sort of a heart condition; and you know what—the doctor said for him to take three drinks a day. It's supposed to relax your arteries. Only this old gentleman was a strict prohibitionist and said no, he wouldn't do it."

She staggered, lost her balance, and bumped against the wall. She said, "As though three drinks a day was any trouble. Three drinks a day isn't what I call trouble. Talking about trouble, what would he do if his little boy got drowned, and then was beaten against pilings? Now, you may disagree, but that's what I call trouble; not having to take three drinks of whisky a day." She laughed loudly, pushing her hair up, and said, "When Mr. Daigle told me, I laughed until my sides ached."

Christine put a bowl of ice cubes on the tray and brought it into the living-room. Mrs. Daigle downed a drink of straight bourbon, took a swallow of water, and went on. "What I came here for was to have a little chat with Rhoda; but, of course, I didn't know she had all these social obligations. I thought she was like any other little girl that stayed home and minded her mother, and didn't go traipsing over town to see people just before suppertime. I'm sorry I interfered with Rhoda's social life. I hope you'll pardon me, Christine. I offer you my deepest apologies. I'll apologize to Rhoda, too, when she comes back."

"Are you comfortable?" asked Mrs. Penmark. "Shall I turn the fan more in your direction?"

"I've talked to so many people about Claude's death. I wanted to talk to Rhoda, too. There's nothing wrong about that, is it? She must know something she hasn't told; maybe something she thought wasn't important, and forgot. But everything that has to do with Claude is important to me. I wasn't going to contaminate her in the slightest degree, I assure you. I was just going to rock her in my arms, and ask her a few simple questions."

"Perhaps another time would be better."

"I'm not intoxicated in the slightest degree. Kindly don't talk down to me, Mrs. Penmark. I've been through enough without that. . . . But Rhoda knows more than she's told anybody, if you'll pardon me for being so presumptuous as to disagree with you. I talked to that guard, remember. It was a long, interesting conversation, and he said he saw Rhoda on the wharf just before Claude was found among the pilings. She knows something she hasn't told, all right."

The telephone rang, and Christine answered it. She heard Mr. Daigle's worried voice. He wanted to know if his wife was there. He'd been phoning all over town, trying to find her. Mrs. Penmark said she was, and he promised to come at once and pick her up. Mrs. Daigle, hearing the conversation, said, "Did you tell him I was drinking and making a spectacle of myself? Did you tell him to call the patrol wagon, dear Christine?"

"You heard what I said. I only said you were here."

"That's what you said aloud—yes. But what were you thinking? You were thinking, 'How can I get rid of this pest?' That's what you were really thinking. . . . For your private information, let me tell you something. I don't care what you think of me. Understand? I don't know who you think you are, being so high and mighty, and thinking you're better than other people. You may fool some with that mealy mouth, but you look like 'Ned in the Primer' to me."

"If that's what you really think, perhaps you'd better not come here again."

"I wouldn't come here again for a million dollars laid out in a line. I wouldn't have come this time, if I'd known about Rhoda's social life. I didn't live on Easy Street when I was growing up, the way you did. I lived on the Road of Hard Knocks, as the fellow says," She poured herself another drink, downed it, and continued. "You think you're important, don't you? Going around being *kind* to people. Nobody asked you to come to my house the night Claude was killed. Nobody asked you to come that second time, either. I wondered ever since why you came that second time. You had something on your mind, but didn't say what it was. I said the same to Mr. Daigle, but he said I was out of my mind."

She got up, and stood swaying beside her chair, steadying herself, with her index finger pressed against the upholstery. "I won't wait for Mr. Daigle," she said. "I'll go home by myself. I know where I'm not wanted, and I'm not wanted in a place where people have all these social obligations, if you get what I mean."

"Please sit down, Mrs. Daigle. Your husband said he was leaving at once. He'll be here any moment."

"'Let her come around and snoop as much as she wants to,' I said to Mr. Daigle. 'Let her be kind, too, if that suits her. Christine's got everything coming her way,' I said. 'She's the lucky one.'"

"I don't consider myself the lucky one. Please believe me."

Mrs. Daigle said, "Pardon my mentioning it, because I know personal remarks aren't considered good form, but you're not looking well. You're looking sort of—well, sick and *sloppy*, if you know what I mean. Come over to my house and I'll give you a free beauty treatment, if you're pressed for ready cash. Call me up sometime this week, and we'll get together. I don't charge my friends anything. It won't cost you a nickel."

The doorbell rang again, and this time Dwight Daigle was there. He said, "Come, Hortense. It's time to go home."

Hortense wept noisily. She came up to Mrs. Penmark and embraced her, resting her head on her shoulder. She said, "You know something! You know something, and you won't tell me!"

Mrs. Penmark said she would not go to the library again, that there was little left for her to learn about her mother, but next morning she woke wanting to know the details of Mrs. Denker's electrocution. She did not return this time to the garden and the pergola; she went into one of the small rooms reserved for the research worker and took out the daily newspapers that covered the period she sought to know about. She read steadily for the next few hours. . . . Her mother's death in the chair had been a sensation that had been featured everywhere. There was a photograph of her mother at the moment of her death. A reporter had smuggled in a camera, concealed somehow behind a button, and at the instant the current hit Bessie Denker and hurled her against the straps, the picture was snapped.

She studied the picture with concentrated attention. Everything was there for the eye to see—the black mask that covered her mother's face; the bound hands raised from the wrist, trembling and out of focus from movement; the fingers spread apart like the talons of a predatory bird; the thick, dead-white, hairless legs, strapped down and bulging outward under the power of the current. . . .

She sat for a long time, the picture before her eyes. . . . She had been foolish to wonder what Rhoda's end would be. She

knew now, for Rhoda, unless something were done, would repeat the idiotic pattern of her grandmother's life, making the
necessary allowance for time and circumstances. She, too, for
Rhoda was very clever indeed, would escape for a long time; but
she would be caught and destroyed at last. . . . And in that interval between accomplishment and detection, she would destroy
everything she touched; she, too, would end up in a blare of publicity and sentiment—in the gas chamber, at the end of a rope, or
lunging forward as the current struck her and hurtled through
her blood. Clearly, at that instant, she saw the picture of her
daughter's end, and, covering her face, she turned away and
murmured, "God have mercy on us!"

Now, she no longer wanted to read, or even to think about
her mother, and she returned the old papers to their custodian.
She got her things together in preparation for departure; but
Miss Glass came into the room and said, "I've been thinking
about your book—particularly the end. Have you decided yet?"

"Yes, I think so."

Miss Glass smiled in a self-deprecatory way, and said she had
a confession to make, an apology to offer. She'd done a thing
which, now that she thought it over, she saw clearly she should
not have done. She knew how jealously authors must guard their
plots, but she'd been so interested in Mrs. Penmark's situation
that she'd told it to others. It had happened this way: her sister,
with whom she lived, had strong literary feelings, and there was
a little group to which they both belonged that met each week to
ponder trends in writing. Now, at this last meeting, she'd outlined Mrs. Penmark's plot, since it illustrated a point which had
been raised. It was an indiscretion beyond doubt, although she
was sure none of the people present would be dishonest enough
to use it for their own.

At any rate, to make a long story short, she'd spoken of the author's difficulty in finding an ending for the novel, and the group had discussed every possible solution. It had been like a jury discussing an actual case, really. They'd debated the possibilities of psychiatric treatment, reform school, or blind faith in the future; and in the end they'd taken a vote. It had been unanimously decided that the only possible way to end the book was for the mother to keep her secret, kill the child, and then commit suicide.

She ended, "I hope I wasn't indiscreet in repeating what you told me; but after all you didn't say you were speaking in confidence."

"It doesn't matter at all. That ending had occurred to me, too. Perhaps, it's the one I'll have to use."

That night Mrs. Penmark made a holograph will, as follows:

*Upon my death, I leave my jewelry and my 1912 Utrillo landscape to my friend Monica W. Breedlove as a memento of my constant affection. To my husband Kenneth Penmark, whom I've loved to the exclusion of all other men, I return the Modigliani drawing he once gave me with the earnest wish that he find a more worthy recipient for it; that he forgive me if he can, and marry again. My bank balances, my stocks, my bonds, and all other property I possess at my death, I leave to Thelma Jessup, widow of Leroy Jessup, who lives at 572 General Jackson Street.*

She dated the will August 3rd, 1952, signed it, and put it in the drawer of her desk that she kept locked, saying to herself, "It's all I can do in atonement."

When she'd finished the will, she sat for a long time thinking. She knew now what she was going to do; the conflicts that had torn her apart so long were stilled at last. There remained only to do it as sensibly, as simply as she could. She walked about the apartment, thinking out her moves with the same dispassionate concern that she'd once brought to the balancing of a family budget. Everything must be done in calmness, and with discretion; each detail worked out in advance. . . . Insofar as she was concerned, it did not matter too greatly; but Rhoda must not suffer, and she must not be afraid; she must not even be aware of what awaited her. . . .

She unlocked the drawer of her desk and read parts of the sick, imploring letters she'd written her husband; she burned the letters in the fireplace; she shoveled up the ashes and flushed them down the drain. She went through her papers methodically, tearing up old letters and photographs which she'd once thought of saving for Rhoda's amusement or instruction when the child was older, and could appreciate them; and when she'd obliterated her past as best she could, she smoked a cigarette and went to bed, her mind at peace once more. She awoke refreshed and serene, and looking into the hand mirror on her dressing-table, she was appalled at the things that had happened to her.

That morning she left the child with Mrs. Forsythe—it could hardly matter now, since the work of Bessie Denker was to be wound up so soon—and went to the beauty shop near the square. It was there, smiling vaguely to herself under the dryer, that she worked out her final plans, and fixed the day for the death of herself and her daughter. When she came back to her apartment, there was a letter in the box from her husband; she read it over and over, knowing it would be her last contact with him. Things were shaping up nicely, he said. He hoped to be home around the middle of August. He missed his wife and child, and could hardly wait to see them again. He hoped he'd not have to leave them again for a long time. To Christine he sent his undying love.

She took his photograph, brought it to the light, and looked at it for a long time. "That's such a *nice* thing to say!" she said in a sweet, detached voice. "It's such a *pleasant* thing to say!" She touched his lips with her own, and then, sighing with a sort of impersonal regret, she went on with her plans.

She had known from the beginning that she could neither use physical violence on the child, nor mutilate her in any way. The sensible thing to do, then, was to give the child the sleeping pills that Mrs. Breedlove and the doctor had prescribed for her own discomfort, but which she had not taken, as though she'd always known they'd fit somehow into her emergency. But it would be difficult to get Rhoda to take the pills without suspecting her motive in tendering them, for Rhoda had the same primitive instinct for avoiding danger, the same ability to sniff out and avoid the set trap, that animals possess.

She considered and discarded several plans to get the child to take her death potion without suspicion or anxiety; and at last, to lend normal credibility to her design, she took the little girl to a doctor for an examination. The child's appetite was not good; she'd seemed listless and pale of late; she wondered if there were anything the matter with her. The doctor examined the little girl, and later, when he was alone with Mrs. Penmark, he said her daughter was as healthy as a child could be.

On their way home, Christine said, "The doctor thinks you need vitamin tablets. We'll stop here and get them."

She bought the tablets in the child's presence. Later, she took the tablets from their container and substituted the sleeping pills. That night when Rhoda was in bed, she said, "I suppose you may as well take the tablets now. This is as good a time as any."

But when Rhoda saw the number of tablets her mother had measured in her palm, she said, "You don't take all those at one *time*, do you?"

"I asked the doctor that. I didn't know, either. He said you usually took them one at a time, after meals; but your condition was a little different, and he thought it better to take them all at once."

Rhoda said, "Let's see the bottle, Mother."

Mrs. Penmark gave her the bottle, and after the child had examined it, read the label, and verified the fact that the tablets in her mother's hand were identical with those still in the bottle, she said, "Well, all right, Mother," and took the first of the pills.

After each tablet, she took a small swallow of water; and Christine said, "These will make all the difference. They'll solve everything for you. . . . Now, you must take them every one. There are only a few left, now. You must try and take them all."

Then, when the child had swallowed the last of the sleeping tablets, Christine sat beside her. "Do you want me to read to you?" she asked.

The child nodded. She was in the middle of *The Five Little Peppers and How They Grew*, and her mother, finding the proper place, read softly. She thought the child would never sleep; she wondered how long she could keep up her manner of deceptive calmness; then, after a long time, the eyes of the child inevitably closed.

She sat beside her daughter a long time, watching the soft, placid signs of her breathing, thinking how innocent the child looked, how free of the dark, terrible instincts that were in her; then all at once she felt these things were not true, that the things the child had done could exist only in her own imagination; but she pulled herself up sternly and said, "I'm imagining nothing. It is all true."

She bent above her husband's photograph, and looked at it

with love and great longing. His face brought back so many memories, the knowledge of so much they'd shared together, that she feared she'd break down in tears and wild anxieties again; but she did not, and saying aloud to him, "She is not going to destroy you, as she's destroyed me. And she's not going to die publicly as my mother did, with millions reading of her last words, her last thoughts, her last gestures of pain, with their morning coffee. That is not going to happen. That can never happen now." Then touching the photograph with her fingers, turning away in regret, she said in a soft, placating voice, "If you knew, I'm sure you'd forgive me in time."

She kissed the child once on her brow. She unlocked the drawer of her desk for a final time. She stood with the pistol in her hand, inspecting it idly, as though she did not understand its purpose. And then, standing before the mirror in her bedroom, she raised the pistol and put a bullet through her brain.

Mrs. Breedlove, playing contract with her brother and two others, strangers they had just met, laid down her cards, and said for the third time, "I'm worried about Christine. You can say what you please, Emory, but there's something wrong. I've called her a number of times tonight, and her phone doesn't answer."

"Maybe she doesn't want to answer her phone. Maybe she's gone to the movies. Why don't you quit worrying and let poor Christine mind her own business?"

"Christine *always* answers her phone. And she doesn't go out any more at night alone. You know that as well as I do. . . . No, Emory: there's something odd about it."

"Who is this Christine you're talking about?" asked Mrs. Price. "Is she a relative?"

"She's a neighbor," said Mrs. Breedlove. "But I'm fond of her, and of her little girl, too. She's such a lovely woman—so gentle and simple; so completely unaffected."

She shuffled the cards, and when she'd dealt, she said stubbornly, "If she went out, as Emory suggests, Mrs. Forsythe, who lives across the hall from her, would know. I'm going to telephone her this minute."

Emory laughed indulgently and said, "What do you do with women like that? She's been that way ever since I can remember."

"Well, I don't know," said Angeline Price. "I think she ought to call Mrs. Forsythe." She looked at Mrs. Breedlove, and they nodded in agreement. Emory glanced at his watch and said, "It's eleven o'clock. If you're going to catch her before she goes to bed, you'd better hurry and do it." But Mrs. Forsythe said she hadn't seen Christine or Rhoda since just before suppertime. They had not gone out. Of that she was positive. But perhaps they'd just gone to bed early.

Monica said, "Will you ring her doorbell? I'll wait here until you do."

When Mrs. Forsythe returned, she said she'd rung the bell repeatedly. She'd also pounded on the door, and had called Christine's name; but there had been no response at all. "Is there anything wrong?" she asked. "Do you want me to do anything?"

Mrs. Breedlove turned back to the card table; but after a little while, she threw down her hand and said, "I'm going over there and find out what's the matter." Turning to Emory, she added, "If you don't want to come, you can stay where you are. But I'm worried and I'm going to find out."

Emory said, "You know I'm not going to let you drive to town by yourself this time of night." Then, laughing self-consciously, he added, "Let's get started if we're going."

As they approached the apartment house, Johnnie Kunkel, who had to be home by twelve, was pulling up to the curb across the street, having just taken his date home. Mrs. Breedlove called him, and he joined them on the walk. They went first to the front door, and Mrs. Breedlove knocked and rang the bell. Mrs. Forsythe joined them, clutching her kimono to her throat.

Monica said, "Johnnie, do you think you can climb up to the back balcony and get in the kitchen? Break the window if it's locked. Then go straight through the house, and unlock the door for us."

He opened the door at length, and Monica called out in a frightened voice, "Christine! Christine! Is everything all right?"

They went first to Mrs. Penmark's bedroom, where a light still burned, and huddled together at the door; then they backed away, turning on lights all over the apartment. Mrs. Forsythe ran to the child's bedroom, and when the others joined her, she said, "Rhoda is still alive, but we must get help quickly." To Johnnie Kunkel, who stood with his mouth half open, she said impatiently, "Pick up Rhoda and take her to the hospital in your car. Drive as quickly as you can. I think there's time to save her, but we must hurry." Then she added, "Wait! Wait! I'll come with you!"

After the funeral, Kenneth Penmark sat in Mrs. Breedlove's living-room. Rhoda was out of the hospital, and was staying with Mrs. Forsythe until arrangements could be made for her future. She'd said that morning at the funeral that she'd keep Rhoda as long as necessary, for this particular emergency, or forever, if Kenneth would agree. He told her his mother and sisters were to arrive next day, and no doubt Rhoda would go back with them.

But now, sitting beside Monica's big fan, he said, pressing his nervous hands against his head, "Why did she do it? Why, in God's name, did she do such a thing?" He turned to Monica and said, "She was closer to you than anyone. Did she say anything to you that would give you an idea why she did it? There must have been some reason."

Mrs. Breedlove said, "I don't know why she did it. I've thought of it until I'm almost prostrated. I can only say I don't know. I've retraced everything she did, and everything I know. I talked to Reginald Tasker and Miss Octavia Fern, and they haven't any idea, either."

"There was a reason. Christine didn't do things without a reason. I can't understand it. I can't—"

"I think she stumbled onto something too terrible to endure. When she was at the hotel with me, I begged her to let me cable you to come home, but she wouldn't hear of it. She said it didn't concern you at all. She seemed to be so much better these last days. But I shouldn't have left her alone. I shouldn't have. I shouldn't have."

"Do you think she was insane?" asked Kenneth.

"No, I do not. I most emphatically do not."

"Christine wasn't crazy," said Emory. "She was worried sick."

Kenneth sighed, and again he pressed his palms against his forehead, as though to quiet some unbearable pain in his head. Then Mrs. Forsythe came in with the little girl, and Rhoda went at once to her father, to embrace him. He took her in his arms, and she smiled, tilted her head; and then pulling away, she danced across the carpet. She raised her chin a little, showing her shallow dimple, clapped her hands charmingly, and said, "What will you give me, if I give you a basket of kisses?"

"Come, darling," said Mrs. Forsythe. "You aren't strong yet.

You mustn't tire yourself." Then, looking significantly at Kenneth, she added, "She's too young as yet to understand what happened. She's such an innocent child in many ways."

But the little girl was not to be diverted from her game. She did a little pirouette, curtseyed, and said, "What will you give me, Father? What will you give me if I give you a basket of kisses?"

There was a moment's silence before Kenneth said, "I'll give you a basket of hugs." And then, as though the last vestige of his reserve were broken, he covered his face and wept with a harsh, tearing sound.

"Come, Rhoda," said Mrs. Forsythe. "Come, my darling." She took the child's hand and led her to the door. "Let's go downstairs and cut out paper dolls. Your father is tired out from his long plane trip. We'll come back later when he's rested."

Then turning to Kenneth, as though in reproof of his grief, she said, "You must not despair, Mr. Penmark, and become bitter. We cannot always understand God's wisdom, but we must accept it. Everything was not taken from you as you think. At least Rhoda was spared. You still have Rhoda to be thankful for."

## About the author

## About the book

## Read on

Insights,
Interviews,
& More...

# Author Biography

WILLIAM MARCH was born William Edward
Campbell in 1893 in Mobile, Alabama, the
second child and eldest son in a family of eleven
children. He left home at the age of sixteen after
his family moved to a small sawmill town where
he was forced to drop out of school to work as a
filing clerk. In the years that followed, March
made up his high school deficiencies and briefly
enrolled in the University of Alabama Law
School before moving to New York in 1916 and
enlisting in the Marines during World War I.
In 1918, he was wounded at the French front
and left the military with the Distinguished
Service Cross, the Navy Cross, and the Croix de
Guerre.

After the war was over, March began working
for the shipping company Waterman, a job that
he held for eighteen years. In 1933, he published
his first novel, *Company K,* a book largely based
upon his wartime experiences. Following a
psychological breakdown he suffered while
working in Germany, March returned to New
York and wrote five books over the next eleven
years. These books—*Come in at the Door* (1934),
*The Tallons* (1936), *Some Like Them Short*
(1939), *The Looking-Glass* (1943), and *Trial
Balance* (1945)—did not sell particularly well,
but by 1946 March had gained enough
confidence to quit his job and concentrate on
writing full-time.

Soon afterwards, March suffered a more
serious breakdown, and spent six months
recovering in a Southern sanitarium. By 1950,
he had moved to New Orleans and was living a
far calmer and more stable life than during his
chaotic years in New York. When *The Bad Seed,*

universally regarded as his finest work, was published in April 1954, March was already seriously ill. He died of a heart attack soon after, on May 15, 1954, and thus was never able to enjoy the book's significant success. ∾

# "Terrifyingly Good":
## The Contemporary Response to *The Bad Seed*

DESPITE THE RELATIVE OBSCURITY of William March's earlier novels, *The Bad Seed* attracted a flurry of press attention when it was published in 1954, both because of the sensationalism of its subject and the psychological depth of its execution. As these excerpts from the contemporary reviews of 1954 show, critics were almost unanimous in their acclaim of March's ability to evoke a mood of terror and suspense, and to sustain such tension throughout the novel. While some reviewers took issue with the hereditary theory of Rhoda's otherwise inexplicably evil character, the general consensus, also shared by the book-buying public of the time, was that *The Bad Seed* was one of the best novels of the year, if not the decade.

> ❝ Critics were almost unanimous in their acclaim of March's ability to evoke a mood of terror and suspense. ❞

"Dark, original, ultimately appalling, William March's extraordinary new novel is, on the obvious level, a straightforward, technically accomplished story of suspense. The manner of its telling—the dispassionate, exact, almost starched prose, with its occasional glints of sardonic humor—is an impressive achievement in itself. It lends some credibility to a narrative against which the imagination rebels; and towards the end, as horror is piled upon horror, it saves the book (or does it?) from falling headlong into absurdity . . . This is a novel bound to arouse strong responses, to generate vehement discussion, and so not easily to be forgotten."
—Dan Wickenden, *New York Herald Tribune*

"Let it be said quickly: William March knows where human fears and secrets are buried. He announced it in *Company K,* a novel published twenty years ago and equaled only by Dos Passos' *Three Soldiers* as a sampling of men at war. He has proved it again and again in the other novels and short stories, all of them floored and walled in what Clinton Fadiman decided to call 'psychological acumen.' But nowhere is this gift better displayed than in *The Bad Seed*—the portrayal of a coldly evil, murderous child and what she does to both victims and family. In the author's hands this is adequate material for an absolutely first-class novel of moral bewilderments and responsibilities nearest the heart of our decade."

—James Kelly, *New York Times*

*" The Bad Seed* would have been a stronger novel without this false premise—the granddaughter of a murderess is no more likely to be a murderess than the granddaughter of a seamstress, or anyone else. Apart from this flaw, however, *The Bad Seed* is a novel of suspense and mounting horror, which the reader who can close his eyes to March's unnecessary premise will enjoy as the work of one of the most satisfying of American novelists."

August Derleth, *Chicago Sunday Tribune*

"I am too ignorant of heredity to know whether his solution is in fact a solution; what struck me about it was something else: that it was mechanical and, being so, reduced a terrifying ▶

66 Let it be said quickly: William March knows where human fears and secrets are buried. 99

◄ novel to a neat horror story; the moral issue had been burked. All the same, Mr. March's novel has great distinction, and his humanity and humour are delightful."
—Walter Allen, *New Statesman and Nation* (UK)

"Mr. March unfolds this tale of pure evil in a cool, matter-of-fact tone that has a chilling impact. Granted certain improbabilities, *The Bad Seed* is an almost impeccable novel of suspense."

—*Atlantic Monthly*

66 Mr. March unfolds this tale of pure evil in a cool, matter-of-fact tone that has a chilling impact. 99

"Marvelously as all this is told, there is one weak spot in it; not all readers will accept the author's putting the whole load on heredity—on the 'bad seed' that has skipped a generation and appeared again. Nevertheless, when it comes to managing horror expertly, Mr. March knows exactly what he is doing. So he does, too, when it is a matter of seizing the reader's attention and holding it."
—J. H. Jackson, *San Francisco Chronicle*

"I'm afraid Mr. March's last [book], *The Bad Seed*, won't help his reputation much. In many ways, it is a delightful novel, in others, a studiedly frightening one, but it is not completely effective. It is beautifully written; the dialogue is sharp and true, and Mr. March's cynical look at a small group of the citizens of a town that may be Reedyville (he doesn't say) is a pleasure to behold. His thesis, however, is a questionable one."
—Merle Miller, *Saturday Review*

# The Bad Seed
## on Broadway
## and at the Movies

PERHAPS SEEKING TO CAPITALIZE quickly
upon the notoriety and success of William
March's novel, Maxwell Anderson adapted the
book for the stage almost immediately after its
publication. Anderson was already a very well-
established playwright, having won the New
York Drama Critics' Circle Award in both 1935
(for *Winterset*) and 1936 (for *High Tor*), along
with the Pulitzer Prize for Drama in 1933
(for *Both Your Houses*). With Reginald Denham
directing Anderson's script, the play opened
on December 8, 1954, at the 46th Street Theatre
on Broadway, less than a year after the novel was
published. Including its move to the Coronet,
the play ran for a total of 334 performances,
and was a critical and commercial success.
Nancy Kelly, playing Christine Penmark, was
the adult star of the show, winning a 1955 Tony
Award for Best Actress in a Play, but it was
nine-year-old Patty McCormack as a chilling
Rhoda that audiences remembered most. With
her blond pigtails and empty blue eyes, she was
a disquieting vision of horrible evil wrapped in
its most beguiling disguise.

Kelly, McCormack, and the majority of the
cast reprised their roles in the 1956 movie
version directed by Mervyn LeRoy, who, in his
forty-year Hollywood career, produced or
directed more than seventy films, including
*Home Before Dark, Quo Vadis,* and the 1949
version of *Little Women*. The result was less even
than the play; some audiences found the film
suitably frightening, while others were distracted
by its stilted and melodramatic style. Kelly's acting
was generally considered to be overwrought, and

**❝ With her
blond pigtails and
empty blue eyes,
she was a
disquieting vision
of horrible evil
wrapped in its
most beguiling
disguise. ❞**

overall the movie feels far too much like a filmed play to be considered a classic of the screen. Additionally, because of Hollywood's moral codes of the time, LeRoy tacked on a bizarre happy ending in which Rhoda is punished by an unexplained bolt of lightning. Even stranger, during the closing credits Kelly is shown slinging McCormack over her knee and spanking her, a sequence that makes little sense artistically, let alone logically.

There was also a 1985 TV-movie version, which restored March's and Anderson's grimly ironic original ending, but was generally considered inferior to both the play and original film. David Carradine played Leroy Jessup, the unfortunate handyman, and Lynn Redgrave tried her hand at the Monica Breedlove role, while the rest of the cast was filled out by relative unknowns. ∾

> 66 Because of Hollywood's moral codes of the time, LeRoy tacked on a bizarre happy ending in which Rhoda is punished by an unexplained bolt of lightning. 99

# From Page to Screen

WHILE THE PRACTICE OF adapting novels and works of narrative nonfiction into film is commonplace, it is often the book that has the longer-lasting legacy and reputation. However, there are certain instances, such as *The Bad Seed*, in which the movie has become the dominant version of a given story—when the film adaptation is so popular that its literary inspiration has become somewhat obscured in our cultural memory, usually through no fault of the book itself. Below are some HarperPerennial titles that have been overshadowed by their more famous celluloid siblings, but remain excellent works of literature in their own right. Reading them will undoubtedly provide a deeper appreciation of the film versions—and may even inspire some fans to utter those familiar words: "The book was *so* much better!"

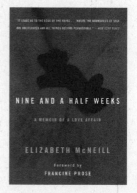

### NINE AND A HALF WEEKS

by Elizabeth McNeill

This is a love story so unusual, so passionate, so extreme in its psychology and sexuality that it takes the reader's breath away. Two ordinary, civilized people meet casually and begin an affair that soon turns into a sadomasochistic experience of frightening intensity. Unlike Pauline Réage's *Story of O,* this is not fiction or fantasy; it is a true account of an episode in the lives of a real man and real woman, originally published anonymously in 1978, and then reissued after the release of the movie in 1986 with Elizabeth McNeill's name on the jacket.

From the beginning, the sexual excitement of the central couple depends upon a pattern of domination and humiliation. As the affair progresses, they play out ever more dangerous and elaborate variations on that pattern and by the end, the woman has relinquished all control over her body and mind. Elizabeth McNeill tells this story with beautiful economy; her very coolness of tone makes the sensations she describes all the more powerful.

The movie version, starring Kim Basinger and Mickey Rourke, attracted a huge amount of controversy for its elaborately staged sex scenes, yet the book is both more explicit and less sensationalistic. Bound neither by Hollywood's ratings restrictions nor the commercial impulse to titillate, McNeill's narrative offers a far deeper, more nuanced look at a frighteningly destructive relationship. While some viewers insist that the movie is a masterpiece of erotica, the opinion of many others may echo that of *New York Times* critic Vincent Canby, who wrote: " '9 ½ Weeks' . . . is pricelessly funny without having many laughs. It's *Story of O* as it might look if conceived as a two-hour television commercial." The praise for the book, however, is nearly unanimous, and McNeill's words seem to have aged far better than Basinger's and Rourke's acting.

" This is a love story so unusual, so passionate, so extreme in its psychology and sexuality that it takes the reader's breath away. "

"It leads us to the edge of the abyss . . . where the boundaries of self are obliterated and all things become permissible."

—*New York Times*

*ENDLESS LOVE*

by Scott Spencer

Endless
Love

SCOTT SPENCER

One of the most celebrated books of its time, *Endless Love* remains perhaps the most powerful novel ever written about young love. Riveting, compulsively readable, and ferociously sexual, it tells the story of David Axelrod and his over-whelming, eventually uncontrollable love for Jade Butterfield.

The lives of seventeen-year-old David and fifteen-year-old Jade are consumed with each other, and their dreams, their desires, and their young sexuality take them farther from the real world than they understand. When Jade's concerned father suddenly banishes David from the Butterfield house, the stunned young man believes that only a heroic deed will win back the family's favor, leading him to set a "perfectly safe" fire to their house with the intention of staging a daring rescue. What unfolds instead is a nightmare, and David enters a dark world of obsession in which his once-innocent love has become a disease. As everything around him falls apart, he continues his punishing and endless pursuit of the one thing that remains most real to him: his undying love for Jade and her family.

First published in 1979 and universally regarded as one of the best books of the year, *Endless Love* is an engagingly dark and complex novel, characteristics the far more famous, yet largely inferior, 1981 film mostly fail to capture. As the influential *New York Times* film critic Janet Maslin wrote at the time: "There are two sorts of people who'll be going to see 'Endless Love'—

those who have read the richly imaginative novel on which the movie is based and those who have not. There will be dismay in the first camp, but it may be nothing beside the bewilderment in the second."

Brooke Shields proved to be the lone bright spot in Franco Zeffirelli's inconsistent, superficial reworking of Spencer's brilliant book, and it was her performance that helped to boost visibility of the film—possibly at the expense of the novel. Readers who do not overlook Spencer's powerful work will be rewarded with an engrossing psychological portrait of the ugly side of love, and a work of the highest literary merit.

"Scott Spencer writes about love's tenacity with such passionate intensity that I was for a time obliged to suspend all possibility of disbelief. From his remarkable opening sentence he had me in thrall."

—*Newsweek*

> ❝ Readers who do not overlook Spencer's powerful work will be rewarded with an engrossing psychological portrait of the ugly side of love. ❞

### THE STEPFORD WIVES

by Ira Levin

When Ira Levin, the author of *Rosemary's Baby* and *The Boys from Brazil*, published this scathing satire of consumer conformity and suburban blandness in 1972, the book's success was almost instantaneous. Both a domestic and international best seller, this slim novel has now sold more than 500,000 copies worldwide, and continues to win over new readers with its subtle plotting and deceptively simple style. The story follows ▶

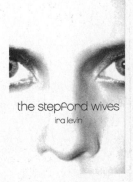

the stepford wives
ira levin

> ◄ Joanna and Walter Eberhart's move to the village of Stepford, where they discover that all of the women in the town seem to love nothing better than cleaning, cooking, and pleasing their husbands. Joanna becomes disturbed by their vacuous, bizarrely cheerful manner, and, along with two like-minded friends, attempts to investigate the cause of the women's strange lack of personality. The truth, it turns out, is far worse than she ever imagined.

❝ *The Stepford Wives* skewers the desires of the average American man. ❞

With its now-infamous final narrative twist, *The Stepford Wives* skewers the desires of the average American man and reveals the latent misogyny at the dark heart of many of our most common male fantasies. The original movie version, directed by Bryan Forbes and starring Katharine Ross, Paula Prentiss, and Peter Masterson, was released in 1975 and became one of the highest grossing movies of the decade, racking in $4 million in domestic sales alone, extremely impressive earnings for the time. Forbes plays up the thriller elements of the story, sometimes falling for horror-movie clichés such as convenient lightning crashes and gothic mansions, but remaining mostly successful in establishing an atmosphere of taut suspense. Fine performances by all of the leads helped the movie receive a positive contemporary critical response almost as impressive as its stunning economic windfall.

Frank Oz's 2004 remake, as *New York Times* critic A. O. Scott notes, takes a different approach to its effective, but rather dated predecessor: "The first 'Stepford Wives' exploited the horror-movie implications of [its] premise, rather than its comic possibilities. Mr. Oz and Paul Rudnick, the screenwriter, swerve maniacally in the opposite direction, whipping up a gaudy, noisy farce that perpetually threatens to spin out of control and eventually does." While Matthew Broderick, Nicole Kidman, and Glenn Close all give capable performances, the film itself is too loud, glitzy, and manic to make much of a lasting impression. Levin's sly, measured novel has none of these problems, and remains one of the most simultaneously funny and chilling satires of the last fifty years.

## *SERPICO*

by Peter Maas

Originally published in 1973, *Serpico* is the tough, taut story of the cop who stood up to a corrupt system. A working-class, Brooklyn-born, Italian undercover officer with long hair, a beard, and a taste for opera and ballet, most of all Frank Serpico was a man who couldn't be silenced— or bought.

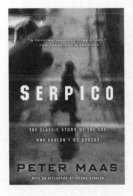

For years a culture of corruption had pervaded the New York City Police Department. Police payoffs, protection, and shakedowns of gambling rackets and drug dealers were common practice and the so-called blue code of silence protected the minority of crooked cops from the sanction of the majority. But Serpico refused to go along with the system. The only oath he swore was to enforce the law, and it didn't say against everybody except other cops. And for this, Serpico would nearly pay with his life.

Maas tells Serpico's story with verve and ▶

66 Maas tells Serpico's story with verve and grit, and the screen version released later that year . . . didn't lose either of those qualities. 99

◄ grit, and the screen version released later that year, directed by Sydney Lumet and starring a young Al Pacino in what would be his breakout role, didn't lose either of those qualities. Both the film and the book are gripping, relentless, and propulsive, and neither should be missed.

"Maas's reportage is detailed and of high narrative quality . . . [full of] tension and drama."

—*Rolling Stone*

Don't miss the next book by your favorite author. Sign up now for AuthorTracker by visting www.AuthorTracker.com.